Ralph Compton: One Man's Fire

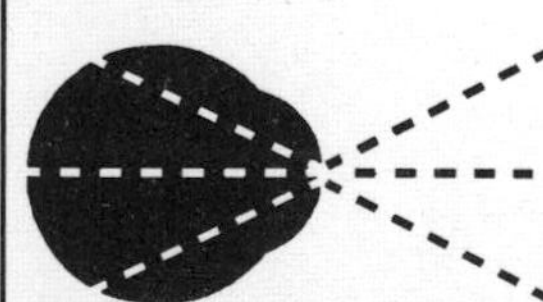

A RALPH COMPTON NOVEL

RALPH COMPTON: ONE MAN'S FIRE

MARCUS GALLOWAY

THORNDIKE PRESS
A part of Gale, Cengage Learning

Detroit • New York • San Francisco • New Haven, Conn • Waterville, Maine • London

Thorndike Press, a part of Gale, Cengage Learning.

Thorndike Press® Large Print Western
The text of this Large Print edition is unabridged.
Other aspects of the book may vary from the original edition.
Set in 16 pt. Plantin.

LIBRARY OF CONGRESS CATALOGING-IN-PUBLICATION DATA

Galloway, Marcus.
Ralph Compton : one man's fire, a Ralph Compton novel / by Marcus Galloway. — Large print ed.
p. cm. — (Thorndike Press large print Western)
ISBN 978-1-4104-5401-0 (hardcover)— ISBN 1-4104-5401-0 (hardcover)
1. Large type books. I. Title. II. Title: One man's fire.
PS3607.A4196R33 2012
813'.6—dc23 2012035810

Published in 2012 by arrangement with NAL Signet, a member of Penguin Group (USA) Inc.

Printed in the United States of America
1 2 3 4 5 6 7 16 15 14 13 12

THE IMMORTAL COWBOY

This is respectfully dedicated to the "American Cowboy." His was the saga sparked by the turmoil that followed the Civil War, and the passing of more than a century has by no means diminished the flame.

True, the old days and the old ways are but treasured memories, and the old trails have grown dim with the ravages of time, but the spirit of the cowboy lives on.

In my travels — to Texas, Oklahoma, Kansas, Nebraska, Colorado, Wyoming, New Mexico, and Arizona — I always find something that reminds me of the Old West. While I am walking these plains and mountains for the first time, there is this feeling that a part of me is eternal, that I have known these old trails before. I believe it is the undying spirit of the frontier calling me, through the mind's eye, to step back into time. What is the appeal of the Old West of the American frontier?

It has been epitomized by some as the dark and bloody period in American history. Its heroes — Crockett, Bowie, Hickok, Earp — have been reviled and criticized. Yet the Old West lives on, larger than life.

It has become a symbol of freedom, when there was always another mountain to climb and another river to cross; when a dispute between two men was settled not with expensive lawyers, but with fists, knives, or guns. Barbaric? Maybe. But some things never change. When the cowboy rode into the pages of American history, he left behind a legacy that lives within the hearts of us all.

— Ralph Compton

CHAPTER 1

Wyoming Territory, 1883

The wagon was supposedly secured against any attempt to rob it. At least, that's what was said by all the men hired to protect it before it had left Omaha. Enough iron plates were fixed to the sides to make it necessary to add an additional pair of horses to the team pulling the monster on wheels. Slits had been crudely cut into the plates so any of the three men riding inside could fire at anyone foolish enough to approach the wagon without permission. The man who might grant such a boon rode up top in a seat partly surrounded by a thick wooden shell that wrapped around the driver's back and sides. Another man sat beside the driver, carrying a shotgun that had been stored among several other weapons in the box at the driver's feet. Strictly speaking, the wagon should have been close to impenetrable. To the young man gazing down at it from atop a ridge south of the trail, it was a big fat egg dying to be cracked apart.

"What do you think, Eli?" another man asked from behind the younger one. He had a thickly muscled torso wrapped in a duster that had been with him through more hard days than most men saw in a lifetime. Dark brown eyes gazed out from behind narrowed lids set within a heavily scarred face that looked like something a goat had chewed up and spat out. It was difficult to discern which dark streaks on his chin and cheeks were dirt and which were wiry stubble.

The younger man kept a pair of field glasses close to eyes that were the color of a sky smeared with mist from an approaching storm. His voice had a faraway quality when he replied, "I think I can take her."

A second pair of anxious men crouched behind the first two, and hearing that didn't do anything to alleviate their situation. The bigger fellow with the dirty face waved back at them as if he were shooing away a pair of annoying hound dogs. "Either one of you messes this up," he snarled, "and I'll use yer carcasses to trip up the team pulling that wagon."

Both of the other men settled down quick enough.

"You sure we can take that thing?" the scarred man asked. "Looks like a rolling fortress."

Eli lowered his field glasses to get a look at the wagon with his own eyes. Smiling at what he saw, he said, "You brought me along this far, Jake. You about to stop trusting me now?"

"Ain't about trust. It's about a job that we can or can't do. I won't charge into a slaughter just so you can scratch that itch you always got for stealing."

"That itch has served this gang pretty well so far."

"Sure has," one of the men farther down the rise said. He was definitely older than Eli, but carried himself like the youngest of the bunch. A wide, round head made his eyes look more like holes knocked into a pumpkin with a roofing nail. White knuckles were wrapped around a Spencer rifle, and every muscle in that arm trembled at the prospect of putting the weapon to use.

"Shut up, Cody," Jake snapped. "When I want your opinion, you'll know about it." Once Cody was sufficiently cowed, the scarred man hunkered down and gazed down at the trail where the wagon was still rolling. "How many men you think are on that thing?"

"There's two up front," Eli said. "Couldn't tell you for certain how many are inside."

"Hank?"

The fourth man in the group was the most raggedy of them all. He resembled a scarecrow thanks to his wiry build as well as the tattered clothes he wore. Even his long hair was stringy enough to look more like strands of wet straw plastered onto his scalp. Three guns were strapped under his arms and at his hip. For all Eli knew, Hank could have had three more besides the .44, .45, and derringer. Ever since he'd lost his left eye, he seemed one twitch away from gunning down anyone in his sight. That twitchiness made it awfully hard for anyone to sneak up on him, and he prided himself on being able to get to anyone before he could be hurt again. Those things made him a perfect spy. "There's five in all," he said with absolute certainty. "If you see two up front, that leaves three in the wagon."

"You'd stake our lives on it?" Jake asked. "Because that's what we'd be doing."

"I watched them load up myself."

Jake showed Eli an ugly grin and slapped the younger man on the shoulder. "All right, then. I suppose we should get moving before all the money in that wagon gets away."

Eli looked down at the trundling wagon as if it were a fat, limping goose on Christmas Eve. "No danger of that. We'd be able to hear it from a mile away even if we did let it get out of our sight."

"How much money are we talking about again?" Cody asked.

Jake was looking down at the wagon hungrily as he told him, "At least twenty thousand. You hear any different, Hank?"

The scarecrow man shrugged. "They loaded up a few strongboxes. If I could get into them things, we wouldn't need the young'un."

Patting the youngest member of the gang once more on the shoulder, Jake said, "That's right. Eli here can crack open the Devil's own coin purse. Ain't that so?"

"Yeah," Eli said. "It is."

Neither Jake nor any of the other men in the gang knew for certain whose money was down there. They'd heard rumors of a bank shipping funds to cover a payroll or provide a loan to a large customer with deep pockets, but none of them had cared enough to ferret out the truth. There were even rumors that some businessman was shipping a bribe to a politician, but when there was a large batch of cash involved, speculations were bound to arise. Those fires were stoked even higher when that money was ferried about in a rolling spectacle like a crudely armored wagon. More than likely, the money was just a payroll being shipped by a company that had been robbed one too many times already. All most of the gang cared about was that the money was inside the wagon and there was lots of it.

But there was a different kind of glint in Eli's eyes when he stared down at that trail. It was a dull, yet intense thing that hinted at a hotter fire deep beneath his surface. "Yeah," he said. "Let's get moving."

The gang mustered like a disciplined army regiment. They kept low so as not to skyline themselves before enough of the ridge was between them and the men riding on the wagon below. When it was safe to move faster, they broke into a run toward the horses that were tethered to trees nearby. Having already scouted out the area while waiting for the wagon to roll by, all of the men knew their way down the narrow path around the ridge, through a stand of trees, and across a short stretch of bushes that had been turned into scorched brambles by an unforgiving sun.

It was no surprise for Jake to fire the first shot, and when Hank joined in, Eli's world became a mush of cacophonous sound.

Despite the horse's jostling movement, he kept his eyes locked on the wagon. Even as the animal wove between pits left by deep puddles or jumped over a fallen tree, Eli kept his eyes glued to the wagon. As soon as the ground in front of him leveled out, he snapped his reins and rode ahead of his outlaw pack.

"You two move around to the other side of that contraption!" Jake shouted. "I'll see to it the kid don't get himself killed!"

Cody and Hank peeled away to circle around the back of the wagon. Compared to the horses that had swarmed around it, the iron-encrusted vehicle might as well have been standing still. It was far from defenseless, however, as rifle barrels poked out from the slits in its side to spout smoke and lead at the gang. Bullets hissed through the air past Eli's head, causing him to duck down as if that would be enough to keep him safe for the remainder of the journey. Before the rifle rounds could get any closer, they were diverted toward a greater threat.

Howling like a mad dog, Jake gripped his reins in one hand and a .44 Smith & Wesson in the other. Rather than fire wildly at the wagon, he gazed along the top of his barrel as if he had all the time in the world to take his shot. When he squeezed his trigger, sparks flew from the edge of one of the slits in the wagon's armor and angry curses echoed within. More shots cracked through the air on the other side of the wagon as the second half of the gang was greeted by another batch of riflemen. Eli tapped his heels against his horse's sides and surged forward as the spark in his eyes grew to a roaring flame.

"Bring this thing to a halt!" Jake bellowed.

The driver responded with a barking command directed at his team. The horses pounded their hooves against the rocky ground even harder as leather straps slapped against their backs. The shotgunner emerged from behind the wooden barricade atop the wagon like a target in a shooting gallery to unleash a smoky payload from one barrel and then the other. Jake had already veered away from the wagon by the time hot lead ripped through the air, and he fired at the shotgunner, clipping his shoulder and spinning him around to collide with the driver. Both men wobbled atop the wagon before becoming entangled in the reins. Once that happened, the team was pulled to the right, causing the entire wagon to lurch.

Eli was close enough to see in through one of the rifle slits by now. When the man behind the weapon poking out through the opening looked his way, Eli had plenty of time to grab hold of the rifle and yank it from him. He could have taken it away completely if the slit had been just a bit wider. As it was, the rifle clanged against iron while the man inside struggled to regain control of it. The driver's predicament caused the rattling iron monstrosity to swing away from Eli, taking the rifle barrel from his grasp and causing something of a panic for Hank and Cody on the other side.

Jake fired two more shots before snarling, "Bring this thing to a stop or I will!" Although the driver had gotten his team pointed in the right direction again, the wagon had slowed to something slightly better than a crawl. This allowed Jake to grab on to a post at the front corner of the wagon as if he meant to hop from his saddle and onto the driver's lap.

With the blood pounding through his veins amid the hammering rhythm of his heart, Eli felt as if he were charging down the trail at a breakneck speed instead of keeping pace with a wagon that was barely moving at all. Now that Jake had gotten under the driver's skin, the wagon slowed even more. The riflemen inside were still ready for a fight, but were preoccupied by Cody and Hank. That meant Eli was able to get back to the slit on his side a second after the rifle barrel poked through it again. Still rattled from his last confrontation as well as the unpredictable movements of the wagon itself, the rifleman on Eli's side pulled his trigger before he even had a target.

No bullet chewed through Eli's skull, but a mighty loud screech pealed through his ears. Apart from his hammering pulse and the dull thump of his own horse's hooves against the ground, he couldn't hear a thing. And yet, not so much as a hint of panic showed on his face as he pointed one of his .38s at the rifle slit and shouted at the man on the other side. Eli only had a vague idea of what he said, but it was enough to get the man to relinquish his grip on the weapon.

The wagon came to a halt and the gang surrounded it like a pack of dogs vying for the biggest chunk of a discarded hunk of meat. Eli was still mostly deaf as he came up alongside the wagon and stared in through the slit. His eyes were searching for one thing, but found another as all three men within the armored box turned to face him. The pair that had been dealing with Cody and Hank still held their rifles and the man on Eli's side had gotten to the pistol holstered at his hip. They all looked through the slit back at Eli and struggled to get their weapons pointed in his direction. From the corner of one eye, Eli could see the shotgunner on top of the wagon swing his weapon around to aim at him.

For that brief instant, Eli felt as if he'd drifted outside his own skin to watch everything from afar. Even if his ears hadn't been ravaged by the close-range gunshot, he doubted he would have been able to hear much of anything. He recalled folks talking about something like that when they'd been about to die. Their bodies drifted up and everything got real quiet. It was said to have been peaceful. As far as Eli could tell, he was about to find out firsthand.

Just as well, he figured.

Once more, the gang acted like a well-oiled machine. Jake brought the shotgunner down with one shot while Hank stuck the barrel of a .44 in through a slit on the other side of the wagon and pulled his trigger. The gunshot sounded like a muffled thump to Eli's tortured ears, and the bullet rattled around inside the wagon like a pebble being shaken in a tin can. All three riflemen flopped onto their sides or bellies in their haste to clear a path for the bullet or any more that might be following on its heels.

Even Eli could make out the dull murmur of those men's excited voices, but he couldn't see any blood. When he felt the rough hand slap down on his shoulder, Eli twisted around while bringing his pistol up to bear.

Jake took his hand away and stepped back. His other hand kept his .44 pointed up at the driver while Cody made his way to the top of the wagon. Although Eli couldn't make out the words coming from Jake's mouth, there was no mistaking the victory etched into the gang leader's smile.

Chapter 2

The wagon was stopped, the men driving or protecting it had been disarmed and tied up, the dust had settled, and yet not everyone in Jake's gang was happy. Throughout the entire process of steering the wagon off the trail so it could be detained and searched without being interrupted by any random passersby, Hank had been glaring at Eli as if he meant to bore through the other man's skull using nothing more than mean intentions. When Eli emerged from the wagon with a strongbox in his hands, he was grinning from ear to ear. Hank's reaction couldn't have been more different.

"What is wrong with you, boy?" Hank snarled.

The wagon driver and riflemen had been tied with their ropes laced between the spokes of one of the front wheels. Jake stood with one foot propped on the driver's shoulder in a casual show of dominance while using his bandanna to rub some of the grit from his face. "Leave him alone. He did real good back there."

"Yeah. Real good at almost getting killed!"

"What concern is that of yours?" Eli asked without taking his eyes from the prize in his hands.

Hank's one good eye twitched as he surged forward to bump against the strongbox in Eli's grasp. "If you get killed in the middle of a job, that puts things into confusion. It leaves us one man short and gives these ones here a chance to get a leg up on us."

Looking toward the men tied to the wheels, Eli asked, "You were worried about them getting over on you? And here I thought you were so dangerous with all those guns you carry."

"I am! And don't you forget it."

"Sure. That's why you flew off the handle and started firing into that wagon like it was a barrel full of fish. The plan was to keep some men alive so's they could be questioned in case we need help getting to the money."

"If you need so much help getting to the money," Hank grunted, "then I don't see why we brought you along."

"Come on, now, boys," Jake said after

stuffing his bandanna into a pocket. "This is a happy occasion. Everything went just fine."

Hank's eye shifted back toward Eli. "No thanks to him. Didn't you get a look at his face when he poked his nose into that wagon? It's like he didn't care about catching a bullet."

"He was just trying to see what we were up against. Ain't that right, Eli?"

Transfixed by the process of gently setting down the strongbox and running his fingers along the mechanism that kept it shut, Eli could barely spare enough time or effort to nod.

"See?" Jake said.

But Hank wasn't appeased. "We're supposed to work together on the jobs we do. Otherwise, I wouldn't need to be a part of any gang. If one man gets it into his head that he don't care about livin' or dyin', he does foolish nonsense like what we saw today. Too much foolishness when lead is flyin' puts all of us in danger. The kind of danger no man walks away from."

Jake took his foot down and watched Eli carefully. He looked over to Cody, but that one simply shook his big head at him and continued tending to the horses. "We handled things just fine."

Eli's eyes widened when he said, "I know how to get this open."

Hearing that made Jake forget about almost everything that had come before. "That's what I'm talking about! Crack it open, boy!"

Eli worked with the speed and precision of a crazed watchmaker. His gaze was focused on the strongbox's lock as if there were nothing else with him in the world. His hands worked feverishly, occasionally bumping his fingers together but never making a mistake. When he needed a different tool, he reached over to where he'd laid the pouch containing them without having to look away from the iron puzzle of gears, latches, and bars. It was another few minutes before the lock budged, every second of which passed without a sound coming from anything besides the horses or the wind. Even the prisoners knew better than to speak up. They'd only known Jake Welles for a short amount of time, but that was enough to be certain they didn't want any of his undivided attention.

"Almost got it," Eli muttered more to himself than to any of the outlaws gathering around him. By the time the final tumbler fell into place, even Cody was staring down at him intently. Eli set his tools aside so he could place both hands upon the lid of the strongbox. With just a few subtle movements, he could tell that gravity was indeed the only thing keeping it closed.

"Go on," Jake prodded. "Let's get a look."

One of the prisoners cleared his throat and started to speak, but was cut short when Jake wheeled around to bark at him in a vicious noise that could have been hacked up from a wolf's throat. Turning back around to look at the strongbox, Jake still resembled more of a hungry animal than a man.

Shifting so his back was to the wagon and the front of the strongbox was pointed directly at him, Eli eased the lid up so his were the first eyes to see what lay inside. Wincing at what he found, he flipped the lid all the way up so the most possible sunlight was cast into the iron container.

"What in the hell?" Jake grunted.

Hank chuckled while nodding with grim self-satisfaction.

Cody leaned forward and took another longer glance before muttering, "It's empty."

"You don't think I can see that?" Jake snapped.

"But . . . it ain't supposed to be empty, is it?"

Jake's eyes narrowed into fiery slits as he said, "No. It isn't."

Eli picked up the strongbox, felt inside, and then turned it around so he could examine it from all angles. "Maybe there's a false bottom."

"Yeah," Hank chuckled. "I'm sure that's what it is."

Eli closed his eyes, ran his fingers along the interior of the box, and then did the same for the exterior. When he stood up, he weighed the box in his hands and then let it drop. As he stomped toward the wagon, he passed the prisoners tied to their respective wheels. Although the bound men reacted as if they'd been scalded by hot water, Eli didn't cast so much as a glance at them. When he emerged from the wagon holding another strongbox, the driver stammered, "I . . . I tried to tell you before."

Once again, Eli closed his eyes so he could weigh the box in his hands using nothing but his remaining senses to tell him what he needed to know. The result he came to didn't bring him any comfort. "This one's empty too," he said while looking to the driver as if the man had just sprouted from the ground. "Isn't it?"

"Y . . . yes. That's what I m . . . meant to —"

The driver was cut short by a laugh that was hacked up from Hank's throat like a fetid chunk of the previous night's supper. "Ain't that just the way?"

Eli threw the strongbox down with enough force to put a dent into the ground. "I suppose you knew all about this, Hank?"

"Nope. You're the big expert when it comes to cracking safes and the like."

"And you're the man we're supposed to trust when it comes to gathering information. How come you didn't know about this?"

"I was told to watch the men piling into that wagon so we'd know how many guns we'd be facing. I did my part."

"Yeah," Cody grunted. "He did his part."

Shifting his focus to the simpleminded outlaw, Eli said, "If we need to know about saddle soap or picking our teeth, we'll ask you. Until then, shut your trap!"

A single gunshot blasted through the air, causing the prisoners to tuck their heads in close to their chests and the three outlaws to turn while reflexively reaching for their pistols.

"You all through with your bickering?" the gang leader asked as he holstered the gun he'd just fired.

Eli turned his back on the others so he

could storm back to the wagon and retrieve one of the two remaining strongboxes.

"I was talkin' to you as well, boy!" Jake bellowed. "Answer me or the next shot knocks a hole through your head."

"See?" Hank grunted. "He don't care about anything but himself."

"You're not exactly the charitable type yourself," Jake pointed out.

"Maybe not, but I never done nothin' that cuts into our profits. Someone went through a lot of trouble to put that rolling contraption together and they'll notice when it don't arrive in Seedley."

Another strongbox hit the dirt beside the wagon, followed by the final one the wagon had been carrying. Eli kicked them aside as he shifted his efforts to the wagon itself.

Like a single ship that managed to sail straight in turbulent seas, Jake strolled over to the driver and lowered himself to one knee. "There was supposed to be a ton of greenbacks on that wagon of yours," he said calmly.

"Yes, b . . . but . . ."

Jake's hand was still wrapped around his Smith & Wesson and he raised it as if his arm were a cumbersome mechanism attached to his shoulder. "Just looking at that wagon tells me two things. First off, someone with a lot of funding went through a lot of trouble to protect your cargo. Secondly, that cargo must be pretty valuable to necessitate that sort of care. Those things bring me back to my first point." Thumbing back the hammer of his pistol, Jake snarled, "There should be a lot of money in that wagon of yours."

The driver sputtered, but was unable to form any words. When he looked over to the other men that were tied up, the only support to be found was an array of trembling, fearful stares.

"All right, then," Jake said as he calmly lifted the pistol to point at the driver's temple. "If you ain't any use to me, you've got to go. This gang's already carrying too much deadweight as it is."

"I think I found another problem," Eli announced. "And it's got to do with more of Hank's end of the job."

Hank made his way over to the wagon, moving every bit like a scarecrow that had been blown off its post to flop angrily through its field. "I've had my fill of you! If Jake won't cut you loose, then I'll be happy to —"

"Shut up," Jake said in a tone that was just as deadly as the gun in his hand. "You were to find out all the information you could about that wagon. Them strongboxes being empty is a pretty big piece of information."

"But he's the strongbox expert!" Hank replied while pointing a finger at Eli.

With a humorless smirk, Jake said, "Yeah. He opens things that're locked, which is what he did. What's your excuse?"

Just when Hank thought he couldn't be cast in a worse light, Eli said, "I think I discovered some information myself." Eli had climbed onto the wagon, hanging on to a post at the front corner that had been used by the shotgunner to get to his spot on the driver's seat. Hanging there like a monkey on a tree, Eli tugged at a joint where the iron plate was lashed to the post. "Whoever put this thing together wasn't necessarily rich."

"How do you figure?"

"It's not a bad job, but any one of us could've done it. It's just a bunch of flattened plates fastened to posts by ropes or rings. There's some bolts and such here and there. Solid, but nothing too complicated."

Nodding as if he were admiring a finely crafted front porch, Jake looked to the driver and said, "Time to stop sputtering and start stringing some useful words together."

Once the driver started to speak, he could

barely contain himself enough to stop. "I don't know who put the wagon together, but they made it to withstand a battle. I could've driven that thing in the middle of Pickett's Charge without getting so much as a scratch to show for it. As for those strongboxes, they are supposed to have money in 'em. Just not until after we made our stop in Seedley."

"That's a whole lot of wasted ammunition spent to protect an empty wagon," Hank said.

"Our orders were to protect the wagon no matter what."

"Why bother when it's empty?"

"Because," Eli said, "if the wagon was taken before it got to Seedley, whoever took it could just ride in and pick up the same money these fellas were meant to get."

"That's right," the driver said with a nod that made it look as if his head had become unhinged. "The men waiting for us in Seedley are looking for the wagon, not me or my boys."

Jake beamed proudly as he looked at Eli. "Always did like the way your mind worked, boy. Is there anything to keep us from taking that wagon the rest of the way into town?"

"Sure," Cody said. "We don't know where

in town it's supposed to go. We slip up too much and we'll tip our hand."

It wasn't often that the rest of the gang regarded Cody as anything more than hired help. When Jake and Hank looked over at him, it took them a few seconds to realize this was one of those times. "Gotta be a bank, right?" Jake asked. "Where else would have that much money on hand?"

The driver looked over to the men who'd fired rifles from inside the wagon.

"There's more," Eli said while easing one of his twin .38s from its holster. "It's written all over your face, so out with it."

"We weren't supposed to go to any bank," the driver said. "We weren't even supposed to go into town. We had to stay in the open so as not to be cornered or trapped by anyone like . . . well . . . like you."

"That plan turned out real good, didn't it?" Jake mused.

Shifting his eyes away from the gang's leader, the driver preferred to look up at Eli when he said, "The place we were supposed to go is a ranch outside Seedley."

The next few moments dragged by on leaden feet. Although the outlaws barely moved an inch, they crept in like shadows being cast by a lantern hanging from a moving train. It was Hank who snapped, "What ranch?"

"Don't tell him," one of the riflemen shouted.

Hank put an end to that one's protests along with his life with a well-placed shot from his .45. The report echoed through the air, silencing the other men further so they could all hear the last sigh to emerge from the rifleman's trembling lips. Aiming the smoking barrel at the driver, Hank formed his next two words as if carefully and tenuously sculpting a pile of hot wax. "What . . . ranch?"

"The Lazy V." When the driver said that, he hung his head so as not to look at any of the others tied to those wagon wheels.

The gears were turning inside Hank's head. His eye was narrowed as if it was blocking out anything that might interfere with his thoughts. "Even if we find the place, there's no guarantee we won't be recognized as soon as we ride in."

"That don't matter," Jake said. "Just so long as the money will be there. It *will* be there, right?"

When the driver hesitated, Eli said, "You'd best answer."

"Yeah," the tired prisoner sighed. "It'll be there. Leastways, it's supposed to be there."

Jake's grin widened. "And that wagon will let us get close enough to smell it. Once we catch that scent, it'll be too late for anyone to do anything to keep us from loading up and rolling out."

"There'll be a whole lot of guns protecting that much money," Eli pointed out. "That's a guarantee. And we still don't know how many men we're looking to go against."

"How many men will be guarding that money?" Hank asked. Since the driver was too rattled to answer, he shifted his gaze to the next closest prisoner. He pointed a pistol at him and snarled, "How many?"

The prisoner at the other end of Hank's gun was the same one who'd fired at Eli through the slit in the wagon's side during the raid. Ever since he'd been pulled from that iron box, he barely had the gumption to lift his chin.

"Answer me or I kill you right now."

Knowing all too well that Hank meant what he said, the rifleman told him, "I don't know. None of us do. We were just supposed to ride the wagon in where it would be loaded up."

"So you're saying you *knew* them boxes were empty?"

"Course we did. We loaded them."

"So why all the shooting?"

"Because that wagon is expensive," the rifleman said. "It was built special for this ride and more down the stretch. The men who hired us didn't want anyone else getting their hands on it. Also, they told us to kill anyone who so much as looked cross-eyed at that blasted thing, whether it was empty, full, rolling down a trail, or sitting in a lot."

Never one to shy away from asking a question no matter how it might reflect on him, Cody asked, "Why?"

Always one to revel in pointing out anyone else's flaws or shortcomings, Hank said, "It's about fear, you ignorant wretch. It's why we make sure to knock the tar out of anyone who decides to test their luck against any one of us when we're in a saloon or somewhere else folks might see. It's why we ride in, guns blazing, like a pack of wild dogs when we're coming up to a stagecoach that's about to get robbed. It's why we don't tear down them wanted notices with our faces painted on them whenever we catch sight of one. If folks quake in fear when they see us coming, they'll be quicker to empty their pockets or do whatever else we tell 'em to do."

"Folks are supposed to be afraid of a

wagon?" Cody asked.

It wouldn't have been the first time Hank struck the simpleminded outlaw, but Eli felt the need to step in before it happened again. "Men like us are supposed to think that iron lummox is too tough to crack," he said, "or at least not worth the effort."

"Whoever counted on that sure didn't count on us!" Jake declared. "We ain't afraid of dyin', so we sure ain't afraid of no oversized, lopsided can on four wheels. Ain't that right, boys?"

Hank and Cody voiced their approval, but Eli could only manage part of a nod. That was all fine and dandy with Jake. The gang's leader hunkered down to the driver, looked him square in the eye, and said, "We'll make our way to that ranch and you'll be driving that wagon to get us as close as possible to the money. You do your job well enough and I might tell you when to duck before the lead starts to fly."

"I'll do what I can," the driver muttered. "But I can tell you right now there are plenty of armed men at that ranch."

"I'll just bet there are. And they're all gonna be taught a lesson in what it is to truly be afraid of somethin'."

CHAPTER 3

Four days later

The town of Seedley might have been small, but it stuck out like a sore thumb amid the wide-open, rolling Wyoming terrain. Overhead, the sky stretched out like a lazy colossus to make everything below seem brittle and insignificant. Eli had been born and raised in Georgia. When he'd gotten his first taste of the high country, he never wanted to go back home. There was something cleansing about having such a vast amount of sky hanging over him. Strictly speaking, the sky was usually about the same and there was always plenty of it, but in the Wyoming and Montana territories, it was more than just an airy expanse that shifted from blue to black and occasionally gray. When Eli looked up, he felt as if something much bigger was looking down at him. Sometimes that was a good feeling. At other times, when he felt he had too much to answer for, he couldn't bear to lift his eyes up farther than the top of his horse's ears.

He and Jake sat in their saddles, two miles outside town. As they watched, one trail of dust was kicked up by a horse that galloped away from Seedley to beat a path directly to them. Jake looked at the animal churning up that disturbance and shook his head. "You'd think Hank would've taught Cody a thing or two about sneaking."

"I think he only rides with him to kick him around when he feels the need."

"I've had friends like that," Jake said without the slightest bit of irony in his tone. "You see any trace of the scarecrow yet?"

No matter how well the nickname fit Hank, Jake only used it when the one-eyed gunman was well out of earshot. "Think so," Eli said. "Some birds were flushed out of those trees over yonder. I reckon that'd be his doing."

"You don't seem too keen on getting that money."

"I ain't afraid of them gunmen," Eli said quickly. "No matter how many there are."

"I didn't say anything about the gunmen. You're plenty ready for them. It just don't seem like you give an ounce of spit about the money. Why might that be?"

"Might be because you're mistaken."

Jake shifted in his saddle. "Nah. That ain't it."

"Or maybe you're not as smart as you think you are."

"I know that ain't it."

"Then maybe I'm just in the wrong line of work," Eli said.

"Wanna know what I think?"

"Would it matter if I said no?"

"Nope."

"Then by all means, enlighten me."

"Every man's got a fire in his belly," Jake explained. "It's just not all fueled by the same thing. Hank's fire comes from spilling blood or putting the fear of God into another man. Cody's comes from getting his hands on one of those big round whores he likes so much."

"Or a steak," Eli said. "Don't forget the steaks."

"That's right. That fella sure does love his vittles. You know what stokes my fire, Eli?"

Without hesitation, Eli said, "Money."

"Amen to that."

"Real interesting conversation, Jake. Nice way to pass the time. How about we put an end to it?"

Jake ignored that request and shifted idly in his saddle as if it had never drifted through the air. "What I don't much like is that I can't pin down what stokes the fire in your belly."

"It doesn't matter."

"Oh, but it does. You see, knowing that means you truly know what makes a man tick. Helps you get along with him and, more importantly for our situation, it helps you think ahead to what he might do in most given predicaments."

"I've pulled my weight in this gang."

"That ain't the question," Jake said as his voice dropped to a more serious tone. "I can't decide what bothers me more. The fact that I don't know what gets you to lift your head every morning or the fact that I might have an idea of what it is."

"Sounds like you won't be happy either way."

"If your fire comes from what I think it does, I won't be happy. Not one bit."

Eli sighed and turned so he was facing the gang leader as much as possible. "All right, Jake. Go on and tell me. What gets my fire burning?"

Jake studied him carefully. The silence that followed wasn't for the sake of drama or to prove a point. It was simply a man taking all the time he needed for his thoughts to come to fruition. "I guess it only matters how you act as part of this gang. Long as you stay in my good graces, you can burn however you like."

"And if I don't?"

"Then I'll burn you even worse."

That threat would have sent a chill down most men's spines. Although Eli wasn't foolish enough to discard it, he always knew it was there just as well as a condemned man knew there was a noose dangling over his head. He pointed his eyes toward Seedley and followed the path of dust that was being kicked up along the trail leading from its border.

"When you and I first met up, it was in a jail cell," Jake said as if he were telling a fairy story to a child. "You were full of venom and vinegar, spitting at them law dogs and shaking them bars as if you meant to pry 'em straight up from the floor."

"And you were too drunk to stand up," Eli reminded him.

"You got that right. I knew there was something wild about you. For men in our line of work, that's usually a good thing. The longer you've been riding with us, though, I ain't so sure."

"So cut me loose."

"No need for that, since you do your job well enough. I just worry about when you stop thinking about doing your job and let that fire in your belly grow too high. Kind of like when you charged that wagon."

"I thought that was the plan."

"It was," Jake replied, "but not at the detriment of your own hide. Me and Hank were firing away like demons. Even Cody gets wrapped up in the chaos, but not you. You get quiet."

"You got something against quiet?"

"I do when it's the wrong kind of quiet."

"And that's what I am?"

Jake's lips tightened against his teeth as if he were either gnawing on something small or looking for a piece of raw meat that was stuck between them. Finally he said, "Haven't decided yet. I just hope I made the right choice by allowing you to walk out of that jail cell in one piece."

Years ago when Eli had been locked up with Jake Welles, his biggest concern had been avoiding getting his neck snapped by the wild, enraged drunk. After Jake had sobered up, he seemed like something close to a rational man and offered him a spot in his gang. Now, as he thought back with the knowledge that Jake hadn't been such a flailing lunatic, it chilled him to think of all that power being focused by a sober mind. Those last few words spoken by Jake made Eli think of half a dozen times when the gang leader could have been poised over him while he was sleeping or coiled in a corner. How many other nights had there been when that killer's eyes were fixed on him, fretting endlessly about what was too quiet for his liking? All it took was one bad night for Jake to stomp out Eli's fire for good.

"Cody's almost here," Eli said.

And, like a storm that had suddenly been blown in another direction, the steely intent on Jake's face was replaced by a sunnier disposition. "So he is. Let's see what he's got to say."

By the time Cody reined his horse to a stop in front of the other two, Jake looked as if he were sitting on his uncle's front porch sipping from a glass of lemonade. "Found out a thing or two about the Lazy V," he said. "First off, I got directions on how to get there other than the straight path that was to be used by that driver."

"You been in town for almost two days," Jake snapped. "We could'a found as much just by riding in circles for a spell."

"Yeah, well, I also found out there's at least a dozen men there that don't belong."

That got a rise out of Jake. "Go on."

"Fella who runs a steak house says two groups of armed men stopped in for supper when they got to town. Said they was headed to the Lazy V."

"Sure they weren't the ranch's hired hands?" Eli asked.

Cody shook his head definitively. "The man I spoke to said they weren't from around here and that they were armed."

"Ranch hands can be armed," Jake pointed out.

"These men looked like gunmen. That's what this fella said."

Eli shrugged. "I suppose you were in that steak house long enough to earn the proprietor's trust. That means there's a bunch of gun hands waiting at that ranch. We were expecting as much."

Hooves rumbled in the distance. Since they already knew who'd be coming, none of the outlaws bothered to watch as Hank approached.

Still smirking at how quickly Cody had shown his colors where his love of food was concerned, Jake asked, "What else did you find out?"

"Those armed men are getting anxious. At least twice a day, one or two of them have been coming into town asking about any stages that have rolled through."

One of Hank's boons was that his ears were sharp as a hawk's eyes, and he displayed that feature as he rode up and announced, "I can vouch for that. Even better," he added while bringing his horse to a stop, "I followed the last pair out of town and back to where they met up with their friends. They're honest-to-God gunmen all right. I'd stake my life on it."

"Any of them look familiar?" Jake asked.

"Not as such, but they had the look of them fellas hired by the railroad. You remember those gents we met outside Wichita?"

Jake twitched as if he was feeling the bite from an old pain somewhere beneath his flesh. "I remember them well enough." He gripped his reins tighter. "You figure out more than one way to get to that ranch?"

Cody nodded. "There's a trail that wanders along a river to the east. It snakes up to one side of the property line. Not as easy of a ride and supposed to meander a bit, but it should get one or two of us to the fence without being spotted."

"And over the fence with no trouble since most of those men will be distracted by the arrival of that rattling mess of a wagon." Looking over to Eli, Jake said, "The two of us will come in through the back way and you two will ride on that wagon. Agreed?"

Every instinct at Eli's disposal wanted him

to disagree with that idea. The tension in Jake's voice convinced him otherwise. "Agreed," he said in a tone that didn't even try to pass itself off as enthusiastic.

Fortunately, Jake never cared if anyone was enthusiastic about following him just so long as they did so with a minimum of fuss. "The wagon's back at the camp," he said. "After Cody tells me the particulars about that backdoor trail into the Lazy V, him and Hank will get to the wagon and start driving it down the main trail into the ranch. You think half an hour head start will be enough for us to get there about the same time as you?"

That question taxed the limits of Cody's mental capacity, and it showed in a painful grimace. Before he was forced to attempt an answer, Jake said, "You've also got to untie that driver and make sure the rest of those men are behaving. All of 'em are trussed up in the back of the wagon. Me and Eli will hightail it to that ranch and lie low until you arrive. After you get the driver situated, just take your time in getting there. How long of a ride is it from here?"

"About seven miles," Cody replied.

"Good. Along the way, do what you gotta do to squeeze any more out of that driver. Just come up with something to get that money in the open or loaded onto the wagon. Once things go south, start shooting. Me and Eli will back your play."

"What if the money isn't in sight by the time the shooting starts?" Hank asked.

"Then we kill everyone at that ranch and search the place ourselves."

Eli wasn't sure if it was the fire they'd mentioned earlier, but there was definitely something clawing at his belly as the gang split up and rode away.

CHAPTER 4

When Eli rode alongside Jake down a broken trail that faded in and out of sight like a fat eel wriggling in a stream, he was reminded of why he'd joined up with the gang in the first place. There wasn't anything between him and his goal. The wind caressed his face. The terrain flowed beneath his horse's hooves in a continuous motion. Even the rumbling noises that rushed through his ears became a part of him, entwining with the beat of his heart to make him feel almost glad to be alive. The grin Jake showed to him when glancing over was ridiculously large, and Eli didn't even try to return it in kind. Instead, he nodded and fixed his eyes on the trail in front of him.

"Fence line's just ahead!" Jake shouted above the roar of the two horses. "Seen anyone patrolling the perimeter?"

"No, but that doesn't mean they aren't there."

As if to join in on their conversation, a pair of gunshots crackled in the distance. Both outlaws reined their horses to a stop and sat hunched forward to listen for more.

The only thing in sight was a cluster of trees and bushes that had been sloppily parted to reveal the sorry excuse for a trail they were using. It was dusk, which meant the shadows were almost thick enough to obscure various obstacles that would make riding along that path dangerous. When Eli squinted hard enough, he could see the fence that Jake had already spotted. It was made of thick pieces of lumber that had been partially covered by overgrown weeds and tall grass. Nothing moved in the vicinity of that fence, or anywhere around the two riders for that matter. Even so, they watched and listened for the first hint of trouble.

"You think the wagon was brought down?" Eli asked.

"If it only took two shots, I'll find Hank and Cody's graves and dance on 'em," Jake snarled. "They were probably just warning shots."

"One way to find out, I suppose." Without waiting for Jake's approval, Eli snapped his reins and rode toward the fence. He could hear the gang leader's laughter as he followed in his wake.

The fence was sturdy, but not high enough to be much of anything other than a marker to trace out the ranch's boundary. Both horses cleared it with an inch to spare and landed upon better-tended ground on the other side. The outlaws felt the glory of charging forward when most others would have been stopped by a simple construction of wooden beams. As far as Eli was concerned, this was the true definition of freedom. No fence could keep him from riding on. No law would tell him what he could or couldn't take. No man would stand in his way. The next smile that drifted onto his face was as genuine as they came.

"Halt!" bellowed a tall man wearing a long coat that flapped in a passing breeze. The rifle in his hand, as well as the one carried by the man beside him, was still smoking after firing the rounds that had brought the iron wagon to a shuddering stop.

Hank sat in the shotgunner's position next to the wagon's original driver. Inside, Cody crouched while holding the door shut that led out from the back of the structure. The one-eyed outlaw knew his partner could be there at a moment's notice when he reached over to tap the driver's arm and whisper,

"Easy. Just do what you're supposed to do."

The pair of riflemen in long coats cautiously approached the wagon. Another two in similar garb stood about twenty paces away, while a fifth man wearing a vest and a rumpled Stetson aimed a pistol at hip level at the wagon. The three farthest away held their ground while the first man in the coat did the talking.

"You're late!" he said.

Half a second before he was prodded by the .44 secreted under Hank's jacket, the driver replied, "Had a little trouble the other day."

"What kind of trouble?"

"Broken wheel." When the rifleman stepped forward to examine each of the front wheels in turn, the driver shifted uneasily in his seat. Beside him, Hank tensed and shot a quick look behind him as if he could see through the iron plates to make certain Cody wasn't about to do anything foolish.

"Doesn't look like anything was broken," the rifleman said.

Laughing nervously, the driver told him, "Course it don't. I had it fixed."

"That shouldn't have taken very long. Don't you carry replacements?"

"Come on, now. This thing ain't exactly

speedy under the best circumstances."

Every second that the rifleman remained silent, Hank cinched his grip in tighter around his pistol. His finger caressed the trigger while the rifleman looked up to study him.

"You'd be Kyle?" the rifleman asked.

"No," Hank grunted.

"Wasn't Kyle supposed to be riding with you?"

The driver shrugged and let out a partial squeak before Hank stepped in to say, "There's five of us in all. It's been a long ride and it's my time to sit out where I can breathe some fresh air for a switch. That all right with you?"

Raising his eyebrows, the rifleman glanced back at another man wearing a long coat and said, "I don't know, Matt. You reckon that's okay?"

"I don't care who's up front, who's in the back, and who stayed home to feed the pigs," Matt replied while lowering his rifle as if it had suddenly become too heavy to lift. "There's a lot of loading to be done, and the quicker we get started, the quicker it'll be through."

"You've got a point there." Looking up at the driver with tired resignation, the first rifleman asked, "What's the password?"

"It's . . . uh . . ." The driver started breathing in quicker gulps as sweat trickled down his face.

"Answer the man," Hank urged while reminding the driver of the .44's presence with a gentle nudge. "There's loading to be done."

The driver stammered to himself, not making a bit of sense but enough noise to raise Hank's hackles. Finally he pulled in enough breath to spit out "I . . . I don't recall."

"What's that?" the lead rifleman asked.

The driver explained, "I don't recall the password. It's been a long ride and . . ."

"And we've been passing a bottle back and forth," Hank said with a laugh that would have been unconvincing even if it had been honest. "Tends to rot a man's thoughts, you know."

"And you're the one at the reins?" Matt asked. "Don't seem drunk to me. Just nervous."

The pair of riflemen that had been hanging back moved in while bringing weapons to their shoulders.

"He can hold his liquor," Hank told him. "You want to see some fellas that can't, just take a look in the back of the wagon."

"Aw, for the love of Pete," Matt growled.

"Those guards are passed out drunk? Mr. Cobbleston will have them strung up by their thumbs!"

"Just so long as he knows I was up front where I should be!" Hank said with just the right amount of defensiveness.

In the space of a minute, the riflemen had gone through a series of emotions, starting at cautious, moving through suspicious and threatening, and arriving at angry. There was bound to be one more stop along that path once the rifleman who now approached the back of the wagon opened its door. Those men got just outside arm's reach of the bent metal handle before a shrill whistle cut through the cooling air.

"What is it?" the first rifleman shouted.

The man who'd whistled stood on the roof of a small barn that was most likely used for storage or as stables for those who weren't allowed to approach the main house. "Someone's comin' in from the back twenty!"

"Who?"

"Looks like Akers and Noss!"

The man who'd been dispatched to check the back of the wagon held steady to see what would develop of the situation. He didn't have to wait long before the sound of approaching horses rolled in like a calm breeze. A pair of horses drew to a stop near the barn, and one of the riders spoke to the lookout. Hank couldn't hear what was being said, but their gestures seemed familiar enough as the two men talked to each other. Before long, the man atop the barn turned toward the wagon and shouted, "It's Akers and Noss! They say —"

A gunshot blazed through the shadows encroaching on the barn like a machete cutting through a narrow reed. One of the riders near the barn dropped from his saddle, and the second twisted around while drawing his gun. More shots came from beyond Hank's line of sight to send the second rider to the ground. The man at the barn lifted a rifle and fired as quickly as he could, levering in a fresh round after each pull of the trigger.

Recognizing the arrival of his partners, Hank stomped on the boards beneath his feet to send an echoing thump through the interior of the wagon. The rear door swung open on metal hinges, sending a metallic shriek through the air that was quickly followed by a volley of gunfire.

"Dear Lord!" the driver wailed as he wrapped both arms around his head and dropped down.

Since the driver didn't have a gun, Hank

let him cower. Ever since they'd drawn close enough to see the ranch's front gate, Hank had kept the pistol in his hand covered by the jacket on his lap. Now he swept the jacket aside while raising the pistol and using his free hand to draw another gun from the collection strapped to his waist. He stood up in the driver's seat, smiling down at the riflemen like the Grim Reaper himself while pulling the triggers of his .44 and .45.

The rifleman who'd done most of the talking thus far had been looking toward the barn when Hank's first round hit him. Hot lead dug into his chest through his back, followed by another round that punched through his heart. He hit the ground in a heap, never to move again.

Jake and Eli thundered around the barn, firing up at its roof. The man posted there fired back, but was unable to hit either of the moving targets before being clipped in one leg. The shot wasn't a killing blow, but it caused the man to fall and roll off the roof to land heavily on the ground. He squirmed and moaned in pain, but wasn't about to pose an immediate threat.

Hank continued to fire at Matt and a few of the men closer to the wagon. Now that the initial surprise had hit them like a punch to the stomach, the riflemen scattered and filled the air with even more rounds. Hank stood tall atop the wagon until bullets started to spark against the iron plates near his legs. Dropping down to get a real close look at the trembling mass of driver huddled against the footboard, he said, "Best stay put or you might get hurt."

The driver didn't know what to make of the outlaw's jovial tone and seemed close to breaking down altogether when Hank began laughing like a demon that had just found the hottest coals on which to dance. As Cody fired at the men who'd approached the rear of the wagon, the entire iron structure shook.

"Got 'em both!" Cody shouted.

"Good," Hank replied. "Now let's put the rest of these fools down while they're still in a cross fire!"

Cody's and Hank's guns formed a chorus of destruction aimed at the riflemen who'd stepped up to greet the wagon. Gripping a pistol in each hand didn't do much for Hank's marksmanship, but it plastered a wicked smile on his face. One of the riflemen fell to a bullet that grazed his left side, but not until more ranch hands showed up to aid in the growing battle.

"Where did *they* come from?" Jake

shouted over the roar of his Smith & Wesson.

Eli and the gang leader had steered their horses around the barn after announcing their appearance. He'd seen a few men falling back toward the barn, but more seemed to appear with every passing second. "They must have been hiding inside," he said. "Probably waiting to see if something like this would happen."

Unaffected by the accusatory tone in Eli's voice, Jake said, "Or guarding enough money to fill them strongboxes. Let's find another way in!"

"I'll draw some of them out so you can get inside. Just try to do more sneaking than shooting."

"Too late for that," Jake replied through the smirk he'd been wearing ever since things at the ranch had truly heated up.

Eli gripped a .38 in one hand and his reins in the other. As more gunshots raged around him, his world took on a dullness that made him feel as if his ears had been stuffed with cotton and his joints rusted all the way through. The moment he rode around to the front of the barn, he was confronted by men who couldn't have looked more panicked if they'd been pitched off the side of a cliff. Among those faces, Eli's was serene.

His goal was within his reach. Not in sight just yet, but close enough.

Just then, the barn doors swung open and men charged outside. The men who fanned out to form a firing line weren't like the ones that swarmed around the wagon. They held their ground like soldiers and took carefully aimed shots while everyone else pulled their triggers to make a lot of noise and fill the air with gritty smoke. One man in particular stood taller than the rest. That wasn't due to his stature, which was average among any grown men's company, but because he didn't recoil amid the gunshots or even bend at the knees to present a smaller target to the outlaw gang. Instead, he kept his right arm straight in front of him and sighted along the long barrel of an Army-model Colt. When the gun went off, his arm bent at the elbow to absorb the kick before straightening again for his next shot.

Eli was barely able to garner a quick look into the barn, but saw it had mostly emptied out. Since he didn't intend to go inside, he pointed his horse's nose toward the wagon and tapped his heels against her sides. The gunshot that brought his horse down didn't distinguish itself from the others rolling through the air. He felt the impact roll through the horse's flesh to send ripples beneath his right leg. Despite not having ridden the animal for long, Eli had always had a soft spot where anything on four legs was concerned. As for animals of the two-legged variety, he believed most of them got what they deserved.

The horse reared up and let out a pained whinny. Eli let go of his reins and pushed away before he was thrown. Although he wasn't exactly the picture of grace, he managed to get clear of the horse before she came down, crumpled, and flopped onto her side. If not for the shots still hissing through the air around him, Eli would have examined the horse's wound. Instead, he drew his second .38 to replace the one he'd dropped during the fall and fired before one of the closest riflemen could blow his head off. All he saw was a bulky figure to his left with a gun in its hands. Having propped himself up onto one knee, Eli fired with the .38. He missed, but the shot convinced the rifleman to dive away before pulling his trigger. In response to the gunshots, and possibly cries from Eli's wounded horse, the wagon's team had become wildly anxious. Eli had turned to see if Hank was in a spot to keep them under control when he came face-to-face with a man coated in blood and wrapped in a long, dark coat.

Some of the blood on Matt's face might have come from another man's veins, but a good deal of it had spilled from a wide gash in his cheek. The edges of the wound were blackened and skin was peeled back to form a long, messy groove. It wasn't a serious gash, but would leave a nasty scar after the stitches had been removed. All of those thoughts drifted through Eli's mind as he stared down the barrel of Matt's rifle.

Eli's legs ached after absorbing the impact of his topple from the saddle. Matt lashed out with one foot to sweep Eli's bent leg out from under him, sending him back until the ground thumped against his backside and cool dirt scraped against the palm of one hand. When Eli brought his gun hand up in a reflexive motion toward Matt, he was assaulted by a barrage of warnings from the rifleman. Eli's head was still too clouded for him to make out what was being said, but Matt's intentions were easy enough to read within the glare etched into his features.

Whatever Matt was saying, Eli was certain he'd heard it before.

Stop.

Don't move.

You're a dead man.

Surely, it had to be something along those

lines. Matt wasn't the first man to say that sort of thing to him, but it remained to be seen if he would be the last. As Eli looked up and studied the other man's eyes, he gauged whether Matt had what it took to pull his trigger. When he arrived at his answer, he let out part of a relieved breath. Before the tail end of that exhale could escape his lungs, Matt was knocked to one side by a bullet that clipped the top of his shoulder to rip a portion of his coat a few inches away from its collar. There wasn't a lot of blood, but the impact of the bullet was enough to draw Matt's attention away from where it should have been.

Eli reacted out of nothing but pure reflex. His gun was still in hand and he brought it up. A blind man could have pulled that trigger and blasted a tunnel through Matt's skull. Just thinking about it made his finger itch. . . .

"Stop right there, son," demanded a stern voice from behind and above Eli. When Eli's .38 didn't waver, he heard another sound that was as familiar as the rustle of trees pushed by the winds behind his childhood home. The metallic click of a gun's hammer being drawn back rattled through the air and was followed by the stern voice from before. "You made the right choice by hesitating," it said. "Don't muck it up now."

Gritting his teeth, Eli sighed, "Son of a —" and was cut short by a clubbing blow delivered to a spot behind his right ear.

CHAPTER 5

Eli's dreams were filled with blazing hot fire emanating from the interior of his head and radiating all the way down to the aching joints of his toes. Every so often, he would stir. His feet scraped against a hard, smooth surface, and his hands brushed against something that made them itch. It hurt when he tried to breathe, so he lay still and allowed himself to drift away again.

He awoke to the grating sound of metal scraping against metal. When Eli tried to respond to those noises, he swore he could hear the inner sound of bone scraping against bone. Some of that could have been his body protesting against the commands it was being given, but another part of the rustling that filled his ears was his own breath clawing its way out from his lungs to grab on to a raw spot at the back of his throat, where it hung as if purposely daring him to set it loose.

Unlike the other times he'd been challenged while shifting his weight, Eli responded by defiantly pushing the breath out of him amid half of a grumbled curse. That became a cough, which grew into a hacking seizure, which racked his entire body as painfully as a set of fists beating him senseless.

"Such language," came a voice from not too far away.

Eli couldn't quite place where the speaker was, but he knew she was too far away to get to him. Opening his eyes to find her was a new kind of torture since they'd been sealed shut by a bloody crust connecting lids to his face. Having already committed himself this far already, he didn't see a reason to stop now, so Eli forced his eyes open as far as he could.

His surroundings were mercifully drab. The little bit of light that invaded his senses did so through small windows set too high up in the wall for him to catch any direct rays from the sun. Walls the color of cloudy skies surrounded him, and his foot scraped noisily against a floor covered with layers of grit as he pulled in a leg that had been dangling over the side of a rickety cot. Every sign pointed to him being in a jail cell. There were no chains on his wrists or ankles as far as he could tell, however, which was a good sign.

"You must be starving," the female voice said.

"No," Eli said, despite the fact that her words had sparked thoughts of food that made hunger claw in his belly even worse. "Where am I?"

"Seedley."

"Who are you?"

She didn't respond right away, so Eli tried a little harder to clear his vision enough to put a face to the voice. Through sheer force of will and a few more deep breaths, he was able to make out most of what was in front of him. He focused on the shape of a slight figure standing about three paces away. She wore a simple dress that was a color similar to the gray walls around him. White ruffles sprouted from her wrists and neckline, but nothing as fancy as what a woman might wear to church. Her face was rounded in the cheeks, and her nose was just a little on the bulbous side. Even with the haze still lurking in his skull, Eli could see the kindness in her large brown eyes.

"I'm Lyssa. Are you Eli Barlow?"

Hearing his full name spoken by a stranger rarely led to anything pleasant, although any excuse to hear her voice couldn't be all that bad. "Where'd you hear that name?" he scowled.

"Sheriff Saunders mentioned it."

"Sheriff?"

"That's right," she replied with a nod. "He asked me to keep an eye on you while you rested. You might not want to try and move."

If Eli was what others might consider to be a rational, even-tempered man, he would have heeded that advice, but he was nothing close to rational by most regular folks' definitions. After all, most would rather work hard to squirrel their money away instead of working even harder to find where someone else's money was secreted so he could take it from them. It was just such a defiance in Eli's soul more than anything else that brought him to an upright position while every one of his aching bones screamed at him to stay down.

"You're still healing up," Lyssa said. "Perhaps you should just —"

"Don't tell me what to do!" Eli snapped. "I'll sit up if I want and go where I please!"

"Well . . . you can sit up, I suppose. As for the rest . . ."

Following her meandering line of sight, Eli got a better look at his surroundings. They were cramped, dirty, stank of stale sweat and dirty chamber pots, and were sealed off by a wall of iron bars between him and Lyssa.

"So I am in jail."

"You robbed a stagecoach and were part of a gang that killed half a dozen men," Lyssa replied. "Where else did you expect to be?"

Eli had an answer to that, but didn't think it was appropriate to say to someone like her. "Where's Jake?"

"Who?"

"He should have been brought in with me! Or what about Hank?" When he didn't get anything but a perplexed look from her, Eli squinted through the storm behind his eyes and asked, "Cody?"

"I don't know who those men are."

"Am I the only man in this jail?"

"No. There's Mr. Gleason in the next cell. He fired at a fellow who was juggling sticks at the theater the other night."

Something heavy rattled farther down the hall on the other side of the bars. Eli had to rub the back of his head to make sure something hadn't just come loose inside his skull. "How long have I been here?"

"Three days," replied a voice that was definitely not Lyssa's. It had come from a man who now stepped into view as Lyssa took a step back.

"You've had me locked up in this cage for three days?" Eli asked.

Blinking as if Eli had questioned which way he should look to find the sky, the man replied, "You robbed a stagecoach and —"

"Yeah, yeah. Where would I expect myself to be?"

The man was one of the fellows who'd emerged from the barn during the last moments of the gunfight at the Lazy V Ranch. Now that he wasn't brandishing a weapon and leading a group of men to gun him down, Eli was able to take a moment to get a better look at him. The Army-model Colt still hung at his side and a full beard still covered most of his face. He wore a simple denim shirt with sleeves rolled up to expose thickly muscled forearms. The hat he'd worn that other night was missing, exposing an unruly mop of hair that burst from his scalp at various odd angles. Propping his hands upon his hips, he studied Eli with a pair of clear brown eyes before shifting them over to Lyssa.

"Go ahead and hand that food through," the man said.

"I don't think he wants it, Sheriff," she replied.

"Leave it anyway. He's just posturing."

A knot formed in Eli's stomach that felt

more like a fist gripping him from within. It formed partly from hunger and partly from the fact that the lawman had seen through his snarling facade with such ease. Lyssa eased the tray of food she'd been holding through a narrow gap at the bottom of the bars. The leading edge of the tray scraped against the crude opening, but there was no danger of the hard pile of oatmeal and stale biscuit getting scraped off. If left there long enough, the food could very well have hardened into something more durable than the walls of Eli's cell. She looked up at him, shrugged apologetically, and walked away.

The lawman watched her leave before turning to watch Eli even harder. "She's a good girl."

"So?" Eli grunted.

"So you should treat her as such. She's not the one who broke the law or put you behind these bars."

Eli looked at the food, wanting it even though the meal looked only slightly more appetizing than the filthy mattress beneath him. Rather than give the lawman the satisfaction of seeing him crawl for the scraps he'd been given, Eli pulled himself to his feet and paced to the other side of his cell. It took just under two steps to get there.

"I'm Sheriff Vernon Saunders."

"That supposed to mean anything to me?"

"It does if you have any intention of getting out of that cage." When Eli closed his mouth and glared viciously at him, Saunders nodded and said, "I thought that might get your attention."

"Where's the other men who were at that ranch?"

"You mean your gang or the ones that were killed? The whereabouts of the latter group is six feet beneath the soil just outside town. They were good men, far as I know. Better than the ones that put them under, that's for certain."

"Far as you know," Eli scoffed.

"But you probably weren't asking about them, were you? You want to know where to find Jacob Welles, or them other two. What were their names?"

Fixing his eyes on Saunders, Eli said, "Never caught their names."

"Course you didn't. Not that I expected to get much out of you. What little I've heard says you're a real hard case, Mr. Barlow." As if he were digging the sharp end of a stick into an open wound, he added, "Eli Barlow formerly of Gracen, Georgia. Georgia is a real fine place. The air smells sweet and the ladies have a real nice way of talking. Can't say as I've ever heard of

Gracen, though."

Eli kept his mouth shut while making his way slowly to the front of the cell.

"Must be nice," Saunders said. "Can't see many places in Georgia being too bad."

Once he was close enough, Eli stooped down and picked up the tray. "Why don't you go there, then? Or would you rather I tell you somewhere else you can go as well as what you can do once you get there?"

"Something tells me I know what suggestion you're about to make. If it's what I think it is, you'll be going there long before I do. See," Saunders said while reaching out to place his left hand flat against one of the bars, "you're set to hang in a few days."

"Suppose I slept through my trial?"

"No need for a trial. You're a member of the Welles Gang. Jake, you, and those others have killed folks in three other counties apart from this one. Maybe more. Everyone knows what happened over at the Lazy V, and there's no reason why one of the men responsible for all that bloodshed shouldn't swing for it at the nearest opportunity. The only guff I've been catching since you've been here is why I didn't roust you out of bed and string you up already."

"Why is that, Sheriff?"

Saunders didn't hesitate before saying,

"Because I'm a man who believes in doing things properly no matter what anyone wants."

"So you want to string me up, but properly."

"Of course I do. It's my job. I knew a few of those men that were killed at the Lazy V. Like I told you already, they were good men."

"You said as far as you knew, they were good."

In a tone that was colder than the stone walls surrounding him on three sides, Saunders snapped, "Better than you or anyone else who'd ride with the likes of Jacob Welles. And that's a fact."

Eli thought of a few comments he could make, if only to get the sheriff's goat. He choked them back and carried his tray to the cot, where he sat down upon the threadbare mattress. "Suppose you got me there."

The sheriff allowed his prisoner to take a few bites of biscuit, which sounded like sandstone being ground by a mortar and pestle. When Eli began using the chunk of hardened biscuit to scoop up some oatmeal, Saunders asked, "You still want to know where Jake and the others are?"

"Unless you knocked them in the head harder than you did me, I'd say they're not in this jailhouse."

"You got that right."

Eli looked up with a clump of oatmeal clinging to his chin as if it had been glued there. "They dead?"

"Not as far as I know."

"Then they got away. Good for them."

"They did get away. In fact," Saunders added while dragging a chair from where it had been placed down the hall so he could sit directly in front of Eli's cell, "they were all too happy to ride away after I cleaned your clock. I expected more of a fight once one of their own fell. Gangs tend to get nasty when it becomes clear they're on the losing end of a fight. Sometimes they turn into savage beasts to make sure they pull their partners out of the fire. Sometimes they become crazed rats who chew on anything they can find just to get out of a losing situation. You want to know which it was in Jacob's case?"

Eli looked up, more out of confusion from hearing someone refer to Jake in such a formal manner. That didn't last long and he quickly got back to his meal. "It's your story, Sheriff."

"It was neither."

"That's real interesting,"

At first glance, it might have seemed that

the lawman was nothing more than a dramatic storyteller trying to draw out a loaded moment. When Eli looked up from his food, however, he saw only a man wincing uncomfortably as he tried to get situated on his chair. The oatmeal was warm and had a sprinkling of cinnamon in it, so Eli shifted his attention back to that.

"That gang of yours rode away as soon as they had the chance," Saunders said after a few more grunts. "Didn't try to rescue you or anything."

"Still time for that."

"Haven't heard a peep from them in days. If there was gonna be something along the lines of busting you out of here, I wager we would've gotten a shot fired at us or even spotted one of them scouting out the town. Near as I can figure, nobody even tried to see where we took you once you were sprawled out and sleeping off your headache."

"You're the one who gave it to me," Eli pointed out. "Or are you about to blame Jake for that too?"

"No. That was me." He shifted in his chair and crossed one leg over the other. It wasn't an easy affair and required him to grab his shin, drag it into place, and hold it there. "Come to think of it, I just heard tell that one of your outlaw friends was spotted in Cheyenne. That's only a day or two ride from here."

"Is that so?" Eli asked with mock interest.

"It is indeed. The one-eyed fella. Hank something or other, I believe."

That struck Eli as slightly more interesting than his oatmeal, and the sheriff picked right up on it. "Got word about it over the wire just this morning," Saunders continued. "Near as I can figure, after all the running and hiding Jake must have been doing after leaving you behind, they probably rode straight on to Cheyenne."

"You do a lot of figuring."

"Most of the time, that's all I need to do around here. Apart from the occasional drunk or dispute between neighbors, this is a pretty sleepy town. That changed last week, though, and things seem to be getting more interesting by the hour. Probably even more so in Cheyenne, though. Your friends have anything planned out there?"

Jake had always talked about going to Cheyenne. Hank liked the idea as well and they both would go on endlessly some nights about how the whole town was like one big bank vault that didn't have a lock. What with the gamblers, cowboys, and thieves in that town, there would always be money ripe for the plucking for any man who had the sand to take it. At least, that's what Jake and Hank always said.

As all of this went through his mind, Eli kept quiet. Even so, Saunders grinned as he watched his prisoner. Perhaps he picked up on the way Eli held on to his tin tray as if he were about to crumple it into a ball like so much paper.

"You enjoying that meal?" the sheriff asked.

"Well enough."

"Good, because it'll be tougher to swallow once your neck is stretched at the end of a noose." Saunders grunted while getting up from his chair and hiking up his pants.

CHAPTER 6

That night, when Eli tried to sleep, something apart from the overcooked oatmeal ate at his innards. While that meal sat in his belly like a lump of coal, his chest constricted around his heart as if purposely trying to grind it to a halt. Taking deep breaths didn't help. Neither did rolling over and trying to get some sleep, which only gave him more time to quietly ponder what the sheriff had said.

Eli wasn't stupid. He knew well enough that Saunders could be feeding him a line of manure just to turn him against Jake and the others. Obviously the outlaws had gotten away despite the reinforcements that had been hiding in that barn on the Lazy V. That must have eaten away at the lawman something awful. His best hope for finding the remaining gang members would be in forcing or tricking the one who was in custody to point him in the right direction.

To do that, Saunders would need to convince Eli that turning traitor was a good idea. If this was indeed the sheriff's strategy, he was going to be in for a rude awakening. Eli was a lot of things, but a traitor wasn't one of them. He forced a smirk onto his face, rolled over, and sent a chorus of creaks through the air hanging within the cell.

Eli sifted through his recent memories involving Jake and Hank. It didn't do any good to think about Cody, since that one had never said anything worth remembering. The other two were a different story. Jake did plenty of talking about everything ranging from jobs he'd always wanted to do to the lawmen he'd put into the ground. A common thread was that the gang was at the top of his list no matter what. Hank talked less, but that gave his words a bit more weight. On the other hand, many of those words were spiteful and angry, which meant they oftentimes faded into the background like the constant clatter of train wheels against a track.

No matter how much talk Eli might have either written off as boasting or simply didn't believe, he'd always been confident that the rest of the gang would back him up if it was necessary. The fact that they'd ridden off when he needed them stuck in his craw. So on that end, the sheriff had done his job by sowing his disruptive seeds very nicely. That grated on him even more.

A scant amount of moonlight drifted in through the narrow window near the top of Eli's cell as well as through the windows of the other cells in the jailhouse. All that did was allow Eli to make out a few blocky shapes in the darkness, while his ears greedily hunted for any sound they could find. When the door to the jailhouse rattled slightly, his hand went reflexively to his side but found only the bottom edge of his rumpled shirt, which had been pulled loose from the waistband of his jeans. Wherever his guns were, they wouldn't help him now.

The door was unlocked, opened, and shut again. Light footsteps shuffled across the floor to echo throughout the small building. Even if Saunders was lying to him for some reason in regards to the whereabouts of the rest of the gang, Jake, Hank, or Cody sure weren't in that jailhouse with him. Eli felt like a single pebble rattling inside a dry bathtub, and now that he heard someone coming in and making their way toward his cell in the dark, he felt even more isolated. Since he didn't have a firearm or blade, he balled up his fist and tensed his muscles in preparation for a leap that would take him off the cot and to the floor near the bars in the space of a few seconds.

The steps drew closer. Soon they were accompanied by a subtle sigh that told Eli it wasn't the sheriff sneaking in to get a look at him. A ghostly figure moved down the hall on the other side of the bars, drifting to a stop before shrinking down to something half its original size. Now Eli considered the possibility that he could be dreaming. When the ghost reached milky white hands into his cell, he decided to make his move. Dream or not, Eli Barlow wasn't about to be picked apart like a rat trapped in a hat box.

As soon as he landed from his jump, his feet scraped against the loose dirt and bits of gravel on the floor. If he hadn't been in such a rush, Eli might have been able to steady himself with a minimum of effort. As it was, he flailed for a second and then toppled onto his side. Twisting partly before he hit, Eli caught himself using one arm against the cot and then pushed away to drop onto the floor. The ghost near the bars pulled in a quick breath and started to retract its hands, but Eli scrambled forward to grab one of its wrists. He pulled it toward him until he heard something very solid pound against the cell door. It wasn't a ghost after all. In fact, he was now close enough to smell the visitor's skin, which told him exactly whom he was dealing with.

"It's me, Eli. Lyssa!" she said to give him one last bit of confirmation that he didn't need. "I brought you some more food."

"Yeah," he grunted while struggling to align his body in a more natural pose without letting go of her arm. "And now you brought me the keys. Very kind of you."

She struggled against him, but wasn't strong enough to pull herself loose. The keys that had been rattling in the dark still jangled noisily in the air well away from the bars. When he squinted and concentrated, Eli could tell she was holding them in her other hand and extending them as far away from him as possible. "What are you doing?" she asked through the strained muscles of her neck, chest, and stomach, which all fought to stretch away from him.

"Trying to get out! What . . . were you . . . doing?" Eli asked while sticking his arm between the bars and reaching for the keys. He could feel her taut body struggling for freedom, and now that he was close enough, he could also hear the sobs that were being pressed down by a quickening series of panting breaths.

A rush of thoughts flew through Eli's

mind. Most of them let him know just how proud Hank and Jake would have been to watch him overpower this woman, take her keys, and force his way out of the jailhouse. And then, like a bunch of quail that had been discovered by an overzealous dog, his fighting instinct flew from him. Eli was left feeling empty and tired when he let go of Lyssa's wrist and slumped back from the bars.

His eyes had adjusted to the shadows long ago, but he still could barely see the outline of her head and shoulders when she scooted back to noisily bump against the opposite wall. She sat curled up in the narrow hallway, which was the only corridor running the length of the building past all four of its cells. Both of them were breathing heavily and neither seemed anxious to move.

"Why . . . why did you attack me?" she asked.

"Why were you sneaking in here like that?"

"I wasn't sneaking!"

"Then where's your lantern? Maybe even a candle."

She took a deep breath and let it out in a sigh. "I've been checking in on you every night since you were brought here. You needed your rest, so I didn't want to wake you with the light of a lantern." Her voice became weary as she added, "I don't need a lantern anyhow. I imagine I could walk up and down this hall, sweeping out each cell with my eyes closed."

"Yeah," Eli chuckled. "Me too. You already knew I was up and around, so what brought you here tonight?"

"Thought you might be hungry."

As if to purposely make Eli feel even worse, the smell of warm bread drifted to his nose. "Not oatmeal?"

"I figured you'd want something better."

"I would," he told her. The words drifted through the air like bits of dust swirling near the top of a loft.

She moved again, collecting herself at first and then gathering some items that were scattered on the floor. "It was just some bread and cheese. It's dirty now. Take it or leave it."

"Take it."

Once she had the tray in hand, she stood up and looked down at him. Her voice was shaky but stern when she said, "Move back to your cot."

He did and even went so far as to pull his legs up and lean against a wall. As Lyssa approached the bars again, she kept her eyes on him. Her face and suspicious frown became visible as if she were appearing to him in a dream. What he saw was pieced together from the few details he could make out in the dim moonlight along with what he'd committed to memory. She eased a tray through the opening near the floor, stepped back, and stood in front of his cell.

"May I have a taste?" he asked.

"I suppose."

Eli eased off the cot and walked slowly toward the bars. When he got there, he felt like a dog that was humbly approaching its master after being caught with its nose in the cupboard. Not liking that one bit, he lifted his chin and looked directly at her while picking up the tray like a man. The food smelled good and he could feel warmth coming off the bread when he grabbed it and brought it to his mouth. While still chewing on that, he found a little hunk of cheese and stuffed it in so both snacks could blend into one.

"It's good," he told her. "Thanks."

"You're welcome."

"So, you just thought I'd be hungry?"

"Well . . . weren't you?"

Because of the thick shadows in the jail, he couldn't see much by way of detail on her face and was fairly certain she couldn't see much of his. Even so, they stared as if studying each other under the glaring rays of a noonday sun. "Yes," he replied. "I was. Just seems strange that you'd take such an interest. Especially seeing as what I done."

"You may be hanged in a few days. That's punishment enough. Any other judgment you get before or after that won't be done by me."

"So . . . I might as well have a full stomach before I get dipped into the hellfire?"

Although she barely moved, a quiet giggle drifted through the jail before it was quickly stifled. "Something like that," she said. "Although I wouldn't have put it in such drastic terms."

"A friend of mine used to say that."

"One of those killers who got away?"

"No," Eli replied with a faraway tone in his voice. "Not one of them. A real friend."

He heard a slight rustle as he ate some more of his snack. It came from Lyssa as she eased herself down to sit with her back against the wall directly in front of his cell. That only put her about two paces from the bars, but she might as well have been a mile away.

"So, does the sheriff know you're here?" he asked.

"Of course he does. You think I have my own key to the jailhouse?"

"Are you armed?"

"No."

"Then you took an awful risk coming in here just to deliver food. What if I'd gotten the drop on you?"

"You did get the drop on me," she reminded him.

"No, I mean what if . . ." Although he knew where that thought was headed, Eli didn't want to make it a real thing by giving it words and a voice. Instead, he cleaned it up by asking, "What if things had turned out worse?"

"One of the sheriff's men is right outside," she said. "All I needed to do was scream or make any other sort of noise to attract his attention and he would have come in here to . . ." Apparently, she didn't like where her thoughts were headed either and completed her statement with "I would have been fine."

Eli took a moment to think back to their brief struggle over the keys. It had seemed like a chaotic mess of arms, bars, and straining muscles, but he had to admit it hadn't been enough to draw much attention. He'd wanted to keep as quiet as possible and she had refrained from doing much more than pulling in her next breath. "Why didn't you scream?" he asked.

"You sure ask a lot of questions. Most

men would be grateful for something to eat apart from that horrible oatmeal we serve everyone else."

"I'm curious. Also, a man tends to think about a lot of things when he's locked up inside a box."

She scooted a little closer, perhaps to get a better look at him or maybe to allow him to get a better look at her. Lyssa's face was calm. Despite everything that had happened, she appeared as if she was simply serving him a late-night snack. "All right, then. I'll answer your question if you answer mine. Agreed?"

"Depends on what the question is."

Unafraid of venturing out first, she asked, "Why did you attack me?"

"I wouldn't call that much of an attack. It was more of a surprise with a sharp twist."

She let out an uneasy laugh. "If that's not an attack, I'd hate to see what you would have done to fit the bill."

Eli could tell she was joking, which meant she truly didn't know how much worse it could have been. Jake bragged about the things he'd done to punish a deputy in Amarillo who'd strayed too close to the bars when he'd been making his rounds. Eli wasn't the sort to visit that kind of torture upon someone, but he could have made things a whole lot more uncomfortable without much effort. Rather than get into all of that, he asked, "Did I hurt you?"

She shifted her weight and, from what he could see in the shadows, rubbed her wrists one at a time. "A little."

"Sorry about that."

"Instead of apologizing, why don't you answer my question?"

"You seriously need an answer?"

"Yes!" she exclaimed, and then shot a quick glance toward the front door of the jailhouse. Suddenly she seemed more like a girl who'd snuck into a boy's room instead of someone talking to a wanted outlaw.

"I need to get out of here," he said. "Or have you already forgotten I'm to be hanged soon?"

"Guess I just wasn't expecting something like that from you."

"If you bring food to prisoners on a regular basis, you should be expecting that or worse."

"Well, I don't really bring food in like this to other prisoners. As far as I know, the sheriff doesn't get many prisoners anyway. Certainly not many that are set to be hanged." Even in the dark, Eli could tell she winced when saying that. There was a leaden pause, followed by a meek "I'm sorry to talk about it like that."

"It's all right. So I'm a special case?"

Lyssa must have been hanging her head low, because he couldn't see any part of her face when she said, "That's more than the question we agreed upon."

"I suppose it is. You still owe me one, though."

"Was that all of the answer I'm to get? You attacked me because you needed to get out? I don't think that's all there is."

"It was instinct," he said with a sigh. "I woke up in this cell. My head feels like it was split in two and nailed back together. Your sheriff won't let me forget about the noose with my name on it. I hear someone come in carrying keys. I saw a chance to grab them and get out. I took it. When I saw you, though, I . . . I just couldn't get myself to . . ."

"I know," she whispered while standing up and dusting herself off. "That's why I didn't scream."

CHAPTER 7

A few more days passed.

The ache in Eli's head became a distant thump at the back of his mind. It wasn't the first time he'd taken knocks to the head, which was probably why each new one hurt more and lingered longer than the last. Then there were the headaches that came and went for no reason. Those made everything above his neck feel as if it had been dipped into melted lead. Those could have come from another source that had been with him for a few years and wouldn't go away any time soon. Whether these aches were the same as the ones that caused him to rot from the inside out or they were just lumps from the sheriff's revolver, all he knew was that they got worse the more he tried to make them feel better.

Lyssa brought him his meals twice a day and sat to talk to him while he ate. For the most part, they discussed various kinds of nonsense. Since none of the discussions drifted in the vicinity of past crimes or the men who'd ridden with him, he welcomed them. Spending time on the trail with the likes of Jake and Hank meant Eli had gotten his fill of gruesome boasts and violent plans. He did his share of stealing because it was a way to put food on his plate. Bragging about it was akin to a blacksmith strutting around because he'd shoed another horse. He was a blacksmith. What else was he supposed to do with his time?

When he heard the jailhouse door open late one afternoon, he didn't get his hopes up. Breakfast had already been served and it was too early for supper. That narrowed down the possibilities where his visitor was concerned. The heavier crunch of boots against a dirty floor confirmed his suspicions enough for him to wager an educated guess before anyone stepped into his line of sight.

"Hello, Sheriff," Eli grunted.

Sure enough, Saunders approached the bars with his thumbs hooked over the top of his gun belt. "Hello, yourself. Feeling any better?"

"Fine and dandy."

"Good to hear."

"Why? Because I don't have many days left and I should enjoy them while I'm still breathing?"

The lawman chuckled. "Them threats are wearin' thin, are they?"

"Something like that."

"So I'll stop tossing 'em at you. How's that?"

Eli sat up. "It's a good start. It'd make my day even brighter if you opened that door and stepped aside."

"Sorry, Eli. That ain't about to happen."

"I preferred it when you called me Mr. Barlow."

"And I preferred it when I was in my bed this mornin' with my boots off and my wife in my arms. We can't always live in the sweet spot, you know."

"Yeah. I know. What brings you here?"

It always seemed as if Saunders plucked his chair from nowhere whenever he reached over to grab it. Like every other time he'd gone through the routine, he set the chair down directly in front of the cell and then lowered himself onto it with half a wheeze. "Well, since you asked, I'm here to make you an offer."

"Unless it's got to do with getting me out of here, I'm not interested."

"Come to think of it, that's exactly what's involved."

Eli reflexively scooted to perch upon the

edge of the cot like a bird that was about to take flight. “Yeah?”

“Yeah.”

In the short time he’d known the lawman, there were already a few habits that had cropped up that grated on Eli’s nerves. One was the sheriff’s penchant for repeating certain phrases when he spoke. Another was his affinity for long pauses before getting down to whatever it was he wanted to say. Normally, Eli was content to let the sheriff dawdle as much as he liked. This time, however, wasn’t so easy. “Spit it out, already,” Eli snapped.

“Hank was spotted in Cheyenne again. This time, lurking outside a bank.”

No matter what Eli thought of Hank as a person, he had to respect him for the job he did. Hank prided himself on being able to sneak in and out of just about anywhere without raising an eyebrow and had earned every bit of that pride. If he’d been spotted and word had spread, Hank was either slipping or . . .

“You’re lying,” Eli said.

“You sure about that?”

“Whether you are or aren’t, what do you want me to do about it?”

“Help me track down Jake and the rest of his gang,” Saunders replied.

"You're the one with all the hints and sightings coming to you from whatever sources you're supposed to have. What do you need my help for?"

The sheriff adjusted his position in the chair so he was perched on it in a fashion similar to Eli's on the edge of his cot. "Because," he said, "that one-eyed fella was spotted after some of those men at the Lazy V followed him away from the ranch. They picked up the Welles Gang's trail several times between here and Cheyenne. Caught sight of one man here and there, but it wasn't more than a fleeting glimpse before those killers disappeared like smoke in the wind. I think they're still there, even if those men who sent word to me gave up the hunt."

That was more like it. The relief Eli felt wasn't on account of his former partners being out and about, but because the lawmen on Jake's tail had already lost him. Then a familiar suspicious jab took some of the wind from Eli's sails. "Why would you tell me all of this?" he asked.

"Because, if we're to work together, I thought we should start off on the right foot. All cards on the table and such."

Eli laughed to himself and shook his head. "Only men who rarely play poker are such advocates of showing your cards."

"You got me there."

"I don't trust men who don't gamble."

"Well, I'm taking the mother lode of all gambles right now," Saunders told him. "There are men in this town who've been hounding me to not only string you up, but make a show of it. If they knew I was having a civilized conversation with you like this, they might reconsider my appointment as sheriff."

"Aw, now, that would be a crying shame."

Saunders was losing his patience, but did so with quiet reserve. He stood up with a grunt, removed the hat from his head, and ran his hand through hair that seemed incapable of being anything but tangled. Placing the hat on his head and putting it perfectly in line helped him settle his anxiety somewhat. "If you'd rather I leave you to rot, just say the word and I'll leave. Them local men I mentioned before would be all too happy to string you up and cheer when your feet start to kick."

Although Eli jumped up in a burst that sent a clatter through the jailhouse as his cot was knocked against the wall, Sheriff Saunders didn't flinch. "You can parade all the folks you want in front of me who want to see me dead," Eli roared. "And you can mention that noose all you want, because it don't matter! I'm dead anyways, so I'd rather not be remembered as a man who stabbed his friends in the back before he was put down like a dog."

"You're no dog, Eli."

"Whatever you want to call it, the story ends the same way."

"Doesn't have to."

No matter how much Eli railed within that cell, Saunders stood his ground and calmly watched. Panting from the effort it had taken to shove his cot back, stomp his feet, and holler at the top of his lungs, Eli asked, "Why stand in the way of those men who want to hang me? In fact, why the hell haven't you strung me up yet?"

"Because," Saunders replied as if he was stating the world's plainest fact, "you're not a killer."

"You were at the Lazy V. You saw us at work."

"I was there and yes, I was watching as best I could from inside that dusty old barn. The man who commissioned that iron wagon to be built insisted on all the extra gun hands he could muster to be there to greet you, but I insisted on watching to see what developed before charging out with guns blazing. That way, I could get a look at who I was dealing with before sending them to meet their maker. I saw Jacob Welles live up to every unflattering word that's ever been written about him. Not a lot's known about that one-eyed fellow, but I learned more than enough to shoot him on sight if he ever got too close. That one with the big head, Cody, I believe his name was, he just seems to be wild and stupid. Even so, he fired at anyone the other two told him to. That makes him dangerous. You, on the other hand, just wanted to get at that money."

"How do you know what I wanted?"

"Because I make my living off of being able to read a man based on what he does, how he carries himself, even how he holds a gun in his hand. Every one of those things will tell you plenty if you're willing to look. I couldn't see everything from that barn, but I did see you riding like a man on a mission. Surprised the living daylights out of me and everyone else at that ranch. Even though we were all expecting some kind of foolish charge, you still got close enough to give everyone a fright. Well done."

Eli had felt a wide range of emotions in a short span of time. They'd ranged from boredom, aggravation, and rage. Now he felt genuinely confused.

Picking up on that like he seemed to pick up on everything else, Saunders said, "Even if that barn had been a mile away, I could've seen the joy written across your face when you rode in to scatter all of them guards. You and Jacob were in your element, that's for certain. One big difference being that Welles wanted to spill blood and you were after something different."

"So you can read a man's mind?" Eli grunted. "See what's on his soul?"

"Not hardly."

"Then how do you know what I was thinking?"

"If you were just out for a ride, you wouldn't have been anywhere near that ranch. You're a member of a gang that don't usually have many members. Do you know how many other men rode with Jacob Welles at any given time over the last seven years?"

"Three or four," Eli said.

"That's right, so you must have some talent as well as a propensity for breaking the law."

"I've reached my limit," Eli sighed as he turned his back to the bars and walked toward the back of the cell until he could place both hands flat upon a wall. "I'm sick of hearing you talk."

"See now, this is where you being in there

comes in real handy," Saunders said while banging his knuckles against the front of Eli's cell. "I get to talk all I want and you'll listen. Mostly, I want you to hear the rest of what I have to say because it goes straight back to the offer I made earlier. You know . . . the one where you get to avoid being hanged?"

Eli sighed heavily, knowing there wasn't anything he could say or do to make the lawman shut up.

"The men who wanted that wagon protected represent the interests of a few different shipping companies. They meant to pay a bunch of gunmen to do the job," Saunders continued. "When I caught wind of it, I put my foot down. After all, protecting stages from being robbed is a lawman's duty and having it happen so close to this town made it *my* duty. I allowed them to bring a few of their own in because it was their property being protected, but I insisted on being there with men of my own. Wasn't a popular decision, but I suppose it was too late for them to do much about it.

"When your gang showed up, the idea was for all of you to be killed in such a way that would send a message to anyone else looking to steal from these gentlemen or their ridiculous iron wagons."

"That wagon was as loud as she was slow," Eli grumbled. "When we were moving it after stealing it, we had to fight just to keep the thing from tipping over."

Saunders laughed and settled back onto his chair. "They do tend to flip over on their own. Heard as much from one of the men hired to guard it this far while we were holed up in that barn. And if them bindings holding the plates to those posts are cut or if the posts themselves are cracked, the iron shell drops quicker than a set of britches in a cathouse."

As much as he wanted to hold back, Eli couldn't help laughing at that. He chalked it up to being overly tired.

"Since them wagons look better than they drive," Saunders went on to say, "those rich fellas needed to make certain outlaws thought twice about approaching them in the first place."

"None of us cared much about the specifics of why those guards wanted to drop us," Eli explained.

"Maybe not, but specifics are very important to a man in my line of work."

Although he hadn't been running on the wrong side of the law as long as Jake or Hank, Eli had seen enough to tell him that plenty of lawmen out there were only concerned with the specifics regarding how money would be put into their pockets. Judging by the sorry state of this sheriff's clothes, hair, and boots, he couldn't account for much more than the paltry sum allotted by any small town to compensate a sheriff for his time.

"The only reason I brought all of that up," Saunders explained, "is so you'd know just how anxious those men were to kill you."

"I guessed as much when they were shooting at us."

"Exactly. And by the time we were committed to the fight, we were in it for blood. Your gang didn't leave us much choice. All of that makes it even more curious that you didn't pull your trigger when you had the chance." Saunders leaned forward to prop his elbows upon his knees. "When my deputy got the drop on you, I figured we'd just have one less killer to deal with. When that deputy turned his head at the wrong moment, I prayed he'd live to learn from that mistake. And when I saw you bring up your pistol as quick as you did, I feared I'd have to visit my deputy's family and tell them they'd never see him again. Imagine my surprise when you faltered."

"That's all it was," Eli said while turning to barely look in the sheriff's direction.

"Nothing more than a stupid falter. Shouldn't read more into it than that."

"But there's so much more to read. The way I figure, it must've taken you more effort to keep from shooting than it would to just follow through on what you started. There was nothing for any outlaw to gain from letting that man live and everything to lose."

"So you cracked me in the head for my troubles," Eli said while reaching up to rub the spot that was still plagued by one of many lingering pains. "Much obliged."

"Watching a wolf hold back from ripping a wounded deer's throat out is something special. Expecting that wolf to let that deer walk away is just plain stupidity. I knocked you out before you could do anything to put your head back into that noose."

"Speaking of which . . . ," Eli said warily.

"I don't hang men for crimes they didn't commit. I don't rightly know what all you did before you came to the Lazy V, but I know what I saw. You didn't kill anyone at that ranch, but you're supposed to be hanged for it just so folks can think their lawmen are earning their keep and that a bunch of rich men know how to protect their wagons. I've lived a full life and a lot of it's on account of following my instincts.

Those instincts tell me that if you were the same kind of killer as Jacob Welles and that one-eyed fella, you would have pulled your trigger when you had that deputy of mine dead to rights. Instead, you let him live and I won't put you to death for it."

Eli turned around so he could lean back with his shoulders against the wall and his arms crossed indignantly across his chest. "And you want me to help you catch Jake, Hank, and Cody in return for you speaking up for me. Is that it?"

"That's it indeed."

"If I'm such a good man, then why would I stab my partners in the back that way?"

"Because you're not one of them. Besides that, what I was telling you about them leaving you behind isn't just a load of dung. If they were anywhere near this jail or even this town, don't you reckon those resourceful friends of yours would've found a way to get word back to you?"

Eli didn't respond, which didn't deter Saunders in the least.

"I wasn't just watching you at that ranch," the sheriff said. "I was watching the rest of that gang real good when they turned tail and bolted from the Lazy V. They didn't even look back to see if you were alive or dead, and they never stopped shooting in the hopes that they might kill just one more man on their way out. Some of those dead men were shot so many times they looked like they'd had a stick of dynamite handed to 'em. That's not the work of anyone fighting to survive. That's the work of someone who loves to kill, plain and simple. If you loved killin' so much, you would've done some of it yourself."

Saunders stood up, moved the chair back to its normal spot away from the bars, and faced the cell. "I've known men to break the law for plenty of reasons. Some just like it and some feel it's what they gotta do. You obviously don't like it and you don't have to do it no more, Eli."

"So I should become a traitor instead?"

"You should see to it that those murdering dogs who left you behind get what's coming to them," Saunders replied. "And if that's not enough, you should do what you need to do to keep your neck from being stretched."

"And you can guarantee my neck's wellbeing?" Eli scoffed.

Without batting an eye, Saunders told him, "Yes, sir, I can. I may not be a fancy federal marshal, and this may not be a big city, but Seedley is *my* town and I'm the law here. If a man's to be executed, it'll be for good reason and by the letter of the law."

"A man at the end of any rope is just as dead, no matter what reason brought him there."

"The difference is if the body swinging from that rope was innocent or guilty. The way I see it, my job is to make sure one walks free and the other swings. So far, I've proven to be real good at my job. You should be happy to know that I believe what I see with my own eyes as opposed to what I hear. I've heard some nasty things about Eli Barlow, but all I've seen is a conniving, quick-tempered thief. From what I've been able to gather by talking to a few trusted colleagues, most of the killings committed by your gang was done by Jacob Welles and that fella with the one eye."

"Most," Eli reminded him. "Not all."

"As for the rest, I suppose they could have been killed by them two or you or maybe some other members of the gang that aren't so well known. All I got to go on with those is faith."

"Faith?" Eli grunted as if that was a term that was offensive to his sensibilities.

"Faith in my judgment and instinct. Same faith that tells me you're worth a gamble. You ride with me to track down that murdering gang of yours and I'll see to it that you don't get hanged for what them other men did."

"You say you didn't see me kill anyone at that ranch, so I should walk away no matter what. Ain't that what the letter of the law would say?"

Now it was the sheriff's turn to chuckle. "You're still a known thief and gunman. I'm sure you shot a few men here and there, since that comes with the life you've chosen. Even if you never pulled a trigger in your life, I know for certain you've stolen more money than I've ever earned in any of the five towns I've kept the peace in. You'll go to jail or otherwise make up for the crimes you've committed, but unless I speak on your behalf, there's bound to be plenty of other charges tacked onto your name that probably don't belong there. I'll do everything in my power to make sure you get a real trial and a sentence that fits your crimes. Needless to say, whatever you do while helping me will be taken into account to ease things for you even more."

"That's real honorable of you, Sheriff. Last time I got such a deal thrown my way was when some fella in a fancy suit was trying to get me to buy a cheap watch from the back of his cart."

Saunders smirked at the sarcasm that

dripped from Eli's tone like wet paint from the bristles of a brush. "Then I guess it's time for you to see how far you trust your own instincts. Surely you must need some pretty sharp ones to survive in the company of men like Jacob Welles. What do they tell you about how well I'll stick to my oath?"

Eli didn't have to take any time to study the sheriff. He'd been doing that since waking up inside his cell. As much as he wanted to find a reason to dislike the lawman on nothing but principle, Eli couldn't deny that the man meant what he said. "Well, since I don't have much choice, I might as well take you up on your offer."

"Glad to hear it," Saunders said with a genuine smile. He turned and took a step and a half before stopping to add, "Just so you know, if you try to bushwhack me or otherwise take advantage of my good nature at any point during our ride, I'll make dangling from the end of a noose seem like a real comfortable alternative."

Eli had plenty of finely honed instincts, and they all told him to take those words at face value.

CHAPTER 8

It wasn't until the next day that Eli saw another living soul walk past the bars of his cell. When the jailhouse door swung open, he didn't bother listening for footsteps. He knew Sheriff Saunders would be coming to collect him to make good on the deal they'd struck. If the lawman had left him alone to spend time considering that bargain, he would have been happy to know that Eli hadn't thought about much else. On the other hand, some of the memories rushing through his head reminded him that his days spent with Jake's gang hadn't been a continuous string of bloody deaths and scrapes with the law.

There had been jokes told around campfires, shared experiences that would strike him as funny until his dying day, and genuine moments of friendship that could only be forged between men who'd pulled each other from the fires of hell several times over. But no matter how much Eli pondered or how fondly he reminisced, there was only one conclusion at which he could arrive. Those same men had left him behind, a deal had been struck, and it was in his best interests to honor it. Of course, that didn't exclude the possibility for some creative rewriting of the deal should another opportunity present itself.

The steps shuffled down the hall and Eli was genuinely surprised to see that Sheriff Saunders wasn't behind them. Instead, Lyssa stepped up to his bars carrying a larger tray than normal, which was covered by a clean white napkin. "Brought you some breakfast," she said. "The sheriff tells me you two are to be riding out today."

"That's right."

"Then this is a good-bye meal," she said with a wavering smile. "I cooked it myself."

Swinging his legs over the side of his cot so he could get up and approach the bars, he asked, "You didn't cook the oatmeal and such?"

"That's hardly cooking. It's warming up and stirring. Besides, I've been taking extra-special care of you since you've been awake." She grinned, but caught herself as if the smile and words preceding it had slipped out by mistake.

By now scents from beneath the napkin were drifting through the air to tease Eli's nose. He raised an eyebrow, trying not to give away just how interested he was. "So you went through more trouble this morning, huh? Shouldn't have gone and done that."

"Really? Then I might as well take it back and feed it to the sheriff."

"No!" Eli snapped. He did his best to recover by adding, "That is, I mean you cooked it up for me and I'm hungry, so I should eat it. Is there bacon under there?"

"Yes," she said with a grin that showed she either had a good read on how badly he wanted it or could hear his stomach rumbling from where she stood. Lyssa pulled away the napkin to reveal the plate she held. "Bacon, grits, some toast and honey, and fried eggs."

"Grits?" Eli gasped as he nearly leaped at the bars. "I haven't had those since I can remember!"

"I know," she said with a shake of her head. "We talked about it the other night. Folks around here say they're about the same as oatmeal. Who knows what gets into people's minds?"

Eli hunkered down to receive the plate that was handed through to him. When he got it, he held on with both hands and walked it back to his cot like a preacher taking a chalice back to the altar after giving communion. He sat down, took hold of the dented spoon that was given to him with every meal, and gazed down at the food. "I hardly know where to start."

"Try the grits. Let me know if they were worth the excitement."

"Oh no. I'm saving those. Think I'll have some bacon." The moment his teeth snipped off a section of the crispy strip, he smiled like a kid with a mouthful of candy. "Bless your heart," he said while chewing.

Lyssa waved away the compliment and crossed her arms. "Is it true?"

"Is what true?"

"That you and the sheriff will be riding out?"

"I reckon so," Eli told her while picking up a piece of toast and dabbing it into the soft yolk of an egg.

"Some say you're gonna be rode out and strung up from a tree."

He stopped chewing for a moment and then resumed. "If that's the case, I guess I'll find out soon enough."

Wrapping her arms around herself a little tighter, she said, "I don't believe those stories. If Sheriff Saunders meant to hang you, he'd do it right outside this jail."

"That's good . . . I guess."

"And if he did take you out somewhere else, that would probably be better than doing it here where certain folks would make it even more miserable than it already is for you."

"Lyssa?"

"Yes?"

"Can I please eat my breakfast without so much talk of hangings?"

She lowered her head as a rosy hue flushed into her cheeks. "I'm sorry. I could just leave."

"No," he was quick to say. "I didn't mean that. I'd just like to change the topic of conversation."

"What would you rather hear?" she asked.

Eli was about to dig in to his grits. With his spoon poised over the hot offering, he said, "The weather, your favorite dog, what dress you like to wear, anything you like. Just not hangings and such."

Lyssa pulled up the same chair that Saunders used when he'd sat and spoken with Eli the previous day. She crossed one leg over the other, placed her folded hands upon her knee, and told him about a quilt she was making with another local woman named Henrietta Kaper. Her story began with a description of the quilt along with a brief history of when she'd learned the craft, but quickly turned into a squawking session about how difficult Henrietta was to work with and the various things she said or did to get on Lyssa's bad side.

While Eli savored every last bite of the breakfast and the warm, welcome taste of butter-soaked grits, he also savored the words that she gave to him. Her stories were lyrical thanks to the joyous tone in which they were spoken, and even the biting comments she had in regard to Henrietta were more amusing than mean-spirited. For the span of time it took for her to reach the end of her conversation and for him to clean his plate, Eli felt as if he were anywhere but inside a drab box with bars on the door.

The only thing to top the sound of her voice was the fleeting moment he was given when his finger brushed against hers while he was handing the plate back through the opening at the bottom of the cell door. It was the finest thing he'd ever stolen, and the little grin on Lyssa's face told him she wasn't about to ask for it back.

After Lyssa left, Eli had enough time for his food to settle and churn in his belly before the jail's front door was opened again. This time, there was no mistaking the heavier steps of a man that walked down the short hall. Saunders appeared in front of the cell with a ring of keys dangling from one fist.

"You ready?" the lawman asked.

Eli's breakfast churned a little more. "Does it matter?"

"Guess not." In Saunders's other hand was a pair of handcuffs. He showed them to Eli and then tossed them into the cell. "Put these on and be quick about it."

"Where are we going?"

"Already told you that. Just do as I asked so we can get moving."

Picking up the handcuffs, Eli said, "You sound a bit cross, Sheriff. Anything you want to tell me?"

"Hopefully it's nothing. I'll tell you the rest when we put some distance between us and this town."

The first cuff cinched in around Eli's wrist tight enough to chew into his flesh. That was mainly due to the tension in his body that caused him to squeeze the restraints shut a bit tighter than he'd intended. There was enough chain between each cuff for him to maneuver his other wrist into the open jaws of the second gaping ring of iron. "Our deal still good, just as you mentioned?"

"Course it is," the lawman snapped. "Why

would I lie to a man in your position? If I wanted you dead, I could've done so without wasting so much time and breath in talking to you."

"All right, all right. No need to bite my head off." Eli snapped the cuff shut, making sure to allow some more room for his blood to flow through the veins in his wrist. "When do I get my belongings back?"

The question had been a joke, but Eli was surprised when Saunders leaned over to pick up a sack that he must have dropped near the cell before approaching the bars. "Everything's in here," he said. "Except ammunition for the pistols, of course."

"Of course." Eli held his arms up and out so the sheriff could get a clear look at the chains that were binding them as he said, "I'm ready."

Saunders muttered to himself while fitting his key into the lock of the cell. The door swung open and shrieked as if it had forgotten what it was like for its hinges to move. Even though the sheriff was standing right there watching him, Eli felt as if he was overstepping his bounds when he stepped across the cell's threshold. "Will I be getting my own horse?" he asked.

"Yes, but even on its best day it won't be able to outrun mine," the sheriff promised.

"Do I have to wear these the whole way?" Eli asked while shaking the chain between his wrists.

"You'll get them off when you prove you're worthy. Right now just shut your mouth, step lively, and do what I say. And do only what I say, you hear? Don't listen to anyone else. Don't speak to anyone else. Don't even look at anyone else."

The closer he got to the jailhouse's front door, the more muffled voices Eli could hear beyond it. Behind him, Saunders bristled in a way that was more off-putting than the Colt that was pressed against Eli's back. "Something I should know, Sheriff?" Eli asked.

"Once you step through this door, we'll be turning right. The horses are saddled and tied to a rail. Yours is the black one. You'll get on and wait for me to lead you out. Not one twitch or false move, you understand?"

There was a gravity to the lawman's tone that made Eli stop trying to test the lawman, tease him, or otherwise make light of the situation. He simply nodded and said, "I understand."

As Eli felt the Colt's barrel jam against his spine, he thought back to the friendly tone that had once been in the lawman's voice. Perhaps he'd tested the lawman a bit too much during those conversations. Every man had a limit to his patience, and a sheriff would surely reach his a whole lot quicker when dealing with the likes of him. Saunders's thick arm extended over Eli's shoulder to shove open the door. Since his head was down and eyes averted, the first thing Eli saw were the brackets affixed on either side of the door's frame. His guess was that a thick piece of timber could be dropped in there to keep the door shut and possibly turn the jailhouse into one large cell. Several noises in close proximity caused Eli to raise his eyes again and he was shocked to find no fewer than two dozen men as well as a few women clustered in a large group just a few paces away.

One of the men at the front of the pack stepped forward. He stood just over six feet tall, had shoulders wide enough to bring fallen logs to a lumber mill, and carried a shotgun cradled in the nook of one arm. "You brought him out, Vernon," he announced. "Now hand him over."

Saunders slapped a hand on Eli's shoulder, pinning him in place. The outlaw took that as a direct command and stayed put. "Why would I do something like that?" the sheriff asked.

"Because you know it's the right thing."

"And what if I don't agree with that assessment?"

"Then we'll force you to step aside and take him anyway." The man's eyes narrowed and his grip tightened around the shotgun. "Don't make this any uglier than it already is, because no matter how it happens, we're taking that killer away and stringing him up. Whether there's one grave or two when it's all said and done is up to you."

CHAPTER 9

Sheriff Saunders locked eyes with the man who carried the shotgun and asked, "You really want to go down this path, Mason?"

"You know I don't. That's why I've been doin' everything short of begging you to do your job properly and string that murdering piece of trash up where he belongs."

"I am doing my job. Were you there when the shooting happened?" When nobody answered, Saunders looked around and said, "Unless any of you were there to see what happened, I don't want you telling me what I should or shouldn't do!"

Another man spoke up. He was just under average height, had a slim build, and carried a rifle that was best suited for hunting rabbits or squirrels. "Some of the men that were there are buried out behind the church. You gonna tell us that criminal with you right now wasn't a part of the gang that put those good men into the ground?"

"No," Saunders replied. "I'm not telling you that. I haven't said anything of the sort once in all the times you folks have been questioning me about how I do my job over the last few days. Haven't I been clear with all of you any time you've come along to rake me over the coals?"

"You have," Mason said. "And every one of the times I spoke to you, I told you this moment would be coming unless you carried out that outlaw's sentence."

"My deputy was at that ranch," Saunders said. "Have any of you spoken to him?"

Silence dropped onto the crowd like a curtain. Considering the size of the group gathered in front of the jailhouse, that had a mighty big impact. Even Eli could figure out what it meant for the sheriff's deputy to have made himself scarce at a moment like this.

"What about the other men who rode away from that ranch?" Saunders asked. "Did any of you try bothering them instead of me?"

"They were gunmen hired by some company that don't even have an interest in this town," Mason said. "Besides that, they're long gone. You're our sheriff. You're still here and you work for us."

Saunders wasn't the sort of man to slouch,

but he straightened up even more as he stood toe-to-toe with the shotgun-wielding local. His voice dropped to a harsh whisper, but he could still be heard clear as day in the stillness that had enveloped that small patch of ground. "My duty is to this town," he snarled. "That's a fact. My duty is to the law as well. I do my best to protect you folks' interests, but don't for one single moment think you can get me to jump just by snapping your fingers."

"That's not what I meant, Vernon."

"The hell it isn't! What do you call this, then? You all get an idea in your heads about how I should conduct myself. You get a burr under your saddle when I don't do something exactly the way you think I should. That's all fine and good. You all come to me, griping and spouting off about what you'd rather have me do. That's fine too. What it all boils down to, though, is that I'm the sheriff around here. As soon as I pinned this star to my chest, my word and the law are mighty close to the same thing."

"Comes a time when we gotta take things into our own hands if it's bad enough," the smaller man with the hunting rifle pointed out.

Shifting his focus to him, Saunders asked, "It is, Daniel?"

"Yes! That's how this country was founded. Folks do things the right way, rather than stand by and watch them done wrong."

The rest of the crowd cheered at that while also taking a collective half step toward Eli.

Without hesitation, Saunders placed himself close to the crowd with Eli at his back. "I *am* doing things the right way," he said. "This man didn't shoot anyone at the Lazy V and he sure had the opportunity. You don't think so? Ask my deputy. Even if he's too yellow to stand by me now, he'll tell you this man could have killed him, but didn't pull his trigger. That's how I got the drop on him."

"I heard as much," said a woman in the crowd with her hair pulled into a tight bun and her eyes framed by deeply etched crow's-feet. "And if you could only bring him in because he let you, maybe you're not the sheriff we all thought you were."

"Myra, I know your son was one of the men killed at the Lazy V," Saunders said in a voice that was softer in tone than before. "And if this man here had anything to do with it, I'd tell you. Why would I hide such a thing?"

"That's what we can't figure out," she said.

"There's nothing to figure out." Lifting his chin and raising his voice so his words would carry to every last one of the people in front of him, the sheriff declared, "The reason this man isn't hanging for murders committed at the Lazy V is that he didn't commit any of them."

"Then why ain't your deputy here to stand by you and say the same thing?" asked someone from deeper within the crowd.

"Because," Saunders replied, "he's afraid of being gunned down by an angry mob. And the next time any of you see him, tell him to make himself scarce because if I cross his path again, I'll tan his hide personally."

"Where do you think you're taking him?" Mason asked while nodding toward Eli.

"Finally, someone asks a proper question," Saunders mused. "He's coming with me to hunt down the rest of that gang."

"You trust him over your own deputy for that?"

"After what I've learned about my deputy today, I'd trust just about anyone more than that little coward."

"What do you expect will happen when he finds the rest of his gang? You think he'll just step aside and let you bring them in?"

"Doesn't much matter what he wants or expects," Saunders replied. "Just like it doesn't matter what you folks expect. I've got a job to do and I'll do it. If that's not good enough, no matter who you are, that's just too bad. Now, if you folks will stand aside, time's wasting and the trail's getting cold."

Saunders attempted to walk over to Eli so he could lead him to where the horses were tethered. He was stopped when the crowd, led by Mason and Daniel, flowed outward to assert themselves. "You gonna deny that man there is part of the Jake Welles Gang?" Mason asked.

"I never denied that," Saunders said.

"There's a reward on all of their heads. They're all wanted for murder. You want us to believe otherwise?"

"We just went through this. If this one's wanted for murder in another county, territory, or state, I'll take him there personally so he can stand trial for it. If you want to see a man hang so badly, let me track down the rest of his gang. I'll string them up in a row and you vultures can bring a picnic lunch. Until then, I'm your sheriff and you'll do what I say."

"Not anymore, you're not," Mason

growled as he brought his shotgun up to bear. "You're no longer our sheriff and we won't listen to one more word that comes out of your mouth."

Eli had been in plenty of hot spots when he'd ridden with Jake and he would gladly have stepped into any of those situations instead of this one because back then, he'd at least been armed. Now all he had to do was stand back and prepare for what would surely be the shortest escape attempt he'd ever made.

"Fine," Saunders said. That single word was enough to sink Eli's stomach faster than a canoe that had been on the wrong end of a shotgun blast. "There's an official process to go through to take away my official position. You all start it and I'll face the consequences when I get back."

"You won't be going anywhere," Myra said. She too was holding a hunting rifle. Even though her hands were shaking, she didn't need to be much of a deadeye to hit either one of her targets at point-blank range.

Rather than challenge her, Saunders let his eyes roam over all the faces in the crowd. He placed his hand upon the Colt at his side and nodded solemnly. "You aim to kill me, then?"

"We just want to see justice done to that one behind you," Mason replied. "We don't know why you got it into your head to believe that he's innocent or that he ain't done no harm to anyone outside of the Lazy V. We just know that we've been trying to get you to think straight for days, Vernon. Ever since last spring, you ain't been the same man that took the job as sheriff. You ain't been —"

"I ain't been following your orders to the letter ever since I shot that Mexican fella who turned out to be innocent," Saunders snapped. "Is that what you mean? Well, I ain't about to make a mistake like that again and I don't have to follow your orders. As far as thinking straight is concerned, just because I'm not thinking the same thing as you don't mean I'm out of my mind. Do you honestly think I'm taking this man away from here to set him loose so he can kill or do anyone harm?"

"No," Mason said.

"Then you just want to kill him yourselves? How's that make you any less bloodthirsty than a real murderer?"

Nobody in that crowd was ready to see things from another angle. They weren't there to bargain or to listen. They were there to shout and get their way by force. Eli could tell as much without having met any of them before. He could read plenty in the angry, blinded stares painted onto the fronts of their heads like frowning portraits emblazoned on wooden dolls.

"We got a job to do as well, Vernon," Mason said. "Step aside and let us do it."

"Sorry," Saunders replied in a clipped tone that made it clear he was just as aware of the situation as Eli. "Can't do that."

Mason took a look over his shoulder. For a moment, Eli thought he might be backing down. If that happened, odds were good the rest of the crowd would back right down with him. But when he turned to face the sheriff again, he did so with grim determination in his eyes. "Last chance, Vernon. Hand over the killer and your badge."

"Or what? Go on, Mason. Say it. I want to hear you say the words."

"Or . . . we'll take them both from you."

Saunders had been carrying the sack containing Eli's possessions over his left shoulder. He lowered that arm as well as the sack while squaring his shoulders to face Mason directly. Rather than make a move for his Colt, he reached into the sack, found one of Eli's .38s, and tossed it to the outlaw. Although Eli was more surprised by the move than anyone else, he caught the pistol and fit it into his grasp.

"What do you think you're doing?" Mason asked as his eyes widened. "Have you lost your mind?"

"Since I can't trust anyone that I used to consider my friends and neighbors, I might as well put my faith in the one man here who should back me up."

"You're on that killer's side?"

"If I am, I should be filling you and Daniel there with hot lead right about now, don't you think?" Saunders dropped the sack and placed the palm of his hand squarely upon the grip of his holstered revolver. "And if that man's the mad-dog killer you think he is, he should have opened fire by now as well. Ain't that right?"

"He's got the good sense to know when he's outnumbered," Myra said.

"He was outnumbered at the Lazy V," Saunders pointed out. "So was that whole gang, but they didn't stop fighting. Right about now that speaks higher of them than a bunch of whining cowards who need to cluster in a group of a dozen or more to face off with two men. And just look at you," he continued as if every word put a bad taste in his mouth. "Talkin' like you want a fight, but shifting on your feet as if you don't know what to do with yourselves."

"Don't look at them," Mason said. "They're here because I told them to meet me here if they wanted. They came to show their support."

"All right, then. You're the big man. You take the reins. Since that killer you're so afraid of hasn't pulled his trigger, I guess it's up to you."

Everyone else in the crowd glanced back and forth between the sheriff and Mason. Their allegiances were muddy from the start and became even more so as the seconds ticked away. To show them what they were getting into, Saunders said, "You folks standing around and behind Mason might want to clear a path. If there's shooting to be done, you won't want to get in the way of it."

Mason's confidence waned for the first time when the crowd around him parted like the Red Sea.

"Sure you want to stick to those guns of yours?" Saunders asked with a smirk. "Seems like your followers aren't so eager to keep pushing."

"I've only got one gun," Mason replied evenly. "And it's all I need."

"I've known you for a good while. Never had you figured as someone to lead a lynch mob."

"It ain't a lynching if we're seeing real justice done."

"A vigilante, then," Saunders said. "I met some of them up in Montana. I suppose you could fit that description. Those men are full of talk about justice, but aren't much different than the animals they hunted."

"We're not animals!" Myra shouted. "My son's dead! That man should be dead too!" With that, she raised her rifle and took aim.

Saunders wasn't about to be killed, but he also wasn't about to drop a mourning mother where she stood. He drew his Colt and pointed it downward before pulling his trigger. The pistol barked loudly to kick up a mound of dirt several inches from Myra's feet. Although that was enough to frighten most of the crowd into scurrying away, she dropped to her knees and let her rifle hit the dirt without letting it go, as if the weapon were heavy enough to anchor her to the earth.

The people in the crowd who hadn't already cleared away from Mason did so now as if he were sitting atop a keg of dynamite with a lit match in each hand.

"Drop your weapons and go home," Saunders warned. "This has gone far enough."

Myra seemed unable to let go of her rifle. Tears streamed down her face and powerful sobs racked her entire body.

Daniel's fingers flexed around the gun in his hands. All it took was a warning glare from the sheriff for the skinny local to follow his orders to the letter. He let go of his rifle and had already started running away before it hit the ground.

"Hand him over, Vernon," Mason said. "I've come too far to stop now."

Saunders shook his head. "It's never too late to do the right thing."

Some part of that sent a tic through the man's face. He gnashed his teeth together, shook his head as if refusing to listen to the demons whispering in his ears, and brought the shotgun to his shoulder. Eli reflexively dropped to the dirt and covered his head. Saunders wasted no time before sighting along the top of his revolver and squeezing his trigger. The gun bucked against his palm, sending a shock wave through his arm that was barely reflected in his narrowed eyes. Its single round tore through Mason's elbow, shredding muscle and obliterating the sections of bone it found.

"Damn," Saunders sighed as he watched the other man fall. "Someone help me get him to the doctor."

"Knew you were . . . one of them," Mason grunted.

Saunders had holstered his Colt and knelt down beside him. "One of who?"

"One of them outlaws!"

"That's right," the sheriff said while picking the other man up as best he could without straining Mason's wounded shoulder. It was a difficult task, especially since the other man seemed content to hang like so much deadweight. "You got me pegged. I'm such a smart outlaw that I stayed here in Seedley where I can bring in just enough pay to live in a shack with a leaky roof and eat beans three nights a week."

"Ain't no way to talk your way out of it. You proved where you stand by gunning me down in front of God and everybody."

"You forced my hand, even after I tried talking to you for so long I nearly lost my voice."

"Well, you can lose it for all I care. I don't wanna hear another word you got to say. Not until I see the badge ripped from your chest."

"Sure, sure. Are you gonna work with me or just dangle until you bleed out?"

Suddenly a portion of Mason's weight was alleviated and his body became more level. He winced and choked on a pained grunt as Eli took hold of his other arm and draped it across the back of his neck.

"See?" Mason wailed. "Your friend is tryin' to kill me!"

"I'm just trying to get you to a doctor!" Eli said. "Which way are we headed, Sheriff?"

"See that bridle store across the street? Doc's office is in the tall, skinny building right beside it."

"You're ripping my arm off!" Mason moaned.

"Stop yer bellyaching already," Saunders said. "I've heard enough. You want to lie in the dirt instead of somewhere you can be tended?"

"No."

"Then since none of the others who you had so much faith in are willin' to help, you might want to accept it from whoever's willing to give it."

Mason was moving his feet and standing up more on his own steam now, but was shaky after the gunshot wound. Once he placed some of his weight upon Eli's shoulder, he could allow his arm to dangle so his bloody elbow wasn't taking any undue strain. Before he could be moved another step, Saunders left him to lean completely on Eli.

"Where are you going?" Mason asked.

Saunders didn't feel the need to answer

him. Instead, he approached Myra and lowered himself to place one hand on her rifle and the other on her shoulder. "Take a breath," he whispered to her. "It's going to be all right."

"But he's dead," she sobbed. Her grip tightened once more around the hunting rifle, but the sheriff didn't allow her to bring it up. Still she struggled to reclaim the weapon as if oblivious of what was preventing her from getting it. "He's dead and I'll never get him back!"

"I know."

"It's . . . empty," she wept while gripping her chest just above her heart. "He's gone and it's so empty."

"I know, Myra."

Looking up at him as if she were seeing the lawman for the first time, she said, "Someone's got to pay for losing him."

"Yes," the sheriff told her. "But it's got to be the right someone. He's not it."

Myra looked over to Eli and then back to Saunders. Too weak to say another word, she nodded and allowed him to help her to her feet. She left the rifle where it had landed and shuffled away from the jailhouse.

"Eli!" Saunders shouted. When his prisoner stopped and looked over his shoulder at him, the sheriff said, "If that loud-mouthed, sorry excuse for a vigilante wants help to the doctor's office, one of his so-called friends can give it."

Although he seemed irate at first, Mason redirected his scowl to Daniel and a few of the others who'd been with him in the crowd not so long ago. It took a few long moments, but Daniel eventually moseyed over to offer his assistance. "Git yer hands offa him," he snapped to Eli.

Before any more insults could be leveed at Eli, Mason growled, "Leave him alone. He's the sheriff's burden now. He'd best make sure not to bring him back into town."

"Don't worry about that," Saunders sighed.

Eli came back to the lawman's side amid the rattle of the chain dangling between his wrists. He'd tucked the .38 under his belt so he could help pull Mason across the street, but he removed it now using just a thumb and forefinger to daintily pinch the handle. "You should probably take this before another mob forms up."

"Ain't loaded, remember?" Saunders replied.

Waving the pistol at him as if it were growing too hot to hold, Eli said, "Sure I do, but they don't! Just take it. Maybe you'll gain some favor by making a show of it. I'll act like I'm real scared of you."

"First of all," Saunders told him while snatching the pistol away with enough force to make Eli reflexively flinch, "you should be scared of me. Not only can I kill you at any time, but I've got a town full of folks who'd form a line just to pat me on the back for it. Thanks all the same," he added in a lower voice. "It was good to see you help Mason despite everything that happened."

"And second?"

"What?"

"Second," Eli repeated. "There ain't a first of all without a second."

Saunders grinned as he thought back to his own recent words. "And second, I doubt I'll be gaining any favor with this lot any time soon."

CHAPTER 10

Their ride started off just as Eli had expected it would. They were headed toward Cheyenne using a trail that wasn't as direct as the one he would have chosen, but would get them there well enough. Then again, being an outlaw who'd learned from several other outlaws, Eli knew plenty of trails that lawmen didn't. That was a good portion of how thieves stayed alive for more than a week or so after firing their first shot. But even using a more established route didn't account for them veering off course as they'd done a mile ago. He had let it go at the time because Saunders had removed the cuffs from his wrists and Eli didn't want to annoy the sheriff enough for the restraints to be placed back on. Eli still didn't say anything until he saw a fence marked by a wooden sign emblazoned with a V pointed slightly askew to the right as if it was in the process of falling over.

"What are we doing back at the Lazy V?" he asked.

Saunders steered his horse through the gate that was still hanging halfway open as it had been when Jake and the others were chased off the property. "Looking for tracks."

"Tracks?" Eli asked while casting his eyes back and forth. "What do you need to look for tracks for? Didn't you tell me Hank was spotted in Cheyenne?"

"He was."

"So?" When he didn't get an answer after another couple of seconds, Eli raced a few paces ahead of the sheriff and brought his horse to a stop. The animal he'd been given to ride was a black mare that was either old enough or mangy enough to have patches where her coat was thinning out or simply lighter in color; she seemed more uneven than a poorly made quilt. One thing he'd learned early on was that she didn't like to run. Getting ahead of Saunders caused her to whinny in protest and then breathe heavily when she was finally allowed to stop.

The lawman could easily have ridden around Eli, but chose to give his horse a rest. "What's the meaning of this? You'll keep on riding and follow up on your end of the bargain."

"Which is what, exactly?"

"Which is to do *exactly* what I tell you. Now git!"

"What's the point of wasting time looking for tracks? You think Jake is gonna stay in Cheyenne forever?"

"So you know what he's doing there?" Saunders asked.

"Not exactly, but I guarantee he's not fixing to settle down and raise a family." Cocking his head to one side while studying the lawman, Eli said, "Wait a second. You think I'm holding out on you?"

"Are you?"

Eli let out a long, exasperated sigh. "What happened to all that talk about me being a good person and how well we could work together?"

"I believe I said you weren't a killer. That doesn't exactly lift you into being a good person. As for the part about working together, make no mistake that I'm in charge."

"Oh, don't worry. Nobody can forget that."

When Eli started riding back down the trail leading farther into ranch property, Saunders raced to catch up. It took considerably less effort for his horse to close the gap. She was a beauty with a tan coat and a mane that was mostly dark brown mixed with scattered portions of black. "Are you trying to imply something?" Saunders asked.

"Why would you think that?"

"Because of the tone in yer voice."

"That's always there," Eli replied with a shrug.

"Then maybe because it sounds like you were talking about more than one person just then."

"I was. After the display you put on back in town, ain't nobody going to forget who's in charge. Well done."

Both men were riding slowly toward the spot where the fighting had taken place, but only Eli seemed to be paying attention to his surroundings. "Are you being smart with me again?" Saunders asked.

"No. It reminded me of when Jake and I would ride into a town or step into a bank with guns out for all to see, snarling like dogs and putting the fear of God into folks. We used to call that raising a flag. Does a real good job in laying down the law."

"Let's get one thing clear," Saunders said. "I ain't nothing like Jacob Welles, you hear me?"

"Wasn't meant as an insult. I was just saying you took that bunch of vigilantes and made them back down so good that they won't rise up again."

"Using outlaw tactics?"

"No . . . I . . . I don't know what your problem is, so I'll just put a cork in it and go wherever you point me. You want to look for tracks days after they've been blown away and beaten into the dirt by all them other men who chased the rest of the gang away from here? Be my guest."

The two men rode side by side for a few seconds that dragged like hours. Saunders didn't want to go any faster than a crawl, and Eli was more than happy to tag along. However fast they went or wherever they were headed, it beat being locked in a cage.

"Stop here," Saunders announced.

Eli pulled back on his reins, causing his horse to shudder more than a train engine that was missing half of its bolts. "I think most of the tracks will be farther ahead."

"The ones I'm looking for are right here."

Looking down to where the sheriff was pointing, Eli found imprints that had been pounded into the dirt and dried in place over the last few days. "You sure that's anything important? How many men have ridden up and down this stretch since the shooting stopped?"

"None. This property's been abandoned

since the owner died of some sort of fever a few months back."

"Some sort of fever?"

"Yep," Saunders said as he climbed down from his saddle to examine the ground more closely.

"What kind of fever?"

"Nobody knows for sure. First the old man went stark raving mad, bled from every hole in his head, and then keeled over dead. Then his two sons came down with it, only it was worse. One made it to town. Looked so bad that some folks thought he was the old man come back to life after clawing his way up from his own grave."

"Good God!"

"Yeah. See why nobody cared to come back up here?"

Eli squirmed in his saddle and swiped his hand across his forehead. "If you don't know what fever it was, could we still catch it?"

"Don't think so."

"You don't think or you know so?"

"The doc in town says a fever can only infect a place for so long before it dies out. Since I ain't much of a doctor myself, I'm inclined to believe what he said. Besides, those men who were to meet that rickety wagon didn't seem sick."

"Not yet, maybe. I think I'm starting to feel warm."

"Take your hat off."

"That ain't the point! Why would anyone want to gather here after something like that?"

"They wouldn't," Saunders replied. "Those men from that shipping company or whatever it was didn't bother with the whole story. They were looking for a place to store their horses and gear, and one of the only surviving relatives of this ranch's owner rented it to them. Those shipping company fellas had money to spare and nobody talked 'em out of it."

"What about you?" Eli asked.

"Me?" Saunders replied while running his fingertips along another patch of dried mud thirteen yards away from the one that had originally caught his eye. "I just found a set of tracks that split off from the rest."

"Good. Great. I meant what made you and your men decide to come here and crouch in that barn where . . ." Suddenly Eli lost some of the color in his face. "Fevers can hit animals too. Or if they don't, folks tend to put someone who's got something that might be spread out in the barn. What on earth were you thinking? What did you tell those men of yours to get them to squat in that infested barn with you?"

"I've only got one deputy and he believed what the doctor said as well. None of them other men cared much about what I had to say."

Eli stared at the lawman with his mouth agape. When he saw that expression being leveled at him like the barrel of a gun, Saunders said, "I told you, I heard from a doctor that it should have been all right! What's the matter with you? Are you one of them squirrelly types who thinks he's always sick? My grandpa was like that that. Miserable old cuss."

"Perhaps your grandpa was a smart man."

"Smart or not, it don't benefit anyone to worry so much about dyin'. The Reaper's coming for all of us. Might as well enjoy whatever time you got until he gets around to finding you."

Shaking his head in a similar manner as he would if he'd been told the most ridiculous fairy tale ever conceived, Eli said, "Reaper's coming for some of us sooner than others."

"What's that supposed to mean? You got some sort of condition I should know about?"

Eli deflected one question with another. "Did you find what you were after so we can get away from this place?"

"What are you worried about? You were here just like I was. If there was a fever to be had, you'd already have it."

Somehow, Eli became even paler. "Maybe that's why I felt so bad after being down for so long."

"I think me knocking you on the melon had more to do with it than any fever. These tracks I found are fresh and the rest were put down by your outlaw friends. There's three sets coming from that direction," Saunders said while pointing back toward the area where the shoot-out had taken place. "Two continue toward the fence line this way and the newer ones veer off that-away. There were only four of you who came in with that wagon, right?"

"That's right. Still, I couldn't tell you if those tracks were put down by anyone I know or any of the other men that were here at the time. You were cooped up in that sinkhole of a barn, so maybe you didn't see the men swarming around this place like flies on manure."

"I did see them. In fact, I saw plenty more than you did after you were lying facedown in the dirt. When the rest of your gang high-tailed it out of here, they tore straight over this patch of ground and everyone else tore after them. Not directly, mind you. Your friends were shooting behind them to keep anyone from taking the straight approach, so the rest of us split up to try and circle around from both sides. One group charged for the fence line over there," Saunders explained while pointing to a stretch of grassy terrain to the right of the trail. "And the other went in that direction."

The second route Saunders showed him was a bit rougher since it was studded with scrub and trees. Eli took it all in and didn't have the slightest bit of trouble picturing the chase that had taken place after he'd been knocked unconscious. In fact, he didn't have to stretch his imagination very far at all to be certain he truly had been left behind without a fight. Jake was practical to a fault, and getting killed to save one man wouldn't make any sense to him. Hank didn't need an excuse to cut the gang's numbers down, since that meant his share of any stolen money went up, and Cody was a follower pure and simple. He did what he was told and didn't bother with questions.

"So," Eli grunted as he chewed on the unpleasantness running through his mind, "what does all of this tell you?"

"It tells me that the gang could have split up. Only one of them was spotted in Cheyenne. That means the rest could be meeting up with him later or could even be circling back around to see what you're up to. Any thoughts on which it might be?"

"Couldn't it be that they split up to get away from this ranch before meeting up a mile or two down the road?"

"That could be."

"Which brings me back around to this being a waste of time."

"You think so?"

"Yeah. I just said so, didn't I?"

Saunders smirked like a man who had not only an ace up his sleeve, but three more in his hand to go along with it. "What if I could tell you that these fresher tracks can help us find at least one member of your gang and possibly the ones who set up this massacre in the first place?"

"I'd be pleased as punch," Eli grunted.

"Perhaps you won't be so smug or reluctant to go after them if you knew you were set up for a fall from the start."

"What are you talking about?"

Nodding with the certainty of a fisherman who'd felt a tug on the line he'd cast, Saunders said, "Those men who commissioned that wagon to be built have some deep pockets, but I'll let you in on a secret. That wagon didn't cost as much as you might think to be built."

"I've been up close with that thing," Eli said. "That's no surprise to me. I'm amazed it went as far as it did without rattling apart."

"Some of that money went to hiring the men to protect it, but all of that was just a ruse. The wagon, especially. When I was crouched in that infested barn, I had plenty of time to hear some of those guards talk. Now, they didn't spell out everything they were doin', but they let slip enough pieces of the puzzle for me to get an idea of what it's supposed to look like when it's put together."

While he talked, Saunders led his horse alongside the path that went to the barn. Eli noticed this and pulled back on his reins. "How about you tell me about that picture before we get closer to whatever disease is filling the air around that barn?"

"For Pete's sake! If you don't have the fever yet, you ain't gonna get it now. Will you stop being such a whiny little pup?"

"What if I already have a condition?"

Now Saunders stopped. "What sort of condition? You mean like an ailment?"

"What if I had something like that and didn't want it getting worse? Think that's a good enough reason to steer clear of that barn?"

"Do you have a condition?"

Frustrated with the lack of progress in the conversation, Eli asked, "Is there a good reason to be moseying in this direction instead of toward Cheyenne?"

"I was just getting to that," Saunders replied. "That big clunky wagon is a lightning rod. It draws attention and it does carry money, but there's more to it than that. The men in the barn were talking like they didn't even care if that contraption made it out of here or not. I asked them about it and they told me that thing's the finest piece of bait ever created. It draws outlaws either into ambushes or onto their company's payroll."

"What?"

"You're a thief, Eli. When you see something that heavily armored and that heavily guarded, what's the first thing that goes through your mind?"

"That there's gotta be something good inside."

"And when you took that wagon, was there?"

Reluctantly, Eli sighed, "No."

"Why not?"

"Because they were supposed to be picking the money up here."

"And I can tell you," Saunders said, "with absolute certainty that there wasn't any money here."

"What?"

The lawman grinned from ear to ear, but not in the self-satisfied way that someone might expect. Instead, he looked more like a man who'd kept a particularly good gift as a surprise until the last possible second. "I met the men here as soon as they arrived to organize the party that quickly became a shooting gallery that day. They brought strongboxes and one was filled with some money, but the others were weighted down to feel the same."

"Why would they do that?"

"To draw outlaws like yourself to this spot where they could be captured, killed, or chased off."

"And what did you say about putting them on a payroll?" Eli asked. "Jake would never agree to work for a company when he could just steal from them."

"Wasn't Jake. One of the men in that barn mentioned a meeting with a one-eyed fella back when the wagon made a stop in Omaha."

Eli gnawed on the inside of his mouth as he thought back to the time Hank had spent away from the gang. He was supposedly gathering information, but it didn't take much for Eli to be convinced that the murderous scarecrow was up to something other than that. He let out the breath he'd been holding and held his ground before being led one more step. "You can stop this right now," he said to the lawman. "I already agreed to help track Jake down, and I got my own reasons for doing so. You don't need to try and get me on your side by feeding me all of this."

"No need to feed you anything," Saunders said. "I'm just as curious as you are as to whether or not I pieced together what I heard into the correct picture. Both of us are here to get some proof."

"And you only thought to tell me about it now? That works out pretty well considering how the story serves your purposes."

"Convenience ain't got a thing to do with it. From what I heard, that shipping company likes to get outlaws to spread the word that their armored wagons ain't worth the trouble of trying to rob. They even pay for the service when they can. They pay even more for a member of a gang to hand over one of his own."

Eli shook his head as his stomach clenched tightly. "None of this makes sense. You're trying to tell me a rich company is interested in collecting bounties on wanted men?"

"No." Saunders sighed as if he were dealing with a thickheaded child. "It's all just about them making their wagons look too tough to rob. The iron plates give them the appearance of being too difficult to attack, and the men who still want to charge after them will know the last bunch that tried to do the same wound up dead or in jail."

"And some outlaws take this deal instead of the money being moved?"

"There is no money being moved. Not in that iron piece of junk, anyway. For the outlaws that are approached, it's either no money or a payment from the shipping company in exchange for a clear path to a safe spot somewhere. You saw all the men that were here. You've been in your share of gunfights, I'm sure. Do you seriously think the rest of your gang should have made it out alive?"

Eli's head was swimming. Saunders must have seen as much, because he said, "It's not that hard to grasp. You just gotta shift away from thinking in such easy terms. This had nothing to do with a robbery. It was about two groups of men wanting to make easy money. The shipping company is investing time and funds into making their jobs easier so they can have safer shipments, get more customers using their overpriced services, and become a bigger company. The outlaws are either stupid gun hands who get tripped up to make the company look like they know what they're doing or smart enough to take a handout and walk away from an ambush."

"There's gotta be more to it than that."

"I'm sure there is. Remember, I'm working on what I pieced together from what I overheard."

"And what did you hear, exactly?" Eli asked.

Looking down the trail as if he could see all the way to the spot where he'd huddled in that filthy barn, Saunders said, "I saw them load one strongbox full of rocks while protecting another with their lives. There was mention of a turncoat among the outlaws coming to this ranch and plenty of griping about having to take turns driving or riding in that ironclad contraption."

"That's a whole lot of loose lips among those guards," Eli said without trying to hide the skeptical tone in his voice.

"There were a few. They got even looser once they figured they could trust me."

"You're an amicable sort. I suppose that wasn't so hard."

"It wasn't," Saunders said as he shifted and gritted his teeth as if he despised the words he was about to say. "Especially after I accepted a payment from them to step in line with what they wanted me to do."

"You took a bribe?"

"They said it was compensation for my time, but yeah. I'd call it a bribe."

"Didn't have you pegged as a crooked lawman."

"That's an honest mistake, considering what I just told you." The sheriff wheeled around and approached Eli as if he could not only pull the outlaw from his saddle but lay out the horse with one punch for good measure. His hands balled into thick fists and muscles swelled along his arms and chest as he said, "But if you ever call me that again, I will skin you alive. Understand me?"

"Sure."

"They offered the money to me and it was plain to see my deputy had already taken his payment. That's why I didn't want him anywhere near my jailhouse when I was dealing with you." There was no small amount of regret etched into Saunders's eyes when he said that part. "I didn't take it right away until it became clear that there was more going on than just a simple job guarding some money from a bunch of desperados. After I took the payment, they figured I was on their side, so they weren't so cautious when speaking amongst themselves."

"So that's how you got all them pieces to the puzzle?"

"Yeah, and I ain't proud of it. Taking a payment like that must not seem like much to you, but it means a lot to me. A man in my position gets offered plenty of money for plenty of reasons. The first time a man accepts one of them payments makes the rest easier to take. But it also marks him. Maybe not so anyone can see right away, but it marks him all the way down to the bone. I've seen it."

The sheriff was right. Taking a bribe didn't seem like anything to Eli. He'd seen plenty worse and had even doled out a few payments to crooked lawmen himself. But he also knew what it was like to be marked by an act that he'd wanted to take back. Something like that was near impossible to wash away, but that didn't mean he had to stop trying.

Eli thought about that silently while Saunders went on to say, "I took that money as a gamble. As for rounding up your gang and bringing it to justice that day, well, that just wasn't gonna happen. Not then, anyhow. Arrangements had already been made and a sacrificial lamb had already been chosen."

"And you were the one sent to slaughter that lamb," Eli said.

"Nope. You were to be killed somewhere along the line, that's for certain, but all I was supposed to do was stand aside. When I charged out to knock you upside your head, the men who paid me thought I was just trying to take some initiative or maybe impress them so I'd be approached for future jobs. Honestly, I don't know for certain what they were thinking, but they got a mighty big laugh out of me rushing out to take you down amid all that gunfire. By the time the smoke had cleared, most of the others were either dead or had taken off after the rest of that gang. When I stayed behind to get you tied up and loaded onto a horse, I managed to see them open one of those strongboxes. The one that actually had money inside. The same one they'd opened to get the money to pay me and, presumably, my deputy. It's still here."

"They left it behind?"

Saunders nodded. "Buried it close to that barn and then offered me another stack of bills to make sure nobody else came sniffing around it for a while. Until today, to be precise."

"So that's why you cooked up the story about that fever?" Eli asked.

The lawman's patience dried up in a heartbeat and he snapped, "Forget the fever! Someone's coming to collect that money and I'm betting it's someone who must know more about what's going on. They're coming today."

"And you decide to wait until now to let me know?"

"Why should I trust you so much when I can't even trust my own deputy?"

Unable to argue with that, Eli pointed out, "Two men won't be able to bring a big company with deep pockets to justice."

"I ain't worried about that company," Saunders shot back. "I knew some of the other men that were hired on to act as nothing but fodder when the shooting started here. I'm a lawman and my job is still to go after that gang of yours, and in doing so, I could be able to muck up whatever nasty business that company's got going. Sometimes a man can't fix the bigger problems, so he's gotta be content with fixing whatever's in his reach."

"One man's reach ain't very big."

"But if every man cleans up the small patch he can do something about, the world would be real close to manageable."

Eli couldn't deny that sentiment, but he wasn't able to muster up the same hopeful smile that had appeared on Saunders's face.

"Someone's coming to collect their payment," the lawman continued. "That one will lead me to more of the men I'm after, and those will help me answer for the deaths that happened here. After that, I can't help thinking the company who got all of this rolling will be damaged, but even if they're not, justice will be done for them murders and the Jake Welles Gang. I aim for that to happen, and you're gonna help me."

"That's a long way to go to hunt down three men while inconveniencing a big shipping company."

Saunders didn't hesitate before replying, "There's more to it than that. Hopefully you'll see before too long."

CHAPTER 11

They waited on that ranch for hours.

At first, Eli figured he didn't have anywhere else to be, so he might as well fill his lungs with some fresh air before the sheriff made another unexpected move to muck things up.

Vernon Saunders was crazy. The time spent sitting quietly in or near that barn was enough for Eli to convince himself of that much. Perhaps it was a guilty conscience for taking money under the table from men he barely knew or perhaps it was the fact that he'd taken part in an ambush that wound up with so many men dead and buried. There were dozens of ways for a man to go mad. Eli had seen it happen more than once, and whatever had pushed Saunders over that edge, it was always a bad idea to work with a madman.

As if picking up on the thoughts running through Eli's mind, Saunders rushed over to his side wearing a wide grin and even wider eyes. "He's coming," he whispered excitedly. "Hurry up and hide in the barn."

"Hide? *In there?*"

"I swear on all that's holy," Saunders growled, "if I hear you grouse one more time about that fever, I'll —"

"Fine, I'll go into the barn. Burning up from disease is better than sitting around listening to you."

"And what about sitting in a jail cell?" Saunders asked as he escorted Eli into the barn. "If you're so tired of me, then you're more than welcome to go back into town and test your luck with that lynch mob."

"Least the food was good."

Saunders impatiently waved that off while pulling aside a loose board in one of the barn's walls that he'd obviously known was there ahead of time. "As if it's the food that put that grin on your face."

Eli hadn't realized he'd been grinning, but the thought of his last few breakfasts with Lyssa would have been enough to put one in place. "Who's coming?" he asked.

"You tell me. This is part of the reason I went to such lengths for you to accompany me."

The loose board hung by one nail, which allowed it to pivot down when it wasn't being propped in place by another nail protruding from the wall. When Eli held the board aside and moved his face closer for a look through the hole, he swore he could smell the disease that had probably soaked into every fiber of the structure. Rather than ask for clarification as to how long ago the most recent fever patient had been stricken, he diverted his thoughts with the task at hand.

"What exactly am I looking for here?"

"Single rider coming in from the north," Saunders told him. "Shouldn't be able to miss him."

"Right. *If* he's headed straight for this barn."

"Which he is."

"Sure," Eli sighed. "Unless you're not . . . Wait a second." Straining to push his forehead even harder against the wall as if that would be enough to show him more, he said, "I see the man you're talking about."

"And he's headed this way?"

"Yes." The moment he said that, Eli swore he could feel the smugness rolling off the sheriff like a heat wave. "Where's the money buried?"

"At the base of that post about ten paces in front of you. See it?"

"Yep. What's the plan from here?"

The sound of iron brushing against leather meant Saunders was drawing his Colt. When Eli turned to see what was happening, he found the lawman checking to make sure the pistol was loaded. "The plan," the sheriff announced, "is for you and me to approach whoever that is once he's off his horse and trying to dig up his payment."

"And what if he's just passing through?" Eli asked. "Maybe looking for water or a ranch hand looking for work?"

"Then he's not the man we're after. You'll get to say you were right and I've got rocks in my head. Happy?"

"Most definitely." When Eli pressed his face once more against the wall, he couldn't tell which he was hoping for the most. On one hand, if he'd been offered up as a sacrifice so the rest of the gang could cash in to salvage a payday from a foolish job, he wanted to know about it. On the other hand, it would do him a lot of good to be there once Sheriff Saunders was taught that he couldn't be right all the time. Unfortunately, when Eli saw the rider bring his horse to a stop and climb down so he could start poking around the base of that post, he knew the lesson would have to wait for another day.

"You recognize him?" Saunders whispered.

Eli nodded, bumping his head in the process. "Yeah. I'd be able to spot that overripe head from a mile away."

Cody approached the post, sniffed around it like a dog looking for scraps, tapped the loose earth around it with his boot, and then looked around some more. Even though he didn't seem to realize he was being watched, the outlaw sighed and grumbled to himself while getting down to his knees so he could scrape in the dirt with both hands. Eli shook his head. Leave it to Cody to forget to bring a shovel when his only job was to dig.

"You think you'll be able to do this?" Saunders asked.

"We can take him without a doubt."

"No," the sheriff said. "I mean will you be able to take a stand against your own gang?"

When he turned to look at the sheriff, Eli noticed the Colt was held at hip level and pointed in his direction. All it would take was a twitch of one finger for a round to drill a hole through Eli's midsection. He'd already had plenty of guns pointed at him, so one more wasn't about to rattle him. "I never liked him very much anyway," Eli said.

Saunders holstered the pistol, but kept his hand resting upon it. "We go straight at him.

Nothing fancy and no rough stuff unless there ain't no other choice. Understand?"

"You're the boss. Besides, I don't have any bullets in my gun."

"And that's the way it'll stay."

"Cody may not be the sharpest knife in the drawer, but I can guarantee his gun will be loaded. I do have an idea for a way to get some results without bloodshed, though."

"I'm listening." After hearing the bare bones of Eli's plan and agreeing to it with a nod of his head, Saunders faced the door to the barn and nearly kicked it off its rusted hinges before stepping through. He walked with his head held high and his chest puffed out as though he had an army behind him.

Cody shifted so he was only down on one knee. That way, he could turn toward the barn while granting himself easier access to the pistol at his side. His expression was that of a dumb animal with sharp teeth. Dangerous without a hint of intelligence. He was about to say something, either to explain his presence there or frighten away his unwanted visitor, when he caught sight of a face he obviously hadn't been expecting. "Eli? That you?"

Walking with confident steps, Eli said, "It's me, Cody. What're you looking for under that dirt?"

"I don't know. I just . . . thought somethin' may have gotten dropped during the fight. You know . . ."

Eli shook his head. "You always were too stupid to be any good at lying."

Like most stupid people and bad liars, Cody didn't like hearing that. He bared his teeth angrily and snarled, "I should be askin' you what you're doing here with that law dog! Were you the one who set us up to be gunned down?"

"You and I both know I wasn't the one to set anyone up." Hooking a thumb back at Saunders, he added, "That law dog told me all about the deal Hank worked out."

If surprise was a flesh-and-blood thing, it would have punched Cody in his oversized head and left a scar. He tried to recover with a few blinks and deep breaths, but it was too late. His fingers scraped noisily against something solid as he raked them through the dirt on their way out.

"Go on," Eli said as he drew his .38 and held it at his side. "Keep digging."

The gun in Eli's hand was the focus of Cody's attention. Since it was held in a somewhat casual grip and pointed at the ground, there was no way for Cody to get a good enough look at the cylinder to see if it was loaded or not. Without anything else to go by, he looked back to Eli's face. The expression there told Cody that he could very well be the next thing filling a hole on that deserted property.

"I swear." Cody gulped. "It wasn't my idea."

"I know," Eli calmly replied. "You never came up with any ideas. Why should you start now?"

"To hell with you, Eli! You and yer law dog!"

"Keep digging."

When Cody didn't start moving, Saunders took a step forward. With Eli doing such good work thus far, he'd been content to let him do the talking. He didn't say a word as he raised his gun and fired to drill a hole through the short pile of freshly turned soil next to Cody. The outlaw jumped and grumbled under his breath as his hands scooped deeper into the hole he'd created.

It wasn't very long before the scraping that Eli had heard became louder. "What's that?" he asked. "Better pull it up so we can have a look."

"Hank and Jake both sent me here to fetch this," Cody insisted. "Told me where to dig.

I'm just doing my part. You know how it is."

"Then I suppose they didn't tell you what's inside that box?" Eli asked.

"No."

All Eli had to do was cock his head and give half a grin to let Cody know he wasn't about to sneak that lie past him either. This time, the other outlaw didn't bother trying to defend his statement. "It wasn't me that made the deal," he moaned. "I'm just the one to come and collect the money. Maybe you should ask that one there about money," he snapped while pointing at Saunders. "I hear he took his share to make that massacre happen."

"You mean this money?" Saunders asked while digging into one of his pockets to remove a small bundle of cash. "I'll be using this for expenses to track down the rest of your gang. And the only reason it was a massacre was that you, Jacob Welles, and that one-eyed fella couldn't stop pulling your triggers."

Squatting down with his arms propped upon his knees and his .38 dangling where it could be easily seen, Eli asked, "What's the plan from here, Cody? You supposed to deliver this money to Jake and Hank?"

"No, they'll just let me keep it and ride

off to Old Mexico without them. Of *course* I'm supposed to deliver it to 'em."

"Where are you meeting them?"

Cody's eyes began to wander between the two men in front of him before gazing up to the skies above them all.

Thumbing back the .38's hammer was enough to bring Cody's attention back to earth. "Where are they?" Eli asked. "Answer me."

"Or what? You'll shoot me?"

"What problem could I possibly have with shooting you?" Eli asked. "You and the others handed me over to be killed."

"You don't know that."

Keeping his head cocked, Eli narrowed his eyes and asked, "Don't I?"

That question barely needed a second to sink in. As soon as it did, Cody's rocky facade crumbled away to reveal a sorrowful, vaguely pathetic grimace. "That wasn't my idea either. I swear to all that's holy, it wasn't."

"I believe you." Before Cody could draw any hope from that, Eli added, "But you went along with it well enough. What should I do about that?"

"Take the money in this box," Cody offered meekly. "That'd make Jake and Hank real upset and make you real rich."

"You mean they'll be upset when you tell them about me?"

"No! I wouldn't!"

"Then how would you explain the missing money?" Eli asked. "Aren't they waiting for it right now?"

"Yeah, but . . ." The more Cody tried to speak, the harder he winced. It was almost as if gears inside his skull were grinding.

"Because you've got to tell them something," Eli continued, adding even more logs to the considerable jam inside Cody's head. "You can't tell them you couldn't find it. Even you're not stupid enough to mess up digging a hole."

Cody's eyes snapped open as wide as they could get as he was hit by a sudden inspiration. "I'll tell them the money wasn't here! They'll think them rich fellas double-crossed them. Jake was worried about that anyhow!"

"What rich fellas?" Eli asked.

"The ones who Hank told us about. The ones who offered to pay for us to go after that wagon and take whatever was inside. The ones who wanted us to let everyone know how many guns were guarding that money and how tough that wagon was."

Eli could feel the lawman's self-satisfaction rolling in like fog from a lake at dawn. Twisting his own face into a disapproving scowl, Eli said, "I don't think Jake or Hank would believe they were double-crossed. After all, they trusted those rich men enough to sign on to their plan. They also tossed me away like so much trash, so they had to have a lot of faith in what those men were selling."

Cody thought that over. His lips puckered together and parted again to form the front portion of words that he eventually decided not to utter. His eyes rattled in their sockets, and the considerable amount of forehead above them crinkled into furrows. "Hank never did like you. He always said we should be rid of you."

"But Jake never thought that way," Eli said with confidence. "He and I had plans for some mighty big jobs. Jobs that would make us all rich. Why don't I give you a moment to think about that."

"And I'll want you to take a moment to toss me your pistol," Saunders said. After Cody's gun hit the dirt in front of him, the sheriff tossed the handcuffs over. "And put these on in the meantime. Can I have a word?"

Eli followed Saunders a few steps away where they could speak without being heard by Cody while also keeping an eye on him.

"You really think those cuffs are necessary?" Eli asked. "They didn't do much to keep me from functioning."

"More of a message. I want to know about what that man was saying. Some of it was making sense, but you wrote it off. You think we can trust what he tells us? There's only so far intimidation will take you. After that, a man will say anything he thinks we want to hear."

Eli nodded. "You're right. Time to go with the other plan."

The two men had consulted with each other for less than a minute, which was more than enough time for Cody to get the handcuffs on and not quite enough for him to get to the knife secreted in his boot. When Eli glanced down at the scabbard tucked mostly out of sight, Cody stopped trying to be discreet and lunged for the blade.

Eli rushed at him while bringing the .38 up to bear. He wasn't worried about the outlaw seeing if it was loaded or not, because he pressed its barrel directly against Cody's forehead. "Wrong move. Drop it."

The outlaw did as he was told while showing Eli a glare that could have melted the paint off a boilerplate. That shifted to a more familiar expression of confusion when

Eli tapped Cody's leg to show him the little key held tightly against his palm. "When I stand up," he whispered, "I'll help you to your feet. When I give the signal, we're running for it."

"All right, you two," Saunders bellowed. "Back here where I can see you."

"What signal?" Cody asked.

Eli stood, grabbed one of Cody's arms, and hauled him up. Without missing a beat, he twisted around and pointed the .38 at the sheriff and shouted, *"Now!"*

Whatever Cody might have lacked in intelligence, he always made up for in spirit. This time was no exception, as the outlaw turned away from Saunders and bolted for the closest stand of trees. Saunders fired a few shots at them, which sailed wide or high of their mark. Cody was still breathing heavily with his back pressed against a tree when Eli rushed over to him.

"I knocked him out," Eli said.

Cody took a quick look to find Saunders lying on his side. "When'd you do that?"

"While you were running here. He was forcing me to work with him. I know about the deal that Jake struck and can't blame him or Hank for getting themselves out of a losing situation."

"Sorry about that," Cody wheezed. "I

truly didn't have anything to do with that part."

"I know. We should probably split up," Eli said while unlocking the handcuffs with the key he'd shown earlier. "Tell me where we're supposed to meet Jake."

At first, Cody wasn't ready to say much else. When the handcuffs fell away from his wrists and landed at the dirt near his feet, he was feeling much more charitable. "They're in Cheyenne. I'm to meet them there."

"What's in Cheyenne?"

"The rest of the money that was supposed to be on that wagon," Cody replied with a sneering, almost boyish grin. "Them fellas that set things up with Hank think they're so smart. The money's bound for Cheyenne in a wagon that ain't nothing like the one we captured. It should get to Cheyenne soon, if it ain't there already. Either way, Jake says the men guarding it won't be expecting anyone to hit them after all that happened at this ranch. It was just smoke and mirrors, like a stage show. That's what Hank said."

"Yeah," Eli sighed, trying his level best to keep from showing the disgust he felt. "I just bet it was."

"You gotta know I'm sick about what happened with you and all."

"I know. Where's your horse?"

"Just over yonder." When Cody glanced in another direction to where he'd tied off his horse, Eli cracked the .38 against his big head. The dim-witted outlaw crumpled onto his side, where he lay like a big oafish dog that had found a soft spot to take a nap.

And just as Cody seemed to have found his place, Saunders climbed up out of his and walked over to get a closer look. Nodding while scratching just beneath his hat band, the sheriff said, "That worked better than we'd hoped. Put him down quick and clean."

"I learn from the best," Eli said as he reflexively rubbed the aching spot on his own head that still flared up on occasion.

"Thought you'd let him get a little farther before dropping him like that."

"So did I, but he just had to flap his gums about how sorry he was that I was handed over to those rich men. No matter how bad a liar he is, he could never get himself to stop. I could only stomach so much."

"He tell you where he's supposed to go?"

"Cheyenne. Just like you said."

"Great," the lawman sighed. "Knew that much already. I hope this wasn't a waste of time after all."

"Waste of time? Not hardly." Eli hunkered down to sift through the fallen outlaw's pockets. Having ridden with Cody for as long as he had, Eli knew exactly where to look for the knife as well as a holdout pistol tucked in his left boot. The knife and scabbard found a new home under Eli's belt, and the holdout pistol remained in his hand. It was a .22 that was dirtier than anything else to be found in the outlaw's boot. Saunders eyed it cautiously. "Not only did we confirm what you heard about Cheyenne, but we got some money to help us get there a little quicker."

"I told you I already had confirmation about Cheyenne."

"No offense, but hearing reports that way means less than nothin'. There was a stretch of time when two different newspapers said me and Jake were blazing a trail through the Dakotas or being chased out of Leadville."

"Which was it?"

With a grin, Eli said, "It was Iowa. Me, him, Hank, and this bigheaded idiot lay low after pulling off a string of little jobs in Missouri. That right there is what reliable sources tell you. For the real story, you gotta go to someone who's got a vested interest in knowing the truth. Cody may be dumb, but he sure is vested. Why's there still a sour look on your face? You think I'm lying about what Cody just told me?"

"No. It's that," Saunders said while nodding toward the pistol in Eli's grasp.

The jovial expression Eli had been wearing moments ago quickly faded. "One partner tosses me to the wolves and the next one can't bear to ride with me unless he's got the upper hand *and* outguns me."

"You're still a prisoner in my custody," Saunders said. "What would you do in my place?" After Eli handed over the pistol, the sheriff shook his head and cleared his throat expectantly.

"All right, fine," Eli growled as he handed over the knife as well. "I suppose you're going to hand him over to those vigilantes back in Seedley?"

"I watched him when the shooting started on the day that wagon was brought in here. This one shotgunned at least two men before they knew what was happening. Would you like me to go easy on him because he's your friend?"

Eli looked down at Cody for as long as he could stomach the sight of him. "He's not my friend. He knew what he was getting into when he took up a gun and threw in with the likes of Jake and Hank. Just like the rest of us."

"Then it's settled. Help me tie him up."

CHAPTER 12

Saunders might not have allowed Eli to carry any live ammunition, but he did let him keep Cody's gear and saddle. Cody himself was wrapped up and thrown across the back of his horse. He looked like an overgrown caterpillar lying across Eli's old saddle. Whether he feigned unconsciousness or was truly asleep for the duration of their short ride together didn't matter much. It was a quiet journey to a small town farther down the trail, which they reached just past sundown.

"Glen Becker is a good enough man," Saunders said as they approached a storefront labeled BAKED GOODS & SHERIFF BECKER'S OFFICE. "Good enough to watch over this one until he hands him over to someone else."

"Hands him over to who?" Eli asked.

"If he's got a price on his head, he'll arrange for someone to collect him. If that's too much trouble, he'll send for a federal marshal. They come through here every now and then and are always willing to clear out someone else's trash."

Eli glanced up and down the single short street that looked to contain most of the town's businesses. "Federal marshals come here?"

"Marshals, bounty hunters, judges, there are all sorts of men passing through towns like this one who'd be more than happy to take a wanted man in and claim credit for it. Just like there are plenty of retiring old-timers like Sheriff Becker who'd rather give away someone like your friend than deal with him personally. You saw firsthand what a mess that can shape up to be."

"Only when you break the rules," Eli reminded him.

"Would you rather I stick to the rules?" When he didn't get a response to that, Saunders said, "Didn't think so. Stay put. I'll be right back."

Saunders climbed down from his saddle and then hefted Cody over one shoulder as if he were unloading a sack of feed the horse had been carrying. Midway through the process, Cody woke up and began to struggle. The outlaw made a lot of noise and attracted a whole lot of attention without doing much else. Saunders carried him into the multipurpose storefront and emerged with a bundle wrapped in white cloth. He stuck his hand into the bundle, pulled something out that was the size of a ball, and tossed it to Eli, who caught it and had to toss it from hand to hand to keep from being burned.

"Fresh from the oven!" Saunders announced.

The little ball of bread had a sweet smell that made it impossible for Eli to wait long enough for it to cool. Sure enough, when he took a bite he tasted a hint of honey. "Swapped Cody for some sweet bread?"

"Nah, the bread was a bonus. Ol' Glen's wife is as good a baker as you'll find in these parts."

"What about Cody?"

"I don't know," Saunders replied through a mouthful of bread. "Can he bake anything this good?" Before Eli could look any more disgusted, the lawman added, "You worry more than a fretting hen. Have some more bread. It'll make you feel better."

Oddly enough, a few more bites of the honey bread did make Eli feel better. But he wasn't about to tell Saunders that.

"Sheriff Becker is keeping him chained and shackled to an iron post that's been in that spot longer than the rest of the building," Saunders continued.

"Chained and shackled?"

"Yep," Saunders said with a nod. "Hands and feet, all wrapped up and tied to that post. Satisfied?"

"I suppose. What's to become of him after that?"

Saunders shrugged. "Ain't my jurisdiction."

"I thought you lawmen watched out for each other."

"We do. But we respect each other enough to let another man do his job. Old Man Becker may not be the sort to charge into a fray, but he's handled his share of bad men. Besides, between his sons, nephews, and one grandson, he's got more deputies than I ever had. If memory serves me correct, that hotel right over there is clean and serves some good flapjacks every morning. Let's get us a room so we're fresh for the morning ride."

"A room? As in . . . just one?"

"Don't start grousing about me trusting you again," Saunders sighed. "You're staying in my sight and yes, you will be cuffed to something so I can be sure you won't run away in the middle of the night."

Eli shook his head, but didn't bother

complaining. He'd expected as much as far as the restraints were concerned. In fact, he was surprised he'd been granted as much freedom as he had. When he'd first imagined joining Saunders on this venture, he pictured himself being slung across a horse's back in a manner similar to how Cody had entered town. Eli thought about asking what the name of the town was, but decided against it. Hopefully, they wouldn't be there long enough for it to matter.

The hotel Saunders had mentioned was within sight of the bakery passing for a sheriff's office. For that matter, everything in that town was within sight of everything else. Their room was big enough for both men to be inside it without stepping on each other's feet, and Saunders even allowed Eli to roam free within its confines. The outlaw knew better than to take that as anything other than the test it was. Saunders watched every move he made. When Eli looked down at the street from his window, Saunders moved his hand to within inches of his holstered Colt.

"Town like this one," Eli chuckled, "Jake and the rest of us would ride through and pick what we wanted like a kid with his hand in a cookie jar."

"Those were the days, eh?"

Eli shrugged. "I'd be lying if I said they weren't. Haven't you ever wanted to just draw that pistol and shoot out every window in sight? Knock down anyone who looked at you cross-eyed? Set fire to something just to watch it burn?"

"Sure."

Turning to glance over his shoulder so he could examine the sheriff, Eli asked, "No fooling?"

"Every man's wanted those things. The difference is in who does them or not. Let me guess. It was the other members of that gang who set them fires or gunned down those cross-eyed fellas, but it was you who shot out the windows and took what you wanted?"

Eli kept his mouth shut and stared out the window again. It might have been comforting to have a parent or wife be able to read his soul, but someone like Saunders pulling off the same trick was downright annoying.

"You waiting for someone to ride in, guns blazing, to bust your friend out of jail?" Saunders asked.

"No. I wish I could hear Cody screaming and shaking the bars of that cage, though. Serves him right for sticking a knife in my back and then expecting me to believe him when he lies about it once he gets caught."

"You think Jacob Welles would do any different?"

"Jake's got no reason to lie to anyone," Eli said. "When I see him again, he'll look me straight in the eye and tell me why he did what he did. If I don't like it, he'll either laugh at me or shoot me and be done with it."

"What about the one-eyed fella?"

"His name's Hank."

"All right, then. What about Hank?"

Eli's stare became cold and sharp enough to cut through the window in front of him. "That's easy. Whoever sees the other one first will be the one to walk away."

"Well, nobody's walking anywhere. Not tonight, anyhow. After tomorrow, we won't be riding anywhere either. We're taking a train to Cheyenne and our diversion to that ranch will buy us plenty of time to get there. Whatever move your old gang is making, they won't do it until their third man gets back. And if they truly are getting set to rob a big shipment from them well-armed rich fellas, they ain't about to do it short-handed."

"Do you even truly know who those rich fellas are, apart from some men with interests in a big company?"

"Would you need to know more than that if you aimed to steal from them?"

"I'd need to know a few more bits of information," Eli said, "but I see your point. When'd you find out about the train schedule?"

"Same time I paid for this room. There's a station less than a day's ride from here, and lots of folks stop by on their way to it. There was a schedule at the front desk. Paid a little extra for a boy who works at this hotel to run a few errands for me and buy some supplies. They'll be brought up at around the same time as our supper."

"Room service?"

"Steaks," Saunders said with an expression that was only missing a string of drool running from the corner of his mouth.

"You really went all out."

"Plenty of cash in that box your friend dug up at that ranch. I figure we're putting it to good use by funding our ride to Cheyenne. Whatever's left will be put in the collection plate at the church back home."

Eli shook his head and laughed under his breath. "If that's what you think is wise."

Until that moment, Saunders had been relaxing on the soft bed with one leg up and the other dangling over its side. His back had been resting against the headboard until he sat bolt upright and swung his leg over so both feet were pressed against the floor. "You think that money would be better spent at cathouses and saloons?"

"I didn't say that."

"No, but you're laughing at me with that damn tone in your voice and I don't like it."

"Not laughing. It's just that . . . carrying that kind of money . . . a town like this . . ."

"You think I don't know how to take care of myself?" Saunders growled.

So there was no mistaking his sincerity, Eli turned around to face the lawman and held up both hands to pat the air reassuringly as he said, "I know you can handle yourself. I just meant —"

"You meant I can't watch over a bit of money? Like because I have to get by on a pittance of a wage, I ain't never handled money like that before?"

"Well . . ."

Saunders jabbed the air with his finger to emphasize each of his next words. "Shut yer mouth before I do it for you."

Eli shut his mouth.

"Make yourself useful and help me count the rest of this money. After that, I want you to tell me everything you know about Jacob Welles and whoever's left in his gang.

Is there more than just that one-eyed fella left?"

"You mean Hank?"

"Right. Hank. What's his last name?"

"Only thing I ever called him besides Hank was scarecrow and he didn't like that very much," Eli said. "Truth be told, I couldn't even tell you if Hank is his proper name."

"Is he the sort who would strike a deal with them rich fellas the way Cody was talking about?"

"Yes," Eli replied without a blink. "And it wouldn't be the first time."

After a slight pause, Saunders walked up to the window and stared directly into Eli's eyes. "You still up for this job?"

"Might as well be. I don't have much time left on this earth, so I may as well make the best of it."

"Don't give me that hogwash. I know when a man ain't got nothin' left to live for, and that ain't you no more."

"Right, because I want to ride by your side on this glorious, righteous job of yours."

Saunders shook his head. "You ain't looking to me when it comes to finding a reason to live. It's about that sweet face that's been in your head ever since you got that first home-cooked breakfast in my jailhouse."

"You talking about Lyssa?"

The sheriff's grin widened even more, which seemed peculiar considering the foul mood he'd been in a few moments ago. "Just the fact that you recall her name tells me she means something more to you than just the woman who brought your meals."

"Another reason I brought up my condition at all is that you need to know that I may not be around to back you up once we get to where we're going. The least I can do is prepare you for everything you might have to face. Now, are we going to keep talking about Lyssa or do you want to hear more about the men who will be trying to kill you in another day or two?"

Nodding with the brand of smug satisfaction that had become the lawman's signature, Saunders said, "Go on and tell me about that gang. We'll need to know everything we can when we wade into Cheyenne."

"And what happens after that, Sheriff?"

"Pardon?"

"Let's say we get to Cheyenne on schedule with everything going our way, and that may be asking for a lot, but what then? Even though there's only two of them, it won't be easy locking horns with the likes of Jake and Hank."

"Never thought it would be easy."

"There'll be shooting and when there's shooting, there's bleeding. Could be your blood. Could be mine. Most likely it'll be a little of both."

"You knew that going in, Eli."

"Yes, sir, I did. For us to make it out of there alive, it's going to take a whole lot of work and no small amount of pain. What's so funny?"

Although Saunders was laughing, it wasn't a jovial sort of thing. Instead, he mused to himself while taking in the sight of the man in front of him. "When I came to you about this job before, you were just interested in getting out of that cage and probably thinking of when you could get the drop on me so you could scamper away to take your chances on your own."

Whether he'd been thinking along those lines or not, Eli knew better than to waste breath in arguing.

"Now," the lawman continued, "you're thinking about what might happen after the job's over."

"So . . . what will happen?"

"Depends on how the job goes. If you're asking me about what things might look like between you and Lyssa . . ."

Eli gritted his teeth and stared out the window just so he wasn't facing the sheriff.

"Well," Saunders said, "that's between you and her. She's a good woman."

"I know that much."

"She deserves to have someone watch out for her well-being. At the moment, that someone is me. I won't let her ride off with no thief or piece-of-trash criminal. Any scoundrel who tries that will have one more gun to contend with." After letting that hang in the air like a storm cloud for another few seconds, Saunders made his way back to the bed, where he plopped down and swung both feet onto the mattress. "Now let's hear about that gang of yours."

CHAPTER 13

They talked for hours. Just when Eli thought he'd rattled off all he knew about Jake, Hank, or Cody, Saunders asked him about something else. The sheriff wanted to know everything from the gang's preferences for picking its targets all the way down to the eating habits of its members. When Eli told him another detail, Saunders nodded and soaked it up as if he'd just gotten the keys to the kingdom.

By the time they were both too tired to speak another word to each other, Eli and Saunders were on friendly terms. Not friendly enough, however, for the lawman to allow Eli to sleep without being chained to something solid. He chose to loop the handcuffs through a metal post in the bed's frame. It might not have been nailed down, but the slightest move Eli made was announced by the clanking of chains or the scrape of wood against floor.

It was just past dawn when Eli awoke. He twisted his hands within the cuffs so he could grab the chain and hold it away from the frame so he could shift his weight. Even that caused a creak within the bed itself, so he became still again and watched the form that was collapsed on a chair in the corner adjacent to the window. Apart from the occasional grunt or scratch, Saunders hadn't moved much since he'd fallen asleep in that spot.

Eli closed his eyes because they weren't doing him much good at the moment. What he needed was information on the bed frame, and since his hearing or sense of touch was all he could use, those were what he focused on. Only allowing the chain to graze the post around which it was wrapped, he eased it down its length in the hope that he might find an imperfection or opening that he'd missed during all of his other attempts throughout the night. The post was smooth until it became chipped closer to the floor. There, it snagged on the chain to make a subtle creak that echoed in Eli's ears worse than a gunshot.

He looked over to Saunders and found the sheriff was in the same spot as before. Unfortunately, so was Eli.

The outlaw stretched his arms until his

shoulders ached.

He arched his back to give himself some more slack, which only made the bed creak again.

Saunders still hadn't moved.

Eli fought the impulse to curse and wildly thrash against his restraints. Times like this made him feel like a dog running at full speed until the rope around its neck was snapped taut. Almost immediately after catching its breath, that dog would take another run. Knowing he'd only be harming his cause by acting so wild, Eli drew a breath, relaxed his muscles, and collected himself.

"Give up yet?"

Eli looked toward the source of that all-too-familiar voice. "How long have you been awake?"

"About an hour, maybe. Thought I'd sit still and rest up awhile longer. Usually I get anxious, but you were putting on a good enough show to keep me occupied. Find a way out of them cuffs yet? Maybe a gaping hole in that bed frame that I missed?"

"Remember what I said about wanting to see Jake get his due for stabbing me in the back?"

"Yeah," the sheriff grunted while stretching his arms and legs.

"Forget it. I hope he shoots you somewhere that hurts."

"Aw, you don't mean that."

"Right," Eli snapped. "Goodwill to all. Now unlock these things so I can get some breakfast!"

Saunders kept his chuckling as he fit a key into the cuffs and allowed Eli to sit up straight. Since they hadn't taken anything out of their saddlebags, there was nothing to pack. All he needed to do was check the floor around the spot where he'd spread out the money from the strongbox for it to be counted. He stuck wads of bills in various pockets, some into his saddlebag, and the rest was split in half and stuffed into each of his boots.

"That came in a box," Eli reminded him. "Wouldn't it have been easier to keep it there?"

"Safer this way," Saunders said. "Trust me."

"If you think so. Is today the day I get a round or two for my pistol?"

"You still have that thing?"

"Yes! It may not be loaded, but me and this gun have been through a lot together. I ain't about to —"

"Hand it over."

Eli blinked as if he'd just been rapped on

the nose. "Hand it over? It ain't even loaded."

"Bullets aren't exactly scarce. Hand it over."

"You don't think you'd know if I found some bullets? That's not saying a lot about you as a sheriff, now, is it?"

Keeping his hand out, Saunders said, "And we've both proven to be pretty darn handy using a pistol as a club. If you make me ask you one more time to hand yours over, I'll give you another demonstration."

Eli sighed and reached for the empty .38 tucked into his holster. "I was surprised you let me carry that thing for this long."

"Consider it a test. If you decided to try your luck at any time by making one wrong move toward that gun or anything else, your ride would have ended real quick and those angry folks back in Seedley would have been real proud of their sheriff."

"You would have killed me?"

"That shouldn't surprise you either."

It didn't, but Eli wasn't about to give the lawman the satisfaction of hearing him say as much. "I handed over those weapons I took from Cody, didn't I?"

"You sure did, which means you passed that test with flying colors."

"And what happens when we find someone who needs to be shot?"

"We'll cross that bridge when we get to it. For right now, just enjoy being outside a cage and take comfort from knowing I'll stick to my word. You proved to be amicable enough this far, but don't mistake my kindness for weakness. I'm still watching you, Eli."

"I know. Only time I saw you so much as twitch was when you were asleep. Now I ain't even sure how accurate that was."

Saunders handed over the saddlebags for Eli to carry down to the horses. On the way out of the hotel, they bought a breakfast of fresh biscuits, ham, and some coffee in a pair of little tin pails so they could carry it with them on their way out of town. They ate in their saddles, shoveling in the food while washing it down with coffee that sloshed around in dented tin cups to spill as much onto their faces and shirts as they got into their mouths. Once they'd both finished, they gripped their reins and started riding in earnest.

It was just shy of half a day's ride to the train station in a little town called Mayor's Crossing. They meant to catch a train that pulled into town at five o'clock on its way to Cheyenne. Considering that Cody had been trying to collect his money the previous day and wasn't carrying a train ticket in his pockets, it was likely he'd intended to ride to Cheyenne on his own. That meant Jake and Hank shouldn't be expecting him for a few more days. The schedule was coming together and Saunders was confident in their chances of getting to Cheyenne and rounding up the gang before Jake or Hank knew anything was amiss. He was so confident, in fact, that he missed one particular fact along the way.

"Someone's following us," Eli said.

Riding beside him, the lawman had his sights set firmly on the trail ahead. When he looked back now, Saunders spotted what had captured Eli's attention. "You mean that trail of dust behind us?" the sheriff asked.

"Yep."

"Could be someone that just happens to be riding in this direction. Mayor's Crossing isn't far and it's the closest train station, after all."

"That dust was getting kicked up behind us since we left town," Eli pointed out.

"Could be strange timing."

"Or it could be someone's following us."

Saunders slowed his horse to a leisurely stroll so he could twist around and get a better look. The dust trail hung in the air farther back along the same path he and Eli had taken when they'd traversed that same stretch. Now that he was watching it closer, he could tell that whatever was kicking up that dirt was indeed headed their way. "Doesn't look like a stage," he said.

"But it's more than just one horse."

After a few more seconds, Saunders grunted, "Can't get worked up about everyone we encounter. Like my mama used to say, it's no use worrying until there's something to worry about." When he shifted back around, Saunders let out a slow, grating sigh.

With his eyes still glued to the trail behind him, Eli asked, "What is it now?"

"We may have something to worry about."

Eli turned in his saddle to find another dust cloud being kicked up in front of them. This one was coming from a flat stretch of land off the trail and would cross their path in a matter of minutes. It hadn't been there before, which meant whoever was coming at them from that direction was doing so as quickly as possible. "Maybe someone's in trouble?" Eli offered.

A gunshot cracked through the air, sending a round hissing about a yard away from the sheriff's head. "Someone is in trouble," he said. "That'd be us."

"I'd like to be a help to you, Sheriff, but I'd need a gun for that."

"Just shut up and get riding."

"Where should I go?"

Another shot was fired that came a little closer than the first.

"Just keep moving along this trail!" Saunders shouted as he drew the rifle from the boot of his saddle. "And don't stop!"

As more shots sped at them, Eli could tell there was more than one rifle being fired at them. More than that, the men behind the rifles were trying to box them in between two lines of fire that closed in like a set of pincers. In Eli's personal experience, the tactic worked fairly well. Unfortunately, it seemed to be working pretty well now as well.

When sending a few quick shots at the plumes of smoke that had arisen to mark the spots where the other rifles were being fired, Saunders wasn't trying for accuracy but hoping to get those riflemen to let up for a moment or two. More shots blazed from behind that got close enough to whisper in his ear as they passed him by. When he turned to fire at the riders coming up from the rear, more shots from ahead thumped into the ground near his horse's hooves. The animal reared up and churned its front hooves in the air.

The sheriff was no stranger to being pitched from a horse's back. He managed to get his feet out of the stirrups so he could throw himself clear, but it was impossible to do much firing on his way down. His boots slammed against the ground to send a painful jolt through both legs. Rather than try to fire before collecting himself, he staggered away from the trail and dropped to one knee. More gunshots came from farther down the trail. and when Eli's horse was brought to a halt, Saunders cursed under his breath.

"You two there!" someone shouted from the trail ahead. "We been nice before. You make one more move and we'll put you down for good!"

"Eli?" Saunders called.

"I'm here."

"You hit?"

"No."

"How many are there?"

After a slight pause, Eli replied, "More than enough."

Knowing the outlaw was speaking the truth, Saunders cursed once more and checked his rifle. There were three more rounds he could fire and some spare ammunition in his saddlebags. Whether or not there would be time to reload was a question he couldn't answer. The Army Colt was at his side, and both of Eli's .38s were tucked beneath his gun belt. The .38s weren't loaded, which meant they were useless.

"We got one of you dead to rights," announced the man who'd spoken up earlier. "Whoever you are that got tossed off his horse, you should know one of my boys has got you in his sights as well. Ain't that so?"

From behind him, Saunders heard someone yell, "That's right!"

The lawman didn't need to see all of the gunmen to know they had him surrounded. Their voices were coming from too many directions and they'd already demonstrated they had the firepower to back up their words. That only left one more factor to determine.

"You men are barking up the wrong tree!" Saunders said. "We can part ways now and be done with it or we can keep this up until someone really gets hurt. I don't think you want that."

"We know what we want," the first voice replied. "Hand it over and you two can crawl away."

"This has got to be a mistake. We're just trying to catch a train, is all." Saunders waited for a reply, but heard nothing apart from a restless breeze brushing against tall grass. Soon he heard a rustling of several sets of boots closing in around him.

"If it's a mistake," the first voice said, "then I'll be the first to apologize. Until then, you'd best follow your friend's lead here and give up quietly."

Saunders strained his neck to try and get a look at Eli. Not only did he see the outlaw standing beside his horse with his hands raised, but he also picked out three more armed men covering the outlaw with shotguns and pistols. The footsteps were getting closer and he knew there would only be more guns among them.

Outnumbered.

Outflanked.

His only partner wasn't armed.

Saunders wasn't the sort to swear very often, but this had become the perfect day to rectify that.

CHAPTER 14

"You men are making a big mistake," Saunders growled. He and Eli had been led about a quarter mile from the trail to a spot where some dusty boulders could hide them from anyone else making their way along the main path. They'd been relieved of their weapons and the robbers were poking through their saddlebags.

There were five robbers in all. At least, that was how many had shown themselves after Saunders was disarmed and trussed up like a steer in a rodeo. They carried an assortment of weapons, all of which could make short work of anyone who gave the bandits a reason to be nervous. The man who'd done most of the talking was clean-shaven and covered in layers of grime that must have come from spending a good portion of the day lying in wait with his belly pressed against the dirt. Judging by the condition of all the others' clothing, they'd been lying right alongside him.

"Big mistake, huh?" the lead robber asked. "You hear that, Eddie? We're making a real big mistake."

Eddie was a tall fellow with a darker complexion than the rest of the men. He displayed an incomplete set of yellowed teeth when he smiled and said, "I hear that, Zack. Big trouble." He turned to consult with some of the other robbers, the rest of which still had bandannas covering the bottom portions of their faces. His filthy clothes were wrapped just a bit too tightly around his midsection to make a rounded gut stick out even more.

Zack had a round face, framed by a wide-brimmed hat and a bandanna gathered around his neck. His mouth was curled into a twisted grimace that looked as if he were either sneering or had dipped his bandanna into the bottom of an outhouse. "Only real mistake I can see comin' up is you squirmin' too much when I search you."

"You want to find something interesting?" Saunders snarled. "Pull aside my jacket."

"Don't," Eli warned.

Zack immediately went to his right, which was Saunders's left. "They want to know about their mistake," Saunders said. "I'm about to show them, is all. Other side, you danged idiot."

Still sneering, Zack moved his hand to the other lapel and pulled it aside. Raising his eyes at the sight of the badge pinned to Saunders's chest, the robber let out a slow whistle. "Well, well! What have we here? We got us a genuine law dog, boys! Maybe we did make a mistake."

The remaining robbers all stopped what they were doing so they could step up and take a gander at the sheriff's tin star, filing by as if they'd paid to gawk at a sideshow freak and showing the lawman even less respect. Zack stepped up again when the others had backed away and handed his shotgun up to a man with a solid build and more hair on his arms, face, and neck than a bear. Even though the big fellow wasn't wearing a bandanna, his whiskers were covering an equal portion of his features.

"You ain't a sheriff around here," Zack said conversationally as he stuck his hands into Saunders's pockets.

The lawman didn't respond.

Eli was being searched as well by the one who'd been called Eddie. Since he barely even had any lint in his pockets, the robber was finished fairly quickly.

"And you ain't no *federale,*" Zack continued. "Where do you call home, mister?"

Saunders kept his mouth shut.

Considering how widely the sheriff had spread the money he'd gotten from Cody, Eli was surprised it took Zack this long to find the first batch. When the robber did, he pulled out the handful of cash and stuck it in the lawman's face as if he were scolding a dog by making it sniff its own mess. "See, now? Why didn't you just give this up when you had the chance?" Zack asked. "Instead, you make us go through all this trouble to chase you down."

"Take the money and go," Saunders growled.

Zack handed the cash back to the fellow with the thick beard and continued searching. In a matter of seconds, he found the next stack of bills. "Wanna save me some trouble, Sheriff?"

Not only did Saunders remain quiet, but he lifted his chin so he could glare at the robber directly while doing so.

That didn't go over well.

Zack closed a fist around the money and pounded it against the lawman's chin. The impact rocked Saunders back against the boulder he'd been propped against and sent his hat flying. Zack gave Saunders just enough time to collect the blood in his mouth and spit it at him before punching him again.

"There's more in his other pockets," Eli said.

"Shut yer trap!" Saunders said through a mouthful of blood.

Everything the lawman could see was eclipsed when the big, shaggy fellow stepped in front of him. Instead of using his fist, the bigger man gripped his shotgun, turned it around, and drove the butt into Saunders's face. Surprisingly enough, the blunt impact didn't hurt as badly as the punches he'd been given. Rather than point out how the shotgun hit him flush, Saunders rolled with the blow and allowed his head to hang forward.

Zack reappeared in front of him and hunkered down near the lawman's legs. "You gonna sit still for this," he asked while reaching for one boot protruding from the rope that had been wrapped around the sheriff's legs, "or does Robert need to beat you into next week?"

Turning toward Saunders, Eli grunted, "Might as well check his boots."

Rather than grab the lawman's feet himself, Zack stepped back so two of the others could do the deed for him. Both wore bandannas around their faces and pulled as if they fully intended to claim the sheriff's feet as prizes along with his boots. After no small amount of tugging and squirming, the boots came off amid a flurry of cash. Turning them over brought several delighted shouts from the bandits as they greedily scooped up their prize.

"Much obliged to you, Sheriff," Zack said with a tip of his hat. "Now, if you'll excuse us." With that, he stepped away so he could confer with the rest of his men. Only Robert stayed behind. Although the bearded man stood a few steps away from the prisoners, he remained well within the range of his shotgun. He didn't have to say one threatening word for the prisoners to know what would happen if they got any funny ideas in their heads.

But Saunders wasn't interested in funny ideas. He barely seemed interested in the armed men surrounding him. Even when he scraped his feet against the ground, he seemed more perturbed by the loss of his boots than the money that had been inside them. "Just when I thought I could trust you," he grumbled.

"Excuse me?" Eli said.

The lawman snapped his head around to look at Eli when he hissed, "You heard me. I stuck my neck out to keep you from getting hanged. I took a gamble on letting you out of that cell so you can clear your name. I even went along with you when you told me to pretend you got over on me in front of that friend of yours with the big head. After all of that, you still gotta chime in and tell these . . ." He paused before saying the word that was cocked and ready to fire. Even though Robert didn't seem to be concerned with what the men were saying, Saunders dropped his voice a little more and continued with "Tell these idiots about where they need to look to find what they were after."

Eli shook his head in disbelief. "Are you telling me you seriously thought they wouldn't have found that money?"

"Maybe they would. Maybe they wouldn't. All I know for certain is that they found everything they wanted real quickly because of you."

"Were you that attached to the money?" Eli scoffed. "Even Jake would have given it up eventually."

"How many times do I gotta tell you that I ain't anything like those outlaw friends of yours? And maybe you're a bit too much like them than I thought."

"Wouldn't be the first time you were wrong about something," Eli grunted. After a few seconds passed, he added, "It would have only gotten worse, you know."

"What would? Riding with you? No need to tell me that. I guessed as much all by myself."

"No. The beatings. They would have only gotten worse. They weren't guessing about the money. They knew you had it. Why else do you think they went through such pains to stop us?"

"Maybe they were after our horses," Saunders offered.

"Yours ain't a bad specimen, but mine? That nag ain't hardly worth the nails holding her shoes on. Any horse thief could see as much."

"Then maybe they were just desperados looking to get lucky by stopping whoever they could."

Eli shook his head. "They were waiting for us. They had that trail scouted. There were wagons riding ahead of us. Didn't you see them when we left?"

"Yeah, I saw 'em."

"Then why wouldn't they have taken their chances with them? More to pick from and easier to stop than two men on horseback."

"You're just so damn smart, aren't you?" Saunders spat. "It's just so easy to act like you know everything once it's already panned out."

"I don't know much about a lot of things, but I know plenty about this," Eli said in a whisper that sounded as if it tore apart the back of his throat. "It wasn't so long ago that I was on the other side of these situations. I made my living knowing who to rob and when to rob them. Isn't that sort of experience why you brought me along for this suicidal ride of yours?"

Even if Robert couldn't hear every word that was being said, it was plain to see that he was finding their argument amusing. A wry smirk crept beneath his thick beard without doing a thing to diminish the deadly promise in his eyes.

"You've got your job to do and I've got mine," Saunders said. "Don't make things harder by stabbing me in the back."

Eli fixed his eyes on his feet, which were stretched out in front of him and bound by rope that had been hanging from Saunders's saddle. "You wouldn't have been able to do your job when you were dead or busted up too bad to move. Those beatings would have gotten worse, especially since you decided to show them your badge."

"I been a lawman for plenty of years. I know what I'm doin'."

"Yeah, but it's clear you've done more work with cowboys than true killers."

Glaring at Eli with an intensity that was akin to sunlight being concentrated through a magnifying glass, Saunders said, "I've strung up plenty of killers and gunned down plenty more. You of all people should know better than to question my backbone in that regard."

"I'm not questioning anything, Vernon. I'm just saying you made a mistake by showing all that money back in town. Maybe it was an oversight or maybe it was just a wrong guess, but it cost you. Cost us both."

Still somewhat taken aback by hearing the outlaw call him by his common name, Saunders gnashed his teeth and shifted so he was staring straight ahead. The robbers were wrapping up their conference and beginning to disperse. A few words were still trickling in, which kept the group together while they began to drift over to the boulders where the prisoners were being held.

"Maybe they did know we were coming," Saunders admitted, "but I don't know how that could have been prevented. As for showing my badge, it's like you said with the money. They would have found it on their own anyway."

Eli nodded. "You got a point there."

Nothing more was said because the robbers had arrived at some kind of consensus and were approaching the boulders with steam in their strides. Robert reflexively stepped aside to let Zack and Eddie move past him. The man with the thick beard as well as one of the ones still wearing bandannas over their mouths took positions on either side of the two pointing weapons at Eli and Saunders.

"What town you say you were from?" Zack asked.

When Saunders replied, he did so with his chin held high and his chest puffed out as much as his ropes would allow. "Seedley."

To his own men, Zack asked, "Anyone been to Seedley?"

Eddie nodded. The rest of the robbers shook their heads.

"They know you're gone?" Zack asked.

"Yes, but they're expecting me back."

"How many deputies you got?"

Before Saunders could reply, Eli said, "Three, but the sheriff's been wearing that star on his chest for longer than any of us have been drawing breath."

The robbers shifted their attention to him and Zack asked, "Who did you say you were again? One of his deputies?"

Eli's laugh came up like a piece of undigested meat. "He was escorting me to some prison up north."

The faces that could be seen showed keen interest when they heard that. The men wearing bandannas still showed enough in their eyes for Eli to know he'd caught their attention.

"What prison?" Eddie asked.

"How should I know?" Eli said. "All I know is that every town in this territory and at least three others have been plastering my face along with the faces of my gang on every wall that can hold a nail. Yellow-bellied law dogs like this one here have been saving all their pennies to pay out on the rewards being offered. You know that money you found on him today?"

"Yeah?"

"It's meant to be a loan for some other law dog friend of this one here's so they can pay up if the rest of my gang's ever rounded up." Turning to glare at Saunders as if he were about to spit on him, Eli added, "Fat chance of that ever happening. He was lucky to catch me at all. Bushwhacked me from behind."

"What's this gang you're supposed to run with?" Eddie asked.

Eli relaxed and squared his shoulders as if he were reclining in a padded armchair.

"The Jake Welles bunch. Ever hear of them?"

This time, when the robbers looked at each other, there was something else reflected within their eyes.

"Sure we heard of them," Zack said. "That don't mean you rode with them."

"Rode with them into Missouri last year to cut our way through three banks in as many weeks. Dragged out each safe and busted them open myself."

"Everyone's heard of that run," Eddie scoffed. "I heard of it too. Doesn't prove I was there. What's your name again?"

"Eli Barlow."

More glances were passed back and forth among the robbers. Although he was interested in what was going on, Saunders wasn't quite ready to step in just yet.

"I heard of that name," Zack said. "Where were you caught?"

"Seedley," Eli replied as if he were naming a hated enemy. "Jake and the others got away."

"What others?"

Even though he hadn't inserted himself into this conversation, Saunders could tell that question was loaded with some deadly ammunition. In fact, every one of the robbers watched intently as Eli spoke his reply.

"Cody Beasley and Scarecrow Hank."

Some of the robbers in the back of the group scowled beneath their bandannas, but Zack and Eddie grinned. "Ain't too often I find someone who's heard of that name," Eddie said. "Ain't no lawman in these parts that knows it, that's for certain. Them that calls him Scarecrow to his face usually got a fight on their hands."

"Me and Hank locked up plenty of times," Eli said. "We worked together well enough, so he usually let it slide. Course, there was a time when we were stuck in a downpour in Kansas that ol' Hank wasn't in such a forgiving mood. Cracked me in the jaw with his fist wrapped around that little derringer he carries under his belt."

"I rode with Hank for a while myself," Eddie said.

Eli shrugged beneath his ropes. "Hank rode with lots of men."

"I caught sight of that derringer once. Made the mistake of calling it a woman's gun."

"That couldn't have gone over well."

"It sure didn't," Eddie laughed. "So you say this lawman bushwhacked you?"

"He did. Me, Hank, Jake, and Cody were robbing a stagecoach and it all went south in a rush. This one got lucky, but still wasn't man enough to fire a shot. Instead, he knocked me down and wrapped me up."

"That why your holster was empty and you didn't have anything but dust in your pockets?"

"Yes, sir."

"Seems like you're not too lucky where being tied up is concerned," Zack pointed out.

"Maybe not, but at least you men had the sand to do it without hitting me from behind like a coward."

Saunders might have been keeping his mouth shut, but he was fuming so much that smoke was about to come out of his ears.

Zack handed his shotgun over to Eddie and drew a hunting knife from the scabbard that hung from his belt. Lowering himself to one knee beside Eli, he asked, "So there's rewards being offered for you and Jake and the rest?"

"Ain't there always?"

"And this sheriff was carrying enough to pay them off, huh?"

"That was just to help boost the funds of other local lawmen that're friends of his. Ever since I was caught, everyone else is looking for the rest of the gang. Jake especially. Bounty hunters will be about, as well as posses or vigilantes. Wouldn't cut it if anyone went through the trouble of bringing in someone like Jake or Hank and there wasn't enough in the kitty to pay the reward."

"Friend of mine who was in Cheyenne said Jake was headed that way."

Saunders felt his heart skip a beat, but Eli barely seemed to notice. On the contrary, his expression drifted more toward casual amusement as he said, "We're also supposed to be in Wichita or down Texas way. Don't believe what you hear, right?"

"That's right. That's why I have a hard time believing the sheriff of some town I ain't never heard of is responsible for fillin' the coffers of someone outside his jurisdiction."

"These lawmen all take care of each other," Eli said. "Besides, you got your hands on the money that was stuffed in this one's boots, pockets, and everywhere else. That should tell you all you need to know."

"All I should know . . . like there's more where this came from?"

Eli's only response was a grin and a wink.

"Think you could take us to where it is?"

"One of you knows where Seedley is, right?" Eli asked.

"Yeah."

"Then you know as much as I do. I couldn't have found that mud hole on a map if my life depended on it. You men seem like the sorts that would appreciate knowing where they might find a load of cash. I just hope you might see your way clear to repaying that information with a kindness of your own."

"What'd you have in mind?" Zack asked.

"What do you think?" Eli snapped as all of the friendliness disappeared from his voice. "I been locked up in a jail cell and led around by the nose for long enough. I just want to go my separate way."

Zack held the knife so its blade was less than an inch from Eli's ropes. "We ain't seen nothing to make us think you were lying. Fact is, you've said things that no man other than an outlaw would know. I can tell by the look in your eyes that you're not just another dog who hides behind a badge like this one here."

Where Saunders had been fuming before, he was positively steaming now. Sweat trickled down his face that had nothing to do with the temperature.

"But if I'm just gonna cut you loose," Zack continued, "I'll need something more than just a how-do-you-do."

"Professional courtesy isn't enough anymore?" Eli sighed. "What a sad state of affairs that is."

The blade came up toward Zack's face so he could tap it absently upon his cheek. He then used it as a pointer when he said, "Next time you see Jake Welles or any of the others from that gang, I want you to deliver a message. Tell them Zack Pardow and his boys were good enough to swoop in and relieve this sheriff of his money, which also shortchanges plenty of other lawmen around here of the ability to pay off rewards being offered for their scalps."

Eli's smile was all too genuine. "He'd get a kick out of that."

"Then he should also think highly enough of us to consider taking us on."

"All of you?"

The hardened face that Zack had been showing his prisoners crumbled a bit when he shrugged and said, "Most of us. Any that he'd like riding with his boys."

"I don't speak for Jake, but I can put a good word in."

"That's all I ask." From there, Zack went through the short sawing motions required to hack through the ropes that had been binding Eli from head to toe. After a few strands were cut, the rest loosened and he was able to wriggle free. Zack dropped his knife into its scabbard and offered that hand to Eli, who took it and was helped to his feet.

Eli straightened his clothes and rubbed a few spots that had been cramped or chafed during his most recent imprisonment. When he looked down at Saunders, he found the sheriff looking back up at him with an expression that was best described as cautiously hopeful.

"We're going after the rest of the money that one's sitting on in Seedley," Eddie said. "You're welcome to come along with us if you like."

"I'll pass on that offer. Seen enough of that place already. Watch yourselves while you're there. Plenty of men who'll be ready to pick up a gun if an alarm is raised."

"Deputies?"

"Vigilantes. If this sheriff wasn't good for anything else, at least he was able to talk enough sense into that group to keep them in line."

The robbers all looked back and forth at each other in another silent council. Eli might not have known exactly what they were relaying in all those glances, nods, and shakes of heads, but he'd been a part of enough such consultations to have a pretty good idea.

"Keep him wrapped up tight," Zack said while kicking Saunders with the side of his boot. "If he don't come up with a good way to that money or help us get past them vigilantes, we'll drop him as deadweight and get rich the hard way. You good from here, Eli?"

"Better than good."

"All right, then. Let's not waste any more time. We should be able to get to Seedley, conduct our business, and be out before dawn."

All of the robbers made their way to horses that were tethered nearby. Robert tossed his shotgun to one of the masked men so he could walk over to the boulders, pick up Saunders, and heft the sheriff over one shoulder with a minimum of fuss.

"You'll probably want a better horse," Eddie said.

Eli nodded. "I'll take the sheriff's. Give me my guns and his as well. Also, I could use some ammunition."

That got a healthy round of laughter from most of the robbers.

Approaching Zack with an outstretched hand, Eli took the Colt from him and said, "You did the right thing in letting me go."

"Call it professional courtesy. Just remember what I said about talking to Jake on our behalf."

"I'll do that. One more thing. How'd you decide to come after us? You were following us all the way from that last town, right?"

"You got that right. George back there tends to horses for most of the folks passing through who stay at the hotel or rent a room," Zack replied while waving back to one of the masked men. After that, the man pulled down his bandanna to reveal a face that was a lot younger than Eli had been expecting. It only took a second for him to recall seeing that face outside the hotel when he and Saunders had approached it to rent their room. "That sheriff was waving around a good amount of money when he paid for his room and made arrangements for supplies to be rounded up and brought to him."

"Showed me plenty of cash when he told me to take good care of his horses so they'd be ready to ride this morning," George said. "Even gave me something extra for my troubles. Figured there'd be plenty more where that come from."

Eli didn't outright say the words *I told you so,* but his eyes expressed that sentiment well enough when he met the sheriff's piercing glare.

"Soon as I'm out of these ropes," Saunders growled, "I'll tear you apart with my bare hands."

"Save some of that gumption, law dog," Zack said as he passed him by on the way to his horse. "You're gonna need it."

CHAPTER 15

Eli was extremely happy with himself as he rode away from the robbers who'd had him wrapped up tighter than a corset only a few minutes ago. Not only had he managed to talk his way out of a very unpleasant situation, but he'd pulled himself out of official custody with the sheriff's horse beneath him to boot. It wasn't much of a surprise that so many folks had heard about his old gang. Jake had always insisted on letting folks know who was stealing from them so his name could become a thing unto itself. Eli and Hank hadn't been as happy with that idea and nobody cared to know who Cody was, so it all worked out well enough. When Saunders had described the iron wagon as a lightning rod, he'd acted as if that were a new concept. Eli had ridden with the biggest lightning rod of them all. Other robbers knowing about the Welles Gang was like a school-marm knowing her ABCs.

A sly grin crept onto his face as he slowed his horse to an easy stride. Until now he'd simply wanted to get away from the robbers before they thought better of letting him go. Now that there was a good enough distance between them and it seemed nobody was following him, Eli had to think about where he meant to go. Surprisingly enough, that wasn't as easy as he'd expected.

Most recently, he'd barely been able to take three steps in a row without someone tugging on a chain connected to his wrists or running into a wall of brick or bars. Before that, he'd ridden with Jake and that bunch. As much as Jake liked to talk about being free, he was the only one to truly make that claim. After Eli's face was seen in Jake's presence during a job, he'd been irrevocably connected to that bunch. Eli could come and go as he pleased just as long as he didn't stray far enough to make one of the other gang members nervous. The chain was longer and the walls were a bit farther away, but they were still there.

His mind then drifted to a stretch of time where he'd truly been able to do what he wanted and go wherever he chose. It was one of the most terrifying periods in Eli's twenty-eight years on earth. The horizon flowed out in every direction, making him feel small and his choices insignificant. Before that, his life had been a path that had become nearly too rough to traverse. Every day had been a heavy, grinding thing filled with pain that wore him down to a nub. The unnamed sickness in his skull made his thoughts grind together like gears that could only be oiled by however much whiskey it took to numb him. Every time a doctor shrugged at him where his sickness was concerned set him adrift on open water with no star to steer by.

What Eli wanted to do and what he was able to do had always been two separate things. That's how it was for most folks. What seemed particularly cruel was the fact that his wants and natural gifts couldn't even be within spitting distance of each other. He hadn't started out wanting to steal the money that wound up in his pockets, but he had a knack for it. Locked doors and sealed safes beckoned to him. Men in suits who thought they were comfortable behind armed guards and the letter of the law might as well have spit in his face and insulted his kin. Like a bird that only needed to be pushed from the nest, Eli just had to swipe his first silver dollar to know where his natural gifts needed to be applied.

Ever since he'd gotten the taste for stealing, he knew he couldn't go back to the traditional ways of earning his keep. Considering the condition that gnawed at the inside of his head in painful jabs that lanced behind his eyes or stabbed at the roots of his teeth, wasting time with menial labor seemed ridiculous. As the pain became worse and his lawless deeds weighed him down more, Eli had pulled away from every other aspect of life that he might possibly miss when it drew to a close. That alone was a restraint that cut into him worse than a bit in his mouth. Thinking back on that took away the sweet taste of victory he'd been savoring a few short moments ago. He pulled back on his reins again, bringing his horse to a stop.

Once again, the horizon was spread out like all of creation laid out for him to see. Feeling the dizzying certainty that he was beneath something so vastly greater than him made Eli understand why the good Lord had given men eyes that could only take in so much. Being able to see the rest made his head swim with too many possibilities, too many directions to be taken, and too much space to cover in even a dozen lifetimes. Eli gripped the saddle horn and eased himself down until his boots touched solid ground. Rather than look up at the infinite reaches beyond the clouds drifting lazily between man and God, he focused on dirt and things that sprouted up from it as best they could.

Eli squatted down to place his fingers in the soil. Whenever he'd been lost or in need of advice, he could always rely on the one thing that was always present no matter how far he roamed or how badly he might have twisted things up.

Inspiration never came easy.

Guidance was an even trickier thing.

Although he didn't expect quick answers or some shining path leading him to his destiny, Eli hoped for something more than the windy silence he got. The longer he waited, the more he became acutely aware that he was alone in the middle of Wyoming Territory with nothing more than a stolen horse and filthy fingers to show for it.

Eli's gut twisted into a knot.

All the experience he'd cobbled together throughout his years on either side of the law told him he was a fool to expect anything more than aching knees for the time he'd wasted thus far.

The outlaw in him was still slapping Eli's back to congratulate him on a job well done where Sheriff Saunders was concerned, but the man beneath those things knew the real story.

If Eli hadn't cared whether Saunders had lived or died, he would have chosen different words when bringing Zack and those others around to his way of thinking. He could have gained even more favor by borrowing a gun and shooting the lawman himself. Instead, he'd woven the story about the money in Seedley and where the cash in Saunders's boots had come from. At the time, he hadn't thought much about why he should take such a roundabout way in explaining those things. Eli let out a sigh and cursed himself for being weak. The only thing worse than a lawman dragging him around by a chain was an angry lawman hunting him down after being double-crossed and left to rot in the incapable hands of simple thieves.

Saunders wasn't the only one who could spot a killer by looking one in the eye. That skill was required for any outlaw of Eli's caliber to survive, and he could tell for certain those robbers were capable of filling the lawman with lead and taking whatever trophies they could to impress any other robbers who might not have been there to witness the act for themselves. For some reason, Eli had done his best to avoid that outcome.

Did he consider Saunders to be a good man?

Had he somehow grown to like the sheriff?

While those possibilities might have had some merit, Eli knew there was something else. Something that didn't come to him until he'd given his heart a chance to stop galloping within his chest and his thoughts a chance to settle in his mind after being kicked up like silt at the bottom of an old trough. What weighed even heavier on him wasn't making things easier for himself in the present. That was akin to only laying down enough track for a train to roll around one bend. What Eli was concerned about, whether he'd known it at the time or not, was how things looked for him in the longer stretch.

Being concerned about the future was something new to Eli. When he was a younger man, his future had been either out of his control or too vast to contemplate. Now, with him an outlaw, it had been etched into stone: a play with only two acts. Too certain to question and too short to worry about.

That had changed at a moment when things seemed to have been at their lowest point. During a period when Eli felt the most confined and possessed the least amount of hope, he'd been given a reason to breathe deeper and savor the breath as something more than just a gulp of air. He'd been shown something worth living for. He'd met someone who made it seem worthwhile to change his old ways and forge new ones.

He'd met Lyssa Beihn.

If asked why the woman's face had stuck with him ever since she'd brought him that first meal while he was locked away in Seedley, Eli would have been hard-pressed to come up with a good answer. He'd been attracted to other pretty women, drawn in by the scent of their skin or soothed by their touch, but Lyssa was different from all those passing fancies. She'd seen him for what he was, arrived when he hadn't had the strength to put on a false front or win anyone's favor. After all of that, she still had a smile that had been lovingly crafted just for him. He'd never stopped seeing that smile. Never stopped hearing her footsteps as she drew closer to his side. Never stopped wishing he was worthy of holding her hand.

And there it was.

Eli's eyes came open the rest of the way as the thing he'd been waiting for finally arrived. Lunging at the keys in her hand in one moment of weakness had been an animal's instinct, as well as one of the most shameful moments of his life. It had given him a good look at the man he'd become. Eli hated that man. Although it was too late to keep him from being seen, that man could be changed. The fact that Lyssa had seen fit to speak to him after that sorrowful display told him it wasn't too late for that.

There was still time for him to make a choice that involved action instead of re-action. Time to travel a path that required him to walk on his own steam instead of being dragged by someone else's.

It wouldn't have been an easy choice to make under the best of circumstances, and these were terrible no matter how he looked at them. Sure, he had a horse and open ground in front of him, but that was no longer good enough. Even if he'd given up on holding himself accountable for anything, he now knew there was someone else out there worthy of answering to.

Finding her hadn't been easy. Eli even wondered if it had been a miracle. Having never bought in to such blindly optimistic talk, he honestly didn't know how a true miracle could be defined. His heart told him he wasn't using that word lightly, which was enough for his head to agree. Once that was settled, there was only the question of where he should go from there.

After being sidetracked by some bad decisions made by the outlaw part of Eli's soul, he'd been granted a quiet moment where he was both honored and punished to see who he was and what he needed to do.

Helping Saunders had been the right thing to do.

Allowing his fate to be decided by the likes of Zack and Eddie wasn't even close.

Getting a glimpse of Lyssa had been a blessing.

Winning her favor, a pursuit worth living for.

Throwing away the chance to feel her hand in his was nothing short of a sin. Eli had heard about sins and sinners from folks who tossed those words about with ease, but to one who'd sinned, they meant more. To one who'd walked in the darkness, the shadows were that much deeper. Preachers called swearing in the wrong company or kissing the wrong girl a sin. They called children and misguided drunks sinners.

Eli knew sin and he'd stood beside sinners. Neither of those things was something he took lightly, which was why allowing himself to be anyone other than a person who could look Lyssa Beihn in the eye cut him right to the quick. Now that Eli knew exactly where he'd so recently strayed, why he had to find his way back, and what he needed to do to get there, he just needed to see it through. That was no small thing.

After sinking his fingers a little deeper into the ground, Eli slowly curled them to feel dirt slide beneath his nails and cool pockets of dampness ease against his skin. Eventually, he made a fist. Closing it as tightly as he could, he brought it up and opened it to allow the mush to spatter back against the overturned grass.

Insects that had settled upon his shoulders and arm now scattered as if surprised by the fact that their perch could move on its own. Even his horse shifted uneasily when Eli returned to place his hand on its side. He stroked its brown and black mane until it calmed and nuzzled his arm.

Looking up and toward the ground that had been in front of him, Eli took hold of the reins in his dirty hand and brought the horse around to face the path he'd left behind. Plenty of hurt lay in that direction, but it was the way he needed to go. Riding anywhere else would have just given him something to regret later on.

"Aw, hell," he grumbled while climbing

into the saddle. "I better do this before I realize how stupid it is."

CHAPTER 16

The robbers stopped and started again more times than an engine with a broken piston. If they weren't riding at full speed amid the thunder of hooves, they were drawing to a halt so they could cluster together and whisper among themselves. The most consistent element of the group was Robert. His bulky frame and whisker-covered face was never far from Saunders. Despite the shotgun in the large man's hands, the sheriff took some comfort in the fact that he could at least count on one thing to remain the same.

"What is it now?" Saunders asked after the horses had been reined in for what felt like the tenth time.

Also consistent was Robert's commitment to remaining quiet unless one of the other bandits addressed him. When Saunders spoke to him, which was often, he stood still without so much as looking in the lawman's direction.

"Come on, now," Saunders groused. "The least you could do is let me know what all the deliberation is about. After all, it's probably my life hanging in the balance."

"No, it isn't."

Saunders couldn't help letting out a surprised chuckle when he heard the voice rustle from beneath Robert's thick carpet of a beard. "You're telling me my life isn't hanging in the balance?"

"No," Robert said as he shifted his eyes to look over at the lawman. "I'm telling you it ain't the least I could do. The least I could do would be to pound this shotgun against your skull to keep you quiet."

"Or wrap a bandanna around my mouth. That'd work and that's even less effort than constantly ringing my bell."

Saunders couldn't be certain, but he thought he might have seen a hint of a smirk beneath the big man's whiskers. "Yeah," he grunted. "I suppose that'd be the least I could do."

"So, what are they talking about?"

Surprising Saunders yet again, Robert said, "Which way we should head into Seedley. Or what we might find when we get there. If you got anything to say in that regard, now's the time to speak up."

Saunders nodded, but didn't make a sound.

"Wanna know what's the least *you* could do?" Robert asked. "You could tell us how to get to the rest of that money before Zack asks again. If you see Eddie comin' your way, you'd be wise to start talking even faster. He's getting real impatient and that's when things get ugly."

"Like this isn't ugly enough?"

This time, the lawman's jovial tone had no effect on Robert. He shifted his head to look at him directly and growled, "No. This ain't even close to how much uglier things could be."

Any lawman worth his salt would hear plenty of threats throughout his career. Most of the time, they weren't even empty ones. While no lawman could be frozen by threats like those, he had to know when to be concerned. At that moment, Saunders was concerned. Either he'd been holding on to one last bit of hope or he simply hadn't allowed himself to look at the entire picture, but he'd been able to keep a relatively level head. Rather than allow that one slim advantage to slip away, he steeled himself and said, "Things aren't about to be ugly for just me, you know. I'm a sheriff. A lawman."

"I know. Saw the badge."

"Then you should know it's more than just a decoration pinned to my shirt. It means there are consequences for not listening to what I say and a price to pay for raising a hand against me."

When Robert chuckled this time, it could very well have been a tremor before the earth opened up. "We done a lot more than raise a hand."

"That's right. And before things get worse, you should think about saving yourself."

"Only man that needs to be saved around here is you."

"And once word gets out that you've held me this way or done anything worse, you and the rest of this gang will be wanted men."

"Already are," Robert sighed as if he was stating the color of the sky.

"You must not have killed any lawmen," Saunders replied with an equal amount of certainty. "Otherwise, I would've heard about it. Once a lawman is gunned down anywhere within a week's ride of here, word spreads like wildfire and that's way out here where the grass grows tall. You go anywhere closer to a town of any size, and word will spread even faster."

"Ain't such a bad thing for word to spread about us. Makes the next job easier."

"I'm not talking about a reputation. I'm talking about a death sentence." From the corner of his eye, Saunders could see the rest of the robbers were starting to break out of their group. The other four were still talking, but it wouldn't be long before they were ready to ride again. "Lawmen don't like being the hunted ones," he said in a rush. "You see, we've got a reputation too. It doesn't do us a lick of good for it to be known we can be gunned down so easily. Before you know it, every outlaw in the territory will be running free, thinking they can do as they please."

Robert let out a single, huffing laugh that ruffled the edge of his mustache that hung closest to his upper lip. "We been doin' what we please so far."

"Right. Because you're not in anyone's sights. You men become known as killers with no fear of the law or any man who stands behind it, and that will most certainly change. The prices on your heads will triple. Not only will bounty hunters be looking for a payday, but any other lawman will want to make it known that the law is something to be respected. They'll make an example out of you," the sheriff added in a conspiratorial whisper. "That means you'll be shot full of holes, propped up in a box, and put on display as a warning to any other foolish souls who think they can tear through these parts like a plague. They'll take pictures of your bodies and post them as a message to more would-be gunmen. You ever seen pictures like those? In order for them to do their job, the men in them have to be messed up. Real bad."

Saunders couldn't tell if that registered with the bigger man or not. Robert only budged when Zack came along to pat him on the back and tell him it was time to get moving. Once everyone else was in their saddles, Zack approached Saunders and said, "We're going to Seedley and you're riding up front with me and Eddie."

"If you think I'm going to help you do anything, you're mistaken," the lawman told him. "There isn't even anything for you to take once we get there. I don't know where Eli came up with that nonsense about money lying around."

"See, that's just the thing. Not all of us are convinced of that either. On one hand, I know for a fact that he rode with Jake Welles. I heard about a skinny dude with a baby face riding with him and Hank, and he sure fits the bill. He said some things that no one else would say unless they were part of that gang or at least rode with men who were, and since one of us even heard of a man named Eli riding with Jake Welles, I'd say there was something to that story of his.

"On the other hand, Eddie's been to Seedley and he knows it's got a vigilante problem, which adds even more credence to what Eli said. We got its sheriff under our thumb, which should count for something. At the very least, someone there should be willing to pay some sort of ransom to get you back. We even came up with the idea of using you to walk into the little bank they got in that town and help ourselves. If nothin' else," Zack continued, "you'll make a fine shield if any deputy or hotheaded citizen decides to take a stand against us. Whatever we get from that combined with what we already took from you should make this a pretty valuable little venture. Whatever hand we decide to play, it works out pretty well for us."

"What about me?" Saunders asked.

"Could work out well enough to keep you alive, depending on how you cooperate."

"Me cooperating with you doesn't make me much of a sheriff. My name would be mud in this whole territory."

"But you'd be alive."

Narrowing his eyes and screwing his face into a contemplative grimace, Saunders looked as if he was truly weighing his options. After a few seconds, he shook his head once and said, "Think I'll pass on the offer, but I've got a good one for you. How about you set me loose before you and your boys get in too deep for you to ever get out again?"

When Zack looked to him for backup, Robert said, "He thinks every man wearing a badge will hunt us like dogs if we harm a hair on his pretty little head."

"I never went so far as to call myself pretty," Saunders replied, "but I appreciate the compliment."

Zack wasn't amused. Approaching the lawman and grabbing his neck as if he meant to either lift him onto his horse or throttle him right then and there, he snarled, "If you think you can talk your way outta this, you're sadly mistaken! And if you think we're gonna believe a word you say or be threatened by you just because of a title slapped on you by some mud hole of a town, you're mistaken *again*."

"Then I suppose I should keep my mouth shut."

"Good idea, lawman! You do what you're

told, walk where you're pointed, and keep your manners in line and we should get along just fine. You don't and I'll drop you with one shot to the gut so my boys can finish you off in ways you don't even want to contemplate."

Saunders didn't waver as he stared at the outlaw. Keeping his composure wasn't a very difficult task. All he needed to do was think about one particular thing to draw his entire being into one focused point. He wasn't certain if he would actually make it to Seedley or what would happen once he got there. All he knew was that, if he didn't do something about it, he was a dead man.

"You understand me, Sheriff?" Zack asked, spitting that last word out like a piece of gristle.

Saunders nodded once, causing the outlaw to beam proudly.

"Very good. We're gonna load you back onto that horse and then we're riding back to your town. This goes right and nobody has to get hurt. Not even you. Things start going wrong . . . well, they'll go wrong for everyone. Us, you, and anyone within range of our guns."

As promised, the sheriff was dumped across the back of a horse and the outlaws started riding again. Saunders didn't bother himself with any more details than that. He had bigger problems to solve, no tools at his disposal, and precious little time to get anything done.

He wanted to think he'd been in tougher situations, but that would have been a bald-faced lie.

CHAPTER 17

Saunders had never been very good at poker. That single fact had never really bothered him until now. Mostly, what he wanted was the ability to make his face unreadable by his opponents. As he was carried back along the trail he'd covered what seemed like a lifetime ago, he was certain his rage was pouring out of him like steam from a teakettle. The outlaws were treating him differently, watching him closer, even keeping their guns drawn and ready to fire. Whether that was because of any changes in him or due to their closer proximity to their destination was anyone's guess. Since they still had a ways to go before arriving in Seedley, Saunders could only assume some of the bandits were beginning to grow weary of their unwilling travel companion.

When the entire group slowed to a stop, Saunders felt his heart skip a beat. They hadn't been riding for very long, and after all of Zack's big talk about his plans, he figured they'd be riding well into the night to get back to Seedley that much quicker. There was always the possibility that they'd just needed some time to reconsider their options and see the error of their ways. Then again, that seemed almost as likely as a twister coming along to sweep away the bandits and leave Saunders with his ropes untied.

"Who is that?" Eddie asked.

Since he was draped across the back of a horse, Saunders couldn't see whom he was referring to. Zack rode past him and took a moment to dig for something in his saddlebags. The sheriff could only guess it was field glasses or a telescope, because the outlaw's voice was heavy with concentration when he said, "Looks like that friend of ours changed his mind about joining us."

Eddie hacked up something and spat it onto the ground. "Yeah, well, if he thinks he can just swoop in and get an equal share, he's mistaken."

"There's more riding on this than money. It's a shot at trading up into some bigger jobs."

"With Jake Welles and his bunch? Think I'd rather take my chances when I'm not in the sights of so many lawmen."

"You don't know anything," Zack said amid the distinct clatter of a telescope being collapsed. "Just being able to count a man like Jake or Hank among our friends could mean a lot. Go see what he wants."

"No need. He's coming to us."

"Go meet him, I said!" Zack snapped. "See what he wants before we let him get up close."

Eddie's muttering wasn't clear enough to distinguish every word, but Saunders could tell that it wasn't favorable.

As Eddie's horse broke away from the group, another drew closer. Saunders closed his eyes and listened to the two rhythms of hooves beating against the dry ground to meet somewhere nearby after only a few seconds. Once again, Eddie's voice could be heard along with Eli's. No matter how hard Saunders concentrated on the discussion going on nearby, he couldn't make out more than a few words. Eddie still seemed perturbed, but Eli was as cool and unwavering as polished steel.

"This is taking too long," Robert grunted in a voice that would only be heard by the few men in his immediate vicinity.

Being one of those men, Zack replied, "Give it another moment. Eddie's probably just sticking his foot in his mouth again."

"He does that a lot."

"Yes, indeed."

"Too much," Robert snarled.

In that moment, Saunders decided the big man with the bigger beard was more than just a set of able hands and a shotgun. Because Zack didn't correct him with the speed in which he frequently scolded Eddie, Robert could very well be one of the leaders of this pack instead of just another follower. The sheriff stowed that away for future use as a horse rumbled up to settle beside Zack.

"What's he want?" Zack asked.

"Our law dog there," Eddie replied. "Says he wants us to hand him over."

"Why?"

"I asked, but he wasn't talking. When I told him he'd better talk before I knocked the words out of him, he started making threats."

A deep rumbling laugh churned up from the depths of Robert's gut. When Saunders twisted around to get a look at the bandits, he was just in time to see Eddie puff out his chest and lean forward in his saddle to ask, "Somethin' funny?"

"Serves us right for picking you as a spokesman."

"Send the sheriff to me," Eli shouted from

a distance Saunders guessed to be in the vicinity of ten to twenty yards.

"Shut up, Eddie," Zack grunted. In a louder voice, he stood up in his stirrups and asked, "What do you want him for, Eli?"

"That doesn't matter."

"Sure it does. We got big plans for this one. You know that! If you changed your mind about riding with us into Seedley after that money, just say so. We could loot the whole town with your kind of help."

"There ain't any more money!" Saunders insisted. "How many times do I have to say it?"

"Someone shut him up," Zack barked.

Before Saunders could protest or add anything else to his plea, one of the other two members of the gang that had remained nameless this far rushed over to him and shoved a dirty scarf in almost far enough for the lawman to choke on it.

"I won't ask again," Eli called out. "Either send the sheriff to me or send someone else to talk it over."

"I knew you'd stick your foot in your mouth," Zack said in a harsher, yet quieter tone.

Responding in a hissing whisper, Eddie said, "I didn't do nothin' apart from what you asked."

"Just keep your mouth shut and don't do anything stupid while I'm gone. You," he said while pointing at Robert. "Watch that one there. In fact," he added while glancing once more in Eddie's direction, "better watch them both."

Although Eddie grumbled with discontent as Zack rode away, he wasn't about to say a cross word to Robert. The big bearded man had found his shotgun and seemed ready to use it no matter which target presented itself.

Eli sat with his back straight and his hands stacked on his saddle horn. His eyes were intense slits and his mouth an unmoving line. It wasn't a pleasant expression, but one that wasn't out of the ordinary for someone who'd spoken with Eddie.

Pulling back on his reins so his horse's nose stopped within a few inches of Eli's horse's, Zack shifted his hat so it sat farther back on his head and exposed more of his face. "Whatever Eddie said to make you cross, it don't go for the rest of us."

"Send the sheriff over," Eli said.

"Why would you want that? You ain't fixing to go after that money yourself, now, are you?"

"There isn't any more money."

Zack opened his mouth, closed it before

any flies came in, and then blinked before asking, "What?"

"That money in Seedley," Eli explained. "There ain't any."

"That business about the bounties?"

Eli shook his head. "I was mistaken."

"Mistaken or lying so you can ride back and claim it all for yourself? What happened? Did you catch up with Jake and Hank so you decided the three of you were enough to raid that little town?" Gasping as if he'd accidentally invoked the name of the Devil himself, Zack added, "That's it, ain't it? We ain't enemies here, Eli. We could all work together. You and Jake and Hank would get the lion's share, of course. Just let us come along for the next job you're —"

"No," Eli said sharply. "There's no money in Seedley and no other jobs with me. I came to collect the sheriff and be on our way."

"That brings me back to my first question. Why do you want that sheriff so bad?"

"I've stopped explaining myself to the likes of you."

Studying the darkness etched into Eli's face, Zack nodded. "You still want your pound of flesh after being dragged around by that law dog, huh? Tell you what, then.

You can have him as soon as we're through in Seedley."

"You're not listening to me."

"And you're not using your eyes! You're outmanned five to one. I was trying to be hospitable before on account of our shared interests, but I won't step aside to let one man tell me what to do with my gang. I don't care how many friends that man's got."

Eli wasn't usually the one to toss threats around, but the time had come for him to start doing things he wasn't accustomed to. He gritted his teeth and tensed the muscles around both eyes until his face closely resembled a death mask. "Right now you don't need to worry about anyone I might call friend. I'm the one in front of you and I'm the one you need to be concerned about."

"Is this the same threat you told to Eddie?"

"No," Eli replied. "I told Eddie that I'd knock him off his horse if he didn't remove the smart tone from his voice. I'm telling you if you don't bring me that sheriff, you're going to have a fight on your hands that you most likely won't live long enough to see through to the end."

It had been less than a minute since Zack

had gone to speak with Eli, but the remaining four bandits were about to crawl out of their skins. Only Robert remained in his saddle without straining to get a better look at what was going on between the two men holding court nearby.

"Looks like they're reaching some sort of agreement," Eddie said. "I think Zack is headed back this way."

"Just wait and see what happens," Robert grumbled.

Looking over to the other two men who'd taken positions on either side of Saunders's horse, Eddie snapped, "What's the matter with you two? Don't any of this concern you enough to say anything?"

"They know when to keep their mouths shut," Robert told him. "You should too."

The other two gunmen exercised that prerogative now.

Eddie might have continued his argument just to keep up appearances, but Zack was on his way back. All four of the bandits stopped what they were doing so they could watch for their leader's next signal and became utterly quiet to hear his next words. Eli sat in his saddle as if he'd been constructed from brick and bolted to his horse's back. His eyes were all but hidden in the shadow cast by the brim of his hat, but the intensity within them burned like two smoldering coals at the bottom of a furnace.

Stopping at a point about halfway between Eli and the rest of his men, Zack turned his horse around so its body formed a ninety-degree angle to both other groups. His hand drifted toward the gun at his hip as he shouted, "You should'a kept running after I cut you loose!" With that, he drew his pistol and brought it around.

Eli remained tall in his saddle as he drew the Army Colt that had been given to him. His hand wasn't quicker than Zack's. In fact, Zack pulled his trigger first and sent a round hissing through the air that sailed wide and to the right of its target. Eli didn't flinch as the bullet whipped past him. Instead, he sighted along the top of his barrel and squeezed his trigger in a smooth, deliberate motion that drilled a piece of hot lead through Zack's upper body.

It was a grazing blow, which still nearly knocked the bandit from his saddle. Only a tight grip and powerful reflexes kept him from hitting the ground. Zack fired again and flicked his reins to ride back toward his men. As soon as he cleared a path, gunfire erupted from the other men's barrels.

Saunders couldn't help watching. The sight of Eli sitting in the middle of that hailstorm of lead without making the first move to defend himself was as inspiring as it was terrifying.

One of the silent robbers made the mistake of moving forward to get a cleaner shot and caught one of Eli's rounds square in the chest. He toppled from his saddle as if he'd been kicked by a mule and when he hit the ground, it was clear he would never stand up again.

Since a few of the guns among the robbers were .38s, Eli had been given enough ammunition to reload his own pistols before parting ways with them the first time. Because of that, he reached across his belly to pull one of those guns from its holster and hold it at the ready. The moment the Colt's hammer slapped against the back of an empty casing, he swung a leg over his horse's neck and dropped down. Once both boots hit the dirt, he continued his downward journey until he was in a one-kneed firing stance. The Colt slid from his fingers and he made the border shift to deliver the .38 into his right hand in a seamless transition that allowed him to continue firing seconds after he'd stopped.

"What brought this on?" Robert asked as he and the others climbed from their saddles to take refuge wherever they could.

Zack clamped one hand over the messy wound in his shoulder and snarled through gritted teeth. "He wants the sheriff back. Just kill him!"

"And be quick about it," Eddie said as he took a rifle from his saddle. "He gets loose after this and we'll have Jake Welles's bunch after us."

"I don't care about Jake Welles!" Zack shouted. "Just kill this —" He was cut short by another round that clipped the side of his head. Although it was still not a fatal wound, the impact of a flying bullet against any man's skull was enough to put his lights out for a good, long while. Zack reeled as if from a powerful uppercut and hit the ground on his back.

While he might have been transfixed by the lethal display before, Saunders now pinched his eyes shut as more gunshots closed in around him. He squirmed within his ropes, kicked and thrashed as much as he could, and even shifted his weight in an attempt to get down to where he wasn't on such prominent display. All of the shots blended into a continuous, explosive roar that made it impossible to tell who was shooting or how many shots were landing.

Only a few seconds had passed, which had almost been enough time for the fight to play itself out. Eddie had straightened up with the rifle at his shoulder and was put down by a round that had been fired so close that Saunders could see the smoke rolling from Eli's barrel. That was followed by a second one that sent Eddie to the Promised Land and a third that happened when Eddie's finger clenched around his trigger. By the time Eddie fell silent, Robert was stepping up to make his play.

The bigger man opened his mouth with a scream that was washed away by bellowing thunder from his shotgun. Saunders could feel the earth tremble and could barely make out an agonized cry from a nearby horse that wailed and stomped the ground. Saunders twisted to get a better look and saw Eli stand up from where he'd sought cover. The .38 in Eli's hand went off twice in quick succession, which still wasn't enough to drop the bearded man.

Robert staggered back and into the horse carrying Saunders like a sack of dirty clothes and roared an insult that the lawman couldn't hear because of the ringing in his ears. Before the bearded man could stuff another pair of shells into the shotgun's breech, Eli tossed his empty .38 and grabbed the weapon clutched in Robert's hands. Blood seeped into the bandit's clothes from multiple wounds, providing an explanation for why he was unable to prevent his shotgun from being taken away so easily.

"Walk away!" Eli shouted loud enough to be heard over any amount of ringing.

The foul language erupting from Robert's mouth was loud enough to be heard in the next county.

Eli responded to it by pointing the shotgun at Robert's chest and shouting, *"Run!"*

Staggering away from the horse as more blood seeped from his wounds, Robert somehow remained upright while also finding the energy to reach for a pistol at his hip. Eli allowed him to clear leather before pulling the shotgun's trigger and knocking Robert clean off his feet.

That only left one more bandit. He was one of the men who'd kept a bandanna over his face during most of the time Saunders had been in their company. Saunders still didn't know that one's name, but since the robber tossed his gun and bolted as if an entire tribe of crazed Apaches were hot on his heels, the fellow's name hardly seemed to matter.

Where he had been deliberate and plodding before, Eli now moved with lightning quickness and perfect efficiency. No motion was wasted when he took a knife from Robert's belt and used it to slice through Saunders's ropes. The lawman let out a long breath as the grip around him loosened and he was able to wriggle free like a bug slipping from a cocoon.

Their ears still ringing, neither man tried to talk. Although Zack was unconscious and the other surviving bandit seemed capable of running all the way to the Canadian border, Eli and Saunders quickly gathered up as much as they could from the bandits' supplies, weapons, gear, and ammunition. The horses were accustomed to the chaos of a gunfight and hadn't strayed very far. One of the animals lay on its side, thrashing its legs and pressing its head against a patch of dirt that had been mixed with enough blood to form thick mud. That one had absorbed a shotgun blast meant for him, so Eli was the one to kneel down beside the horse, place his hand gently upon its muzzle, and put it out of its misery.

Eli stood up without taking his eyes from that horse. While there was a hint of pity at the corner of his eye, Saunders swore he could distinguish something else written on his face.

Perhaps it was anger.

Perhaps it was envy.

Chapter 18

"What in the blazes was that?"

It had been several minutes since Eli and Saunders had taken what they needed and set out once more for Mayor's Crossing. Although their progress had been stunted and they'd backtracked a bit, they were still within range of getting to their destination in a good enough time frame to catch one of the trains on their schedule. Hearing that question while hunkering down to fill his canteen from the same creek where the horses were drinking, Eli scowled and looked up at the sheriff. "I was expecting something more along the lines of a thank-you."

"*Thank you?* You want me to *thank* you after handing me over to those trigger-happy idiots and then nearly getting me killed?"

"I came back for you, didn't I?"

"Right! That's the part where I was almost killed."

Eli stood up and placed the top on his canteen. "Would you have preferred staying with them?"

"I would have preferred sticking to the original plan."

"I'm sure you would have liked that just fine, since that was the plan where I was drug around like a dog on a leash so I could catch a bullet or two after double-crossing one of the last men in this territory anyone should double-cross. You'll just have to pardon me if I don't like that one." Eli stuffed the canteen into his saddlebag and tightened the straps. The horse he'd taken after giving the sheriff's back to its rightful owner was Robert's, which was a fine animal indeed. Saunders was happy to get his horse back, but he was anything but happy now.

"You were getting a good deal," Saunders said. When Eli attempted to walk past him to lead his horse back toward the trail, the lawman stopped him with a sharp shove. "I'm not through talking with you yet, boy."

Eli dropped his reins and stepped up to the sheriff. "If this is how you want to play it, then let's go."

"It's not about what I want. It's about what's right."

"The only thing I wanna hear less than you telling me about how lucky I am is a speech about right and wrong."

Without hesitation, Saunders nodded and said, "If you would've gotten that speech earlier, perhaps you wouldn't have wound up another filthy thief stuck inside a cage."

Eli's fist snapped up and around to clip Saunders on the jaw with enough force to snap the sheriff's head back and send a dry cracking sound through the air. The lawman reeled back half a step, braced himself, and then lunged forward with a resounding left hook. The outlaw spun around and dropped to one knee. Looming over him with both hands balled into beefy fists, Saunders growled, "Considering all the reasons I got for beating the stuffing out of you, I'd say you should stay down."

"You say a lot," Eli grunted before driving a punch straight up into the sheriff's gut. "And you never stop saying it!"

That punch took some of the wind from Saunders's sails, but not all of it. Even though he didn't have enough left to stand up straight, he was more than able to lift one foot and drive it straight out to thump his heel against Eli's body to knock him back. "Enough talk, then."

"Now, that," Eli said as he scrambled to get his feet beneath him again, "is the best thing I've heard in a while." With that, he rushed forward. His body remained hunched over and he opened his arms so he could wrap them around the sheriff's midsection after driving one shoulder into him.

Both men staggered backward until Saunders caught a heel on a thick root emerging from the mud alongside the creek. Their momentum carried them even farther past the mud so they could land in the water with a noisy splash. The creek wasn't more than twelve to fifteen inches deep, which meant there was precious little between their bodies and an uneven bed studded with partially buried rocks, branches, and any number of things that had been tossed into the water over the past several years.

Despite having absorbed a few solid blows, the combatants emerged from the water looking refreshed and ready for the next round. Eli, in particular, seemed raring to go as he grinned broadly and tossed his hat toward dry land. "You don't know how long I've wanted the chance to shut that flapping mouth of yours."

Saunders also tossed his hat away and then ran both hands through the scraggly hair sprouting from his scalp. "I think I have an idea, since I've probably been waiting just as long to knock that smug grin off'a yer face."

When Eli swung at him this time, Saunders was ready for it. He leaned back just enough to allow the fist to sail past his chin and then followed up with a short jab to Eli's midsection. Eli twisted at the last moment to absorb most of the punch on his ribs. It hurt, but did less damage than if he'd been thumped in the stomach.

The next several punches Eli threw came in a flurry of wild lefts and rights. The sheriff dodged or blocked each one until Eli snuck in a sharp jab that caught the lawman when he twisted left instead of right. Saunders caught the jab just below his arm. Unlike the blow he'd landed with Eli, this one set up another two punches that landed in precisely the same spot. Each hurt more than the last, and the final one sent a painful jolt all the way through Saunders's torso.

"This would have gone a lot smoother if you would've just let me be a partner instead of an appendage!" Eli said.

"Partner?" Saunders raged as he pivoted on the balls of his feet to snap the back of one fist across Eli's chin. "I had to see if I could trust you first. And just when I thought I could," he snarled while clasping his hands together so he could pound them against Eli's shoulder blade as though he were swinging an axe, "you show me what a mistake that was!"

That backhand had come at him like the end of a cracking whip, and there was no way short of precognition for Eli to avoid getting hit by it. The second blow landed solidly and drove him down to both knees. Eli's hands slapped the water to prevent him from landing facedown in the creek, which also reinvigorated him with a cold splash to the face. After getting back up, he took a step forward to drive a kick into the sheriff's body. He wasn't concerned with where it landed as long as it put a pained look on the lawman's face.

It was all Saunders could do to turn away from Eli and cover himself before that boot landed in the softest of a man's soft spots. It pounded against his hip instead, weakening that leg just enough for him to lose his footing in the slippery creek. Saunders flopped onto his side, rolled away from Eli, and quickly wound up with his head below the shallow surface of the water. When he stood up again, he could hear nothing but Eli's laughter.

"Now, that," the outlaw said, "was worth all the trouble of getting here."

Saunders gasped to pull some air into his lungs and then coughed out the water that had trickled into them. Now that his hair and whiskers were plastered down by the water, two scars running down his left chin to reach a spot near the top of his neck could be seen. They'd been hidden by the whiskers before, and now that they were exposed, the sheriff's feral side was also more clearly visible. He bared his teeth and rushed at Eli amid a spray of water that was kicked up by his churning feet.

Eli might have been laughing before, but that changed as soon as he got a look at the wild man in front of him. The shallow water prevented him from moving too quickly for fear of slipping and breaking his neck, which also kept him in perfect position to be nailed by Saunders. The lawman's charge began similar to Eli's previous move, but ended in a much different way. Rather than simply knock Eli back, Saunders wrapped him up in a bear hug, lifted him from the water, and then tossed him toward the middle of the creek.

At the pinnacle of his arc, Eli let out a surprised yelp and flailed his limbs in preparation for what was bound to be an unpleasant landing. He managed to twist himself around somewhat so a hand and foot were the first things to break the surface of the creek. The rest of his body landed heavily in the water, and once he rolled onto his side, he stayed there.

"Men like you think you can just do whatever you want," Saunders said as he sloshed through the water toward Eli. "You think the law don't apply to you."

"The law," Eli groaned with a pained wince, "is just a bunch of rules set by rich men."

"I look like a rich man to you?"

Eli went through the uncomfortable motions of turning his head so he could look at the approaching lawman. "You look like a self-righteous horse's ass."

Once more standing over him, Saunders placed one foot on Eli's shoulder and shoved him over so the outlaw flopped onto his back. "And you look like a pitiful young man who thinks he's too good for this world."

The only response Eli had for that was to reach out with one hand, grab Saunders's ankle, and yank it out from under the lawman with enough force to send him straight back into the water. Saunders landed on his backside, expelling all of his breath in a grunting wheeze that left him too crumpled to move.

"Now," Eli said in between hard breaths, "you just look wet."

After pulling himself up so he wasn't gulping creek water, Saunders didn't have enough power in his limbs to do much more than get himself right side up. Sitting in the creek with the water up to his waist, he propped his elbows upon his knees and started to laugh. "Ain't we just a sight?"

"Yeah. Jake should be quaking in fear."

That got both men laughing for a short while until they started pulling themselves from the water and making the short walk back to shore. Once there, they each went through the process of wringing out what they could. Saunders grunted as he took a seat on a log and pulled his boots off so he could dump the water from them. "So, why take a poke at me after going through so much trouble to pull my fat from the fire?" he asked.

Eli lowered himself to sit on the ground with the creek on one side and the sheriff directly in front of him. "I got sick of you looking down your nose at me."

"First of all, I wasn't looking down my nose at anyone."

"Sounded like you were."

"What made you think that?"

"You get a tone in your voice," Eli replied without having to think it over.

Saunders scowled and asked, "A tone? You started this whole scrap because of a tone?"

"And . . . you called me boy. I'm not anyone's boy."

"Guess I can understand that," Saunders admitted. "Makes more sense than a tone."

"Depends on what the tone is."

Waving away that topic as if he were chasing a fly away from a picnic lunch, the lawman said, "Secondly —"

"There's always a second with you, Sheriff. And thirds and fourths."

"You gonna let me speak?"

Eli lowered his head and made a benevolent sweeping gesture with one hand.

Ignoring the condescending motions, Saunders continued. "I'd like to know what you were thinking when you handed me over to those outlaws."

"Oh," Eli grunted. "That."

"Yeah. That. What was that nonsense about? I thought we were on the same page."

"Of course you did. You're a lawman."

"What's that got to do with anything?"

Having emptied his own boots of water, Eli sat for a moment and gave his legs a stretch before putting them back on. He looked up at small bunches of clouds chasing each other across the wide blue sky and said, "Lawmen all think their words carry more weight than anyone else's."

"Don't they?"

"See?" Eli chuckled. "There you go. You may have the law behind you, but that don't mean everyone else feels like they gotta step in line. You'd think, since you were men before the badge got pinned to your chests, you'd remember what it was like to be part of the rank and file. But whatever your intentions may be, you all feel like you just have to speak loud enough for everyone to agree with what you're saying."

"So you think most folks don't like to have rules to go by?"

"That's not what I said." Eli leaned forward and gestured with his hands as if he were trying to teach a mule to build a bookshelf. "Rules ain't a bad thing. The law ain't bad either. Just because I break laws for a living doesn't mean I can't see the value in them. The problem is that lawmen take them as gospel and tend to expect everyone else to give 'em the same weight. Gives you all a holier-than-thou tone to your voice."

"You think some of that spite might come from your bad experiences with lawmen who hunt you down and toss you into cages?"

After pondering that for a few seconds, Eli shrugged. "Could be, but it's not just that. You heard about Billy the Kid?"

"Sure. Most everyone this side of the Mississippi has heard of that one."

"Why do you think he stayed ahead of the law for so long? What about Jesse James? He and Billy were famous! Everyone had a good idea of where to find them, but couldn't quite pin them down for a good, long while. Why do you think that is?"

"Those men got what . . ." Saunders said in a tone he immediately recognized as the one that had so recently perturbed Eli. In a more conversational manner, he started again. "Both of them met their end fairly recently and neither one was very pleasant."

"But they put up an impressive chase after pulling off some equally impressive jobs. Seems like someone with that kind of notoriety shouldn't be able to poke their noses out without getting them shot off. Men like them two managed to pull off the trick time and again long enough to make you lawmen look like fools, so I'll ask you again. Why do you think that is?"

"I'm beginning to see what you mean about that tone," Saunders groused. "Makes me want to clean your clock again."

"It's because folks wanted to stand behind men like Jesse or Billy more than they wanted to stand behind you," Eli said as if the lawman hadn't even opened his mouth. "I met Jesse James once and he had a way of talking to folks that made you want to lend him a hand. The lawmen that came strutting around, setting fire to barns just because they thought he might be in there, weren't like that at all. It's a difference in lawmen that makes it seem like they think they're above everyone else. A man like me, long as we steal from the right bank or keep from spilling too much innocent blood, is just following through on things any honest man would like to see done."

"So you and Jake are benevolent champions of the people, eh?" Saunders scoffed.

"No, but we're not strutting around pretending to be better than anyone else."

"Zack and Eddie seemed to do plenty of strutting without having enough to back it up."

"Which is why nobody knew their name or will miss them when they're gone."

Saunders slid his boots onto his feet. "This is all real fascinating. Seems like a way to dodge my original question, though."

"Not at all. You asked why I would go against our agreement and I'm trying to make you see why someone might not feel an agreement is worth keeping just because a lawman struck it."

"All right, then. How about man to man?" Saunders retorted. "We agreed on our plan and you jabbed me in the back the first chance you got. I tried to show you I meant to stand behind my word any way I could. I stood up for you against those vigilantes. I made sure you were fed properly. I swore to give you a fair shake where your legal troubles are concerned."

Ticking off the points one by one, Eli said, "You could have been blowing smoke as far as those promises go. You kept me in cuffs even more than when I was locked up. And you could very well have put those so-called vigilantes up to the task of coming after me just so you could gain my trust by looking like the big hero when you drove them off. As far as I knew, it was all a big hustle just so you could get help in bagging Jake."

"You really are a suspicious cuss."

"Gotta be that way to survive. To be honest, I thought my best chance of survival was in getting away from you as soon as I had the chance. Even if you did mean to stand behind your word, there's no guarantee I wouldn't wind up swinging from the end of a rope anyhow."

"All right, then. Why would that bother you?"

"Why would *dying* bother me?"

Without so much as flinching at what should have been an absurd question, Saunders replied, "Yeah. Why would that bother you? Near as I could tell, you seem ready to meet your maker at the nearest possible convenience. There's a look in your eyes that makes it seem like you're already dead."

Eli didn't have a word to say. Instead, he got to his feet and used one hand to wipe off his face before putting his hat back in place.

"I saw it when you were staring down the barrel of that gun back at the Lazy V before I bushwhacked you. You were ready to die."

"How could you see my eyes?" Eli asked. "You had to sneak up behind me."

"I got a better look than you know," the lawman told him in a quieter, almost haunted voice. "I've seen plenty of others in similar situations and there's a desperation that sets in to keep them alive. I've felt it myself on more than one occasion and I haven't seen it in you until the moment you rode back to burn those robbers down."

"There it is again," Eli grumbled. "Lawman who thinks he knows everything there is to know."

Without rising to the bait that was being offered, Saunders said, "There's a fire inside you, kid, and it ain't the good kind. It's something that's burning you up. Eating you alive."

The smirk Eli had put on a few moments ago didn't last long. It dropped away, leaving only the wet, tired face of a weary man. "Everyone fights to stay alive, like it's something so great. You walk into any saloon and you'll see folks trying to do anything but face what life's got in store for them. You think anyone drinks because the liquor tastes good?"

"Wanting a respite is one thing. Wanting death is something else, Eli."

"We're all gonna get there sooner or later."

"If you're so resigned to it," Saunders said, "then you could have allowed that lynch mob to take you. Or you could have ridden into any number of bullets being fired at you while you rode with the Jake Welles bunch."

"Maybe I just don't want to give lesser men the pleasure of bringing me down. I want to go out on *my* terms. Not at the whim of any lawman and not dangling at the end of a noose while half a town watches."

"Usually a hanging gets a better turnout than that," Saunders scoffed. "There's something else behind that look in your eyes. I may just be a self-righteous lawman, but I seem to be the only one that gives a damn about whether you live or die."

Eli sighed, stared at the creek for a few moments, and said, "I ain't exactly healthy."

"Ain't a lot of us that are."

"No, I mean there's something wrong that even the doctors don't know much about. I get headaches, sometimes bad enough that I can't see straight. Sometimes I feel healthy enough to wrestle a bull by its horns. When I don't, it feels like my head's about to blow off my shoulders."

"You try some kind of medicine?" Saunders asked.

"Tried them all. Once I got sick of feeling dizzy from laudanum or whatever else the doctors threw at me, I just had to learn to live with the pain. That was right around the time I decided to put all of that nonsense behind me and do what I pleased."

"So you indulged in some diversions of the guns blazing variety?"

"Yeah," Eli said. "Something like that. Sometimes I barely have the tolerance to hear a pin drop."

"You never seemed so bad to me. Guess that does explain why you were so squirrelly when it came to that talk of the fever that swept through the Lazy V."

Shuddering at that particular memory, Eli

said, "I've had some practice in dealing with the misery. Serves me well knowing I won't have to put up with it much longer. Doctors say I could drop over dead at any time, and mostly that doesn't sound so bad."

"So you've had it rough. You found out you were sick and ran afoul of someone wearing a badge in wherever you used to call home. Is that why you decided to ride with killers and steal for a living?"

"I don't have to explain myself to you."

"You'll have to explain yourself to someone sooner or later."

The laugh that churned inside Eli was dry as a desert breeze and twice as harsh. "You can spare me the spiritual talk."

"All right, then, explain yourself to me. It's the least I deserve considering what you must know were earnest attempts to keep you from swinging. I understand why you wanted to get away. I figured you'd try to do as much sooner or later, which is why I was watching you like a hawk. But why go on about all that nonsense with the bounty money that was supposed to be back in Seedley? Surely Zack and the rest of them would have found something else to go after sooner or later. You had them hooked without giving them some false treasure to chase."

"Wasn't about giving them anything," Eli grudgingly explained. "It was about keeping you alive."

"Oh, now, that's rich!" After he'd stomped over to his horse and checked to make sure the saddle was buckled tightly, Saunders turned back around to find that Eli hadn't moved from his spot. "You seriously expect me to believe that?"

"I do, because it's the truth."

"And just how does that keep me alive? If anything, all that did was get them worked up about some fat bunch of money that wasn't there. Money, let me remind you, that they all but *needed* me with them to get."

"Right," Eli said. "The idea was to make you more valuable as a hostage because the alternative was . . . well . . . you wouldn't have liked the alternatives much."

"Now who's the one who thinks they know everything? You were tied up right there with me until you started spouting off about all that horse manure."

"Do you have to know another lawman for years to know what might be passing through his mind?" Eli asked.

"No, but that's different."

"Not as much as you'd like to think. Just different sides of the same coin, is all. I've ridden as an outlaw or with them long enough to know what those men were thinking. Because lawmen see most outlaws as wild dogs, it's difficult for you to see such a thing. And because you don't know how a killer's mind works as well as you might think you do, you weren't aware of how close you were to dying before I gave Zack and them others something else to think about."

He might not have thought about it before, but Saunders took a moment to do so now. Finally he had to rid himself of it by fretting with his horse's reins. "You made a mistake. I suppose all that matters is that you thought better of it and came back."

"No!" Eli barked. He stormed over to Saunders and ripped the reins from his hand quickly enough to give his horse a start. "You weren't listening before! All that talk when I was trying to explain the difference between you and me. Did all of that go in one ear and straight out the other?"

"I ain't a child!"

"Then stop acting like one. At least a child has an excuse for not knowing how things work. A grown man should have his eyes open well enough to see that nothing happens because of a greater good. Nobody lives or dies because they deserve to. And there's no guarantee you'll live to see the next sunrise. That goes for everyone no matter how young, old, good, bad, sweet, or surly they may be. You can't believe you were about to be gunned down because you can't imagine such a thing happening for no good reason. Well, I can! I've seen men shot like animals for no reason at all. Sometimes the reason is just that the man doing the shooting likes the way a gun feels when it goes off in his hand or enjoys the sight of blood.

"Those men who had us were going to kill you. They found that bit of money you had and got it into their heads there was more. The more you would have tried to convince them otherwise, the more they would have beaten you to get the answer they were after. And if they didn't get the answer they wanted after a while, they would have started hurting you just because you're a lawman! Why would you bring that to their attention?"

"Thought it might help," Saunders said earnestly.

"Because you think any reasonable man should step in line if a man with a badge asks him to."

"Zack seemed ready to deal. I could have talked him into something sooner or later.

Before we got too far down a bad road, at least."

"Maybe," Eli said. "But that one, Eddie, would have found a reason to gut you, and them others that were too yellow to show their faces would have gone along with him. It's a sad, ugly fact that most men are just looking to be led. If they're already riding with ones like Eddie and Zack and Robert, you can plainly see where they want to go."

"They would've found the badge eventually."

"Yeah, but you had to rub it in their faces. What I was talking about before meant you would have been killed, Vernon! And it would have been an ugly death."

"That why you came back, then?" Saunders asked. "To spare me that ugly death?"

"I didn't come back because I thought I made a mistake. I came back because I had a change of heart." Eli took a deep breath and spoke as if to someone only he could see. "I got away, free and clear, and started thinking about what I wanted to do with my freedom. You wanna know the first genuine prospect that came to mind?"

Through a knowing smirk, Saunders replied, "Lyssa Beihn?"

Eli seemed genuinely taken aback. "That's right."

"See, just because we don't both see the same things, it don't mean one of us is blind."

"Fair enough."

"So you really have it bad for her, huh?"

Eli cast his eyes in another direction. Since his horse was nearby, he decided to walk over and make sure it was ready for the ride ahead. "I want to go back to her, even though I honestly don't know what I would do once I got there. I'm a man who's spent too much time thinking about how things truly are and what truly needed to be done. Romantic interests don't really figure into all of that."

"They rarely figure into any man's plans. I never woke up to see I was with the wrong woman until the right one came along. Now, there's a sticky situation!"

Eli grinned and shook his head. "I don't reckon it was stickier than a man like me coming back to a woman like her with hat in hand. Odds are, she'd turn tail and run after knocking me out with the heaviest thing she could reach."

"Or she could see you for who you truly are. Everyone tends to have one or two sorts of things they can see pretty well. She took a shine to you before I thought you had much to offer. Fact is, she's the one that told me to give you a chance to prove yourself."

"Is that a fact?" Eli asked as the wrinkled corners of his cloudy blue eyes pinched in a bit more.

"It is."

When he turned to look back at the creek, Eli seemed several years younger. "When I managed to get away from you and them robbers, part of me was ready to strike out on my own, maybe lie low somewhere or try to meet up with Jake. But that was what I would have done before meeting Lyssa and it's not what I wanted to show her when I got back. The fact of the matter is that she wouldn't have wanted me to hand you over that way."

"I imagine she'll think pretty highly of you when she finds out what you did."

"I don't know if she ever will find out," Eli said. "That's not the point. What matters is the man I want to be when I see her again. That's what she'll see, just as surely as she would have seen a self-serving thief if I went back to her after slipping away and leaving you the first time."

"So . . . you came back to gun down those bandits, nearly get killed in the process, and cut me loose . . . to impress a woman?"

Eventually, Eli had to admit, "I don't

know if I'd say it was to impress her per se, but . . . yeah."

Saunders slapped the front of his shirt to get rid of some of the water that still trickled over his chest and said, "I can think of worse reasons."

CHAPTER 19

They arrived at Mayor's Crossing several hours behind their original schedule. Some of that time had to be spent riding after sundown, but the sky aided their cause by remaining vaguely illuminated by a warm, purple, and orange glow well past the point when the sun had dipped below the horizon. The last rays of light clung to the Wyoming terrain like spectral hands digging into the jagged rocks and fighting to keep from being swallowed up by a cool, starry night. Still skittish from being picked out of a crowd so easily in the last town he'd been in, Saunders refrained from stepping foot into a hotel. With Saunders having split up what was left of Cody's money, Eli followed the sheriff's lead and spent the night curled up in the corner of the stall he'd rented for his horse at a local stable. The liveryman wasn't keen on the notion, but a bit of smooth talking on Eli's part got him past his concerns without making the pair seem like anything more than a couple of cowboys that were down on their luck.

The two men didn't speak very much throughout that day or night. Instead of it being an uncomfortable silence stretched across several agonizing hours, it was more of a comfortable truce shared by two men who simply didn't have much more that needed to be said. It was the closest thing to peace that Eli had felt since the last time he'd laid eyes on Lyssa Beihn.

"Well," Eli grunted as he shifted and drew in as much hay as he could reach to build something of a nest in one corner of his horse's stall, "at least I finally got my own room."

"And no bars on the door," Saunders replied from the other side of the wooden wall separating the two stalls. "That's gotta count for something."

Coarse pieces of straw scraped against Eli's back where his shirt had come untucked and nibbled like annoying sets of teeth at his elbows. Splintered sections of the wall gouged the back of his neck and poked through his shirt to dig into his shoulder blades. There would most certainly be painful kinks along his spine and in his joints to greet him when he awoke the next morning. The air smelled like the wrong end of a horse, and still, Eli was in good spirits as he drifted off to sleep.

Having arrived with their eyelids drooping low from fatigue, Eli and Saunders hadn't gotten much of a look at the town of Mayor's Crossing until they stepped outside to stretch and take a gulp of fresh air the following morning. Judging by all the campaign signs still hanging as a display from two of the four storefronts to be found along a road that led from one end of town to the other, the town had been founded strictly as a stopover for political candidates of the last two elections. One president, two senators, and three mayors had been through those parts, more than likely to do no more than wet their whistles, shake a few hands, and move on to the next real stop.

The train station was easy enough to find. It was one of the only things on the wide path that could be considered the town's only cross street. For that matter, Eli figured calling the place a town was stretching the definition of the term, but he wasn't there to split hairs. He stood outside the ticket office with his hand resting on the grip of his holstered .38. Eli had to remind himself that not only was his other .38 also in its place at his hip, but both guns were loaded. Saunders was either a man who committed to his character assessments or one of the most wide-eyed optimists there was. Whatever the reason, after their scuffle in the creek the lawman seemed more at ease with him.

Eli was restless and it had nothing to do with the sheriff. More than likely, this was a spot where one of the other men in the gang might have tried to catch a train if they were headed to or from Cheyenne. Eli didn't know whether anyone in the gang had left Cheyenne or had any reason to ride the rails, but the slightest possibility that he might cross paths with them had become more than enough to put him on edge.

"We're back on schedule," Saunders announced as he strode from a ticket office that looked like a large, single-story home. "There's a train due to arrive at noon, which isn't far from now."

"Great."

Saunders scowled at the younger man as he slapped a ticket against Eli's chest. "What are you so glum about?"

"I'll feel better once this is over."

"So will I. Smells like something's cooking over there. Care to have a look?"

It seemed unlikely that there would be any

bloodshed at that train station, but if there was, Eli doubted it would matter where he was when the lead started to fly. "Sure," he said. "Let's eat."

The lunch being served on the other end of the ticket office was an overpriced ham sandwich with a piece of stale cake wrapped in a napkin in a bundle meant for travelers too rushed to find cheaper sustenance in town. What had caught their noses' attention was a thin piece of steak being cooked by a clerk who wasn't in a mood to share. Eli and Saunders ate their sandwiches and wolfed down the cake by the time their train announced its arrival with the scream of a shrill whistle and a trail of smoke in the distance.

The train rattled to a stop at the platform and exhaled a steamy breath or two while men streamed from her sides to gather more coal, wood, or other supplies needed to continue their journey south. Both horses were led up a short ramp into a car with a wide door and a scant amount of hay on the floor. The kid who took the reins couldn't have been more than thirteen, but moved with the efficiency of someone who'd been doing his job for decades. Eli and Saunders gladly handed over their mounts, handed the boy a little extra for a job well done, and stepped onto one of two passenger cars.

Eli thought he might catch some sleep while on the train. Although the motion of the car rocking back and forth as it clattered along was soothing, it wasn't enough to put him completely at ease. With all the thoughts of what could be waiting for them in Cheyenne still rattling inside his head, Eli wasn't about to let his guard down long enough to doze off. Saunders, on the other hand, didn't have that problem.

Less than ten minutes after finding his seat, the sheriff had his arms folded across his chest, his hat down over the upper portion of his face, and his head lolling back and forth to the swaying motion of the car. Deep, grating snores could be heard above the commotion of wheels upon rails, giving a few of the ten other passengers inside the car something to snicker about.

Just seeing the other folks relaxed and enjoying themselves through polite conversation, reading a book, or playing some sort of game seemed strange to Eli. Mostly, he wasn't accustomed to riding on trains. Chasing them and eventually robbing them, yes. Not riding in them. Also, he'd gotten so used to an outlaw's life that it was difficult to recall what it had been like while on the other side of the fence. Most of his days while riding on his own or with a gang were spent worrying about simple things like eating, surviving, staying hidden, and planning the next job.

Targets needed to be found.

Threats needed to be assessed.

Terrain and escape routes needed to be scouted.

Whatever time he had when he wasn't doing any of those things was spent watching for the next person that might try to kill him, lock him away, or string him up. That didn't leave much for reading.

Eli watched the folks on that train with an alternating mix of scorn and jealousy. They seemed simple and oblivious to him. Sheep that didn't know they were in the company of wolves. Too stupid to protect what was theirs because of a childish faith in their common man. But they also seemed very fortunate. They got to enjoy their lives without worrying too much about the uglier things. Death would come for them as it came for everyone else, but it would either be a surprise or a slow, natural process. There was very little concern for how badly it might hurt if they got stabbed in the liver as opposed to catching a blade in the leg. For men like Eli, getting shot was a certainty and he could only hope it wouldn't cost him a limb or make him bleed out slowly like a stuck pig. For the laughing sheep on that train, such thoughts were morbid and peculiar, and for that reason above all others, he envied them.

"Hey, mister."

Although Eli heard the summons from the little girl with the red hair pulled back into twin braids, he stared out the window and pretended to ignore it. His head was aching worse than ever, and pressing his fingers against his temples did little to alleviate the discomfort.

The child would not be assuaged, and her mother was too distracted by the girl's younger brother to prevent her from walking down the narrow aisle to climb onto the seat directly in front of Eli. The bench creaked beneath her negligible weight. Iron brackets strained against the tenuous hold of old screws in the floor as she leaned against the backrest and set her chin on top of the seat to stare back at him.

"Hey, mister!"

There was no ignoring her, so Eli grunted, "Yeah?" while still looking out the window.

"Mister?"

"What?" Catching himself putting more of an edge into his voice than he'd intended,

Eli turned to look at the girl who was addressing him. He came from a small family, which meant he hadn't had much exposure to children after he'd stopped being one himself. Normally, Eli only dealt with them when he was stepping around them on a boardwalk or getting one to quiet down during a robbery. The instant he looked directly at this girl, memories began to rush from the back of his throbbing skull.

Hank had been serving time in a Missouri jail, leaving Eli, Jake, and Cody to run a few jobs on their own. Without Hank to scout or function as part of the main unit, Eli and Jake had needed to rely on Cody a bit more. That never worked out well, and a simple job to steal a batch of horses from a poorly guarded stable outside Joplin turned out even worse.

The owner of the stable was a father who came out calling for his daughter, only to find Jake and Cody leading the horses through a door that had been busted from its hinges. On his way to get the drop on the irate man, Eli stumbled across a frightened little girl who'd either tripped or been hiding in a patch of sloppy mud behind a water trough. She looked up at him with wide, tear-soaked eyes while stretching out a hand in hope that he might help her up or get her to somewhere that wasn't so scary. Instead, Eli had grabbed her arm and walked her over to where her father could see her.

He had his gun in his other hand.

Eli had no intention of shooting her or harming a hair on her head. She didn't know that, of course, and neither did the man who was only protecting what was his when he'd found a bunch of armed men trying to take it. From an outlaw's frame of mind, Eli had done the right thing. He got the father to drop his shotgun and step aside. Nobody was hurt. The girl was tossed away seconds before the gang rode off with some new horses. Even so, it was a moment that Eli couldn't forget no matter how much he wanted to. That was the moment Eli had gone from being a hardened man to becoming the thing that hardened other innocent souls.

It was early in his time with Jake's bunch and became one of many that solidified his position within the gang. That pleading, petrified look in the girl's eyes, combined with his willingness to use her as a bargaining chip, had been one of the first things to tell him he'd ridden too far down the outlaw's trail to turn back any time soon. From that point on, his headaches had grown progressively worse.

The redheaded child on the train to Cheyenne might not have looked exactly like that girl, but he saw those petrified eyes on the faces of nearly every little girl that crossed his path since that day. And in the back of his head, lingering somewhere at the edges of what he could hear, there would always be that timid little voice asking why anyone would want to hurt her or her daddy.

"Mister!"

"What?" Eli asked with a start.

The girl's eyes shifted over to Saunders. "He's snoring. It's really loud."

"Oh. I hadn't noticed."

Her eyes narrowed in disbelief. "How could you not notice?"

"You ever have a dog?"

"Yes."

"Did it ever get sick or eat something that made it break wind for a few hours at a time?"

The girl laughed and looked over to her mother as if she would be in trouble for even listening to such a question. Lowering her head so only the portion of her face above the middle of her nose peeked up, she replied, "Yes."

"After a while, you don't really hear it

anymore or smell the stink. It all just becomes part of everything else." Hooking a thumb toward Saunders, Eli concluded with "He's a lot like that."

It might not have been a valid or an accurate analysis, but it made the girl giggle loudly enough to catch her mother's attention. The woman looked up from the little boy she'd been tending and said, "Maggie! Get over here this instant! Stop pestering that man."

Eli smiled and waved to let the woman know he hadn't been bothered, but the mother was having none of it. She smiled nervously at Eli and then pulled her daughter close the moment Maggie was within her reach. For the next several minutes, the woman gave the little girl a stern talking-to in a harsh whisper. On the rare occasion that she or the girl accidentally glanced in Eli's direction, there was more nervousness in their eyes than seemed to fit the situation.

Perhaps Eli was imagining that in light of the memories that still churned unbidden through his head.

Perhaps little Maggie had a recurring obedience problem that needed to be fixed.

Or perhaps the mother wasn't such an unwary sheep after all.

CHAPTER 20

Cheyenne

Compared to the stopovers and cow towns he'd visited most recently, Cheyenne was enough to overwhelm every one of Eli's senses. The train arrived at a platform populated by waving families and travelers anxiously awaiting their turn to board the wheezing iron beast. When he and Saunders stepped off, they were shoved aside by the little redheaded girl and her brother as they rushed to greet a slender man in a brown wool suit. The mother was visibly relieved to see him, if only for the extra set of hands needed to deal with the two young ones in her charge.

Once they'd gotten their horses, Eli and the sheriff walked away from the station and gazed out at the rest of the city. "Where should we start?" Eli asked.

Saunders pulled in a lungful of air laden with soot that had been spat out from the nearby engine and exhaled in a hacking cough. "I was about to ask you the same thing."

"You're the one leading this expedition."

"And you're the one who knows these men we're after better than just about anybody."

"Imagine that," Eli mused. "Sheriff Vernon Saunders treating a common criminal like a real partner."

"Aw, don't sell yerself short," Saunders said with a wry grin. "I'd say uncommon criminal is more like it."

"Touching. You get us close to where we're supposed to be and I'll let you know if I come up with anything where Jake and Hank are concerned."

They walked away from the train station and led their horses farther into Cheyenne. While most men observed a new town to look for places to eat, names of streets, or interesting landmarks, Eli searched for an entirely different set of details. His eyes drifted to streets that could be more easily blocked off to prevent a quick getaway or were clogged by too many folks walking along either side. He picked out alleys that were dark as opposed to studded with beams of sunlight and looked for signs as to which were more likely open pathways or dead ends. He looked for lawmen or anyone carrying firearms. He also looked for stores that struck him as juicy targets or businesses that might carry sums of cash that were large enough to steal. It wasn't long before Eli began to feel as if a living wall of strangers were closing in on him. It would feel awfully good to climb back into his saddle and strike out for more open terrain.

Beside him, he could see Saunders taking in different sights. The sheriff's attention was drawn to commotion of all sorts or disturbances that might require a lawman's attention whether he was the one designated to tend to them or not. His eyes drifted to some of the same sights as Eli's, but in a more protective manner. Considering such a fundamental difference as this, Eli had to marvel at how he and the lawman could make it this far without one of them doing some more serious damage to the other.

"We should probably not walk out in the open for too long," Eli said.

"You think our chances are good of running into one of your old partners?"

"No, but they're even better that one of them is somewhere watching for a familiar face. Maybe not our faces, but you can bet we'd be spotted."

Saunders gazed up at the windows with

the highest vantage points. "I was thinking they'd be waiting for Cody at a spot they'd arranged earlier."

"One of them would. Probably Jake. Hank would be the one to keep watch."

"You don't think they trust him to get here without being watched?"

Eli shook his head as if he was watching something else play out in the distance. "It's not about trust. It's more about watching to see if anyone was following Cody into town or closing in on him from another angle. If there's any mistrust in play," Eli added, "it's because the rest of us knew Cody wasn't smart enough to go for too long on his own. That's why they sent him out to dig up a box and bring it back. He would've guarded that money like a loyal dog, and if anyone was following him, Cody would lead them in a straight line that was easy to see."

"And what if Cody was caught somewhere along the line? Them other two trust such a simpleminded fool with all that money?"

"They wouldn't if there was more than three left in the gang," Eli said. "Fact is, they're shorthanded. If they're in a town this big, there's something bigger brewing. If they're scouting a bank or whatever like you think, they'll want their two best men doing it. Sending Cody away is the obvious choice. If he messes up, it's the smaller of the two payoffs. If he gets caught or killed," Eli added with a shrug, "no big loss."

"That's cold."

"Yeah, but it makes sense."

"Could you let me know where Hank might be watching from?"

"Someplace high," Eli said. "Maybe a window overlooking a busy street that Cody would have had to cross or a rooftop overlooking a certain spot. He was always the one who did the watching. Hank's best at that."

Now it was Saunders's turn to look up nervously. "You think he might be watching us now?"

"He's one man. Can't watch the whole city. It's doubtful that Cody was gonna take a train, mostly because there are too many people on them or at the stations. That means there isn't much reason for Hank to watch a spot this close to the station. Also, if Hank had caught sight of me, I'd know it. He would have announced himself."

"And if he caught sight of me?"

"Then he'd announce himself in a way you probably wouldn't like too much," Eli said with a subtle nod.

Since it wouldn't do anyone any good to get overly worried now, Saunders asked,

"What about the spot where the gang might be holed up before pulling the job here? Think you could tell me where it is?"

"I can get you close, but that's about it."

"Are you sure?" Saunders asked with a sideways glance that was aimed directly at the man next to him.

Eli stopped and turned to face a window full of suits displayed in a row hanging from a shiny curtain rod. "As sure as I can be. I haven't exactly been able to speak with Jake for a while in case you've forgotten."

"I know that, but this is a job that's still in line with the one that brought you to Seedley. Whatever was supposed to be in that iron wagon is here now. Perhaps you all made an arrangement to come here in case you were separated."

"If we had that kind of organization, I doubt things would have gone so badly at that ranch."

"Most of you got away," Saunders pointed out. "Things could have gone a lot worse. Also, you boys had plenty of time with the driver and guards who were on that wagon when you took it. More than enough to ask some questions in a way to ensure that you got some good answers."

Eli turned to look at Saunders directly. "You were the one who told me I wasn't a killer. You think that still leaves the door open for me to be the kind of man who'd torture someone for information?"

"Not you, but I'd wager at least one of the other men in Jake's gang could manage that sort of thing."

Eli couldn't help wondering if the sheriff had already met Hank. It wouldn't take much more than a handshake for someone to see the cruelty in the scarecrow's eyes or the wicked intentions smeared across his face. Whether the lawman was referring to anyone in particular or not didn't really matter. He had a point.

"I don't know much about this place," Eli said while looking up and down the busy street nearby. "But I do know how we would function before any job. There were certain precautions that were taken, procedures to follow, things to look for that kept us alive once things began to roll. Get me close to the spot where the job is supposed to happen and I can piece together where Jake and Hank might be or what they may be doing. There's just one thing that bothers me."

"Oh, there should be a lot more than one thing," Saunders chuckled.

Ignoring the feeble attempt at humor, Eli said, "When we do get to a point where we're closing in on Jake and Hank, I'll need you to follow my lead."

"Of course."

"I mean follow it without hesitation and without questioning me about why I'm doing what I'm doing. Once we're close enough to them two, things could go real good or real bad in the blink of an eye. Either one of us trips up the other and we're both dead. I don't mean that in any figurative sense, either. Jake or Hank can each kill a man without batting an eye, and when they're cornered, they're even more dangerous."

"You don't have to tell me that. I've seen them cornered before."

"No, you haven't," Eli said crisply as he lowered his head and started walking down the boardwalk as if the ground beneath his feet had suddenly become too hot. "What you saw at that ranch was just them fighting their way out of hostile territory."

"Hostile territory?" Saunders scoffed as he fell into step alongside Eli. "From where I stood, the Lazy V was pretty close to hell that night."

"From where you stood, maybe. For us, it was what Jake would call an unfortunate turn of events."

"I may not be the sheriff of some wild town like Dodge City or Tombstone, but

I've seen plenty of bad nights and unfortunate turns of events."

Eli instinctually matched the pace of the crowd sharing the street with him. He didn't go slow enough to create a snarl in the flow of movement or fast enough to make any waves. Even his posture was perfectly suited to blend in with his surroundings like a lizard that had shifted its skin to a pale shade of brown while sitting beside a sun-baked rock. Although his chin remained tucked in close so his face couldn't be easily seen from any angle, he still did his best to avoid contact with anyone around him. "Once Jake and Hank realize what I've done and who I've come here with, there'll be a turn of events uglier than anything you've seen before."

Chapter 21

The place they were there to visit was a tall, narrow building on a corner with a small sign on which the words McKane Trust & Loan were printed in an elegant script. If Saunders hadn't pointed it out to him, Eli might not have realized the building was there. Much like Eli had blended in with the people walking along the street, so too did the building blend in with its neighbors. If he were to build a place where the real riches were kept, this would have been it.

"I think that's the spot," Saunders said. "McKane Trust Company. That's the place those gunmen mentioned while we were waiting at the Lazy V for you and the rest of that gang to show. Even though they thought they'd bought my allegiance, they still spoke about it as if they wanted to keep it a secret. And before you say what's running through your head, I don't think they let the name drop just to draw me in."

"Why would I be thinking that?" Eli asked, despite the fact that he'd been thinking that very thing.

"I'd heard the others talking about something else before they offered me any money. Couldn't hear much more than a few snips here and there, but the name of this place fits the bill. Furthermore, when I was told one of your partners was spotted in Cheyenne, it was in this vicinity." The sheriff looked around and quickly diverted his line of sight upward. "You think we were spotted yet?"

"Hopefully not." Eli stopped, glanced up and down a street that he still couldn't name, and crossed as if he had important business to conduct after reaching the other side. "Now's the time when you'll have to trust me."

"That's what I expected."

"Keep your head down. Don't look in any direction for too long unless that direction is toward your feet. Stick your hands into your pockets and just find somewhere to be where someone else is standing. If you hear someone call your name, don't look up. Someone calls for a lawman or sounds like they're being torn apart by wild dogs, you just stay put unless the men around you are moving as well. Got me?"

Saunders nodded. "Where will you be?"

"Doing what you brought me to do."

Saunders scowled in a way that made him look every bit the man who could have him strung up by the neck. "That's all you're gonna tell me?"

"That's all I know. This isn't an exact thing that I do. It's what I feel and what my gut tells me. Right now my gut's telling me I need to get moving again before someone's eyes linger on us for one second too long. Believe me, that's as long as it could take for this ride to end in a very bad way."

"Perhaps I should seek out the town law. Some reinforcements might tip the scales back in our direction."

"More men will just slow us down, and more importantly," Eli pointed out, "Jake and Hank will be keeping an eye on the local law. More than likely, if any man wearing a badge decides to look at this building, Jake will know about it and Hank will be ready to rid Cheyenne of a few peacekeepers."

"You have a whole lot of faith in two men."

"No. I'm just not about to underestimate them."

Without wasting another moment to consider his options, Saunders nodded. "Fine. I'll keep my head down. What else should I be doing?"

"Look for patterns around here. Before any big job, that's what I'd be doing. Looking for men who might be guards masquerading as passersby. Watching when windows in the building we meant to hit were opened or closed or used by anyone inside. Studying the nearby buildings for someone watching the place we meant to be. There's bound to be patterns like that around anything that's being closely guarded. Jake or Hank will move in patterns too. Start thinking more like an outlaw and you'll be able to find some."

"Sounds like a lot of common sense to me."

"Is that what you would have done if I hadn't told you?"

After a slight pause, Saunders had to admit, "Probably not."

Eli shoved the lawman away as if he were setting a windup toy along its path. "We'll meet back in this spot."

"When?"

"Can't say for sure. Whenever I'm through scouting. Just keep your eyes open and look for me."

"And what if I see someone following you?"

"Then catch my eye somehow to let me

know. We've just got to improvise with these things."

"Yeah, yeah," Saunders grumbled.

Already, Eli was regretting his decision to come this far. Stepping up to keep Saunders from getting killed was one thing. Continuing to follow the lawman on a suicidal ride against known, cold-blooded killers was another. He could slip away now even easier than before. Saunders was safe and presumably smart enough to know better than to face Jake Welles on his own. If the sheriff didn't go back to Seedley, then he was too foolish to be of much concern anyhow.

There was the matter of seeing Lyssa again. That just wouldn't be possible if Eli cut and ran now. A more practical part inside reminded him that he'd barely spent any time at all with Lyssa, and sticking his neck out this far was a real good way to get his head lopped off. But that was just his survival instinct kicking in again. He had to find his way back to Lyssa. Whatever happened after that could be left to the Fates. That decided, he set about doing what he'd agreed to do.

Cheyenne was a bustling maze of streets teeming with people, horses, dogs, and even a few pigs that must have gotten loose from a butcher. Eli moved like a single fish in a school, taking in everything around him with senses that had been dulled from spending too much time locked in a cage. Taking on Zack and his boys wasn't easy, but it had been a straightforward affair. Stealing, on the other hand, was a dance where each step led into another and led into another and into yet another before the true goal could be seen. That's what had always drawn him to his craft.

When Jake had followed him on outings like this, he'd always said Eli was full of beans. He said there was just a natural instinct or random chance involved with finding the best angle to ride in on a bank or approach a stagecoach. Cracking a safe or coaxing open a lock was definitely a skill, but the rest worked on a gut level. That's what Jake said, but that was only because he didn't know any better.

Saunders had disappeared into the crowd fairly well, leaving Eli to scout on his own. The McKane building was in a busy area with lots of prospects for lookout posts nearby. Plenty of rooftops from which to watch, dozens of windows looking down on the street and out at the building itself, along with countless spots at ground level where a man could keep an eye on the Trust

& Loan without drawing much attention. Eli reflexively wanted to scout the building as he would any other target that was ripe for the picking, but instead he adjusted his sights to look for the best spots someone else might be trying to do that same job.

Right away, he was able to eliminate several possibilities. Businesses that were too busy wouldn't allow the outlaws to come and go without being noticed by a bunch of locals who might ask questions. Men skulking about within places that were too empty would appear out of the ordinary. That still left several possibilities along the street, so Eli fell back on his knowledge of the robbers themselves.

Hank preferred to use homes for his lookout points, but that was only because he didn't mind tying up a family so they could be stuffed into an attic until he was through. Jake didn't like working that way, only because of the extra mess that Hank caused before they got close to finishing the job that had brought them to town in the first place. Although there weren't many buildings that looked like private homes in the vicinity, Eli was able to cross a few off his list.

Doctors' offices were out as well. Cody might not be in Cheyenne, but the others were expecting him, and somewhere in his childhood, that one's oversized head had been filled with demons where doctors and dentists were concerned. Being anywhere near them made Cody too fidgety to be of much use as well as an annoyance to everyone else. Eli smirked as he mentally dismissed one three-level building in a prime position that was shared by two doctors and a dentist on the top floor.

There would be waiting involved, which meant Jake would want to be somewhere he could get plenty of whiskey and, if the mood struck him, a soiled dove or two. Hank also enjoyed the company of working girls, but for reasons other than simple companionship. As far as Eli could tell, Hank had always been a cruel man and unleashed his temper on anyone or anything within his reach. He liked keeping company with working girls, simply because many of them were less likely to complain as long as things didn't get too rough or weren't heard if they did decide to squawk. Saloons were too busy, however, and full of town gossips with tongues loosened by excessive amounts of liquor. Keeping that in mind, Eli looked away from a pair of saloons and was drawn to a billiards hall marked by a small sign hanging from a piece of curvy wrought iron.

The sign read CARD TABLES IN BACK. DAILY DRINK SPECIALS.

Jake would be happy with both of those things.

It was a wide building with two floors lined with several small balconies overlooking the street as well as McKane Trust & Loan. The doors were spaced close enough for them to each lead into a private room. If there was any doubt as to what those rooms were used for, it was expelled by the voluptuous woman with red hair leaning down to wave at Eli while making sure he got a generous view down the front of her dress. She beckoned to him like a siren to a sailor and stretched her upper body even farther over the railing as Eli approached.

"You play billiards, ma'am?" Eli asked.

She twirled her hair around one finger and replied, "We can play something much better if you like."

"Should I come in?"

"I'll meet you inside."

Eli felt every one of his nerves drawing taut beneath his skin. Although he might have wanted to look around for something a little farther back from McKane's, this place was made to order for the rest of his old gang. He knew he could be in Jake's sights at any given moment, so Eli stepped into the billiard hall with his hand placed firmly on the .38 at his side. The second pistol was in its place and he resisted the urge to check them both to make sure they were loaded. He'd checked them plenty of times already, and bullets didn't normally fall from the cylinder on their own. Even with another three pistols, a shotgun cradled in one arm, and a cannon strapped to his back, he still wouldn't have felt safe walking in through that place's front door. Preparing for the worst, he found nothing more waiting for him inside than a beaming smile from a very pretty redhead.

"Well, hello there," she said while walking down a narrow staircase against one wall. "What sort of game were you interested in?"

The sign outside seemed to be legitimate. As advertised, there were half a dozen billiard tables set up in a cavernous single room that seemed to comprise the building's entire first floor. A few men played there while a few more played cards at one of four round tables in the back. Also in the back was a short bar tended by a tall man who watched Eli like a hawk. One hand reached beneath the bar, most assuredly resting on a club or some other weapon meant to dissuade anyone from causing a ruckus.

Eli approached the redhead without trying to keep the nervousness from his smile. Such a thing would only help him more closely resemble someone making what some might call an indecent proposition. "I'd . . . like a game with you," he said.

She smiled right back at him in a sweet, somewhat nurturing way. "My name's Heather," she said while entwining her arm around his. "You'll want to come this way."

Since Heather had taken possession of his right arm, Eli brought his left down so it was close enough to brush against his second holstered .38. The barkeep was still watching him, so he didn't do any more than that. While he'd been nervous on his way in, that was nothing compared to what Eli felt when he was led up those stairs. The walls closed in on both sides, forcing them to each scrape an arm against one side of the stairwell as they stepped upon one squeaking step after another.

"Are you just passing through Cheyenne or did you just dredge up the courage to come in here and visit me?" Heather asked.

"I'm new to Cheyenne."

"Well, then, I'll have to see what I can do to make this trip memorable. My room's this one right here."

Using his memory of what he'd seen from the street as well as his knack for getting a feel for interior layouts, Eli knew this was indeed the room attached to the balcony where Heather had first caught his eye. One quick glance down a short hall was all he needed to see one door for each of the other windows looking out toward McKane's as well as two more facing the other direction. Since Jake or Hank would want a good view, Eli didn't concern himself with those last two doors.

"You look nervous," she said in something close to a purr. Heather kept hold of his arm while working the handle of her door and pushing it open. "Don't be. We can discuss what you'd like and what you can —"

Eli cut her short by pulling his arm free, shoving forward so both of them were in the room, and pushing the door shut using one of his heels. "I'm not going to hurt you."

There was surprise on her face, but this obviously wasn't the first time Heather had been manhandled in such a way. "You'd better not if you want to stay in one piece."

At first, Eli figured she was referring to the watchful bartender downstairs. Then he noticed the curved, slender knife gripped in her free hand. He didn't know exactly where the knife had been hidden, but it was currently poised to disembowel him with one slash. At the very least, he'd get a cut across his belly that would put him into a world of hurt.

"Like I said, I don't want to hurt you," he assured her.

"Then why would you stop being polite so quickly?"

The tone in her voice filled in even more of her character. Eli was now certain that she'd handled herself through much worse than this after falling victim to some less-than-accommodating guests. "I'm in town looking for some old acquaintances of mine," Eli said. "I think they might be staying here."

"You could have just asked me about something like that."

"I needed to be discreet."

She smirked at him without allowing the knife to waver in her hand. "You don't think a woman in my line of work knows about discretion?"

"The men I'm after could already be looking for trouble. They'll be watchful and I had to get out of sight quickly. Are these rooms for rent or are they just for your sort of business?"

"They're for rent as well."

"I think those men may have rented a room or two, so I couldn't dawdle in the hall for very long. Them creaking stairs may have already done me in, so I couldn't take a chance with haggling on prices and such."

Heather studied him carefully. "What do these men look like?" After Eli gave her a quick description of Jake and Hank, she sneered, "Those two are friends of yours?"

"Not friends. Acquaintances."

She must have picked up on the distaste in his voice because Heather nodded slowly and finally lowered the knife. Stepping back so she could put some distance between them without getting too far to cut him, she said, "They're here all right. Been here for a few days."

"Which room are they renting?"

"The one at the far end of this hall on my side."

That made sense, seeing as how that spot would allow them to get a good look all the way down the street in front of them as well as one side of the McKane building. "So you've met them?" he asked.

"I sure have. One came up to me the first night they arrived, spouting a whole lot of tough talk and waving his little gun in my face." Grinning humorlessly, she added, "Not the gun you're thinking of. A derringer. Something some of the other girls working here carry in their stockings."

Hank got no end of grief from the other gang members for carrying that pistol. Not so much because it was out of character for a man to do so, but because he took such offense to anyone calling the size of his pistol into question. "Did he hurt you?"

"He wanted to. I could tell as much before he even reached for that gun of his. Gave him a little cut that he won't soon forget. Judging by that patch over his eye, I wasn't the first."

"No, you weren't." Eli approached the window, took a look outside, and then stood close to the front corner of the room so he could best hear any movement in the hall. "What have they been doing since they got here?"

"One stays in the room and the other prowls around town. Couldn't rightly tell you where they go, since I don't make it my business to spy on folks. Besides, as far as them two are concerned, I'm just as happy to be rid of them."

"I know just how you feel."

Heather's stance shifted into something only slightly less defensive. She was still ready to move if need be, but crossed her arms as if to show she wasn't about to try and draw any blood. "After that first night, they've been keeping fairly quiet. They'll send for one of the girls while the other is out, but I ain't about to step foot in that room. I warned the other girls about them, so they're plenty careful. Hasn't seemed to be any problems, though."

"Are they ever both in there at the same time?"

She thought about it for a few seconds and shrugged. "I don't think so, but I haven't been appointed as their keeper."

"You and anyone else who works here sees plenty," Eli said. Reaching into one pocket, he was careful to move slowly and deliberately until he could ease some of the money he was holding into view. Even after glimpsing cash instead of anything more dangerous in his grasp, Heather wasn't quick to loosen her grip on the knife she still held in one hand. "You're a smart woman," he continued. "You know what it takes to survive among dangerous sorts. You know how to handle yourself. All of that means you can't expect me to believe there's much of anything that goes on in here without you knowing. You may even have your finger on the pulse of this entire town."

"Cheyenne is a big place," she said with a grin. "But I do know a thing or two."

"And," Eli said as he eased the money a bit farther from his pocket, "would you be willing to part with some of that information?"

"For the right price."

"That's what I figured." Eli removed the money from his pocket. It wasn't all that Saunders had given him when handing out some of Cody's cash to cover expenses or incidentals, but it was enough to put a gleam in Heather's eye. "Does this look about right?"

"Depends on what you want to know."

"Let's start with my previous question."

"Far as I can tell," she replied almost instantly, "they ain't in that room at the same time for more than a minute or two. Of course, there are times when I'm too occupied to keep watch, but that's what I've seen."

"What about now?"

"Just one."

"Does he have any female companionship?"

"Did last night," Heather replied. "I didn't see her leave, but she'd be gone by now anyway. Those acquaintances of yours ain't like the ones that usually come in here. They stink of wickedness, and none of us want to be around them any longer than we have to."

"I wouldn't have thought a woman like

you would be opposed to such quaint notions as wickedness."

"A woman like me? You mean a whore?"

"No," Eli said. "I mean someone who holds her own in a rough line of work. That kind of life makes wickedness seem almost too common to be noticed."

Once again, she relaxed. Another step back allowed her to put him out of reach of her own weapon while putting her at the mercy of his if he decided to draw it. Although simple to some, the shift was a show of trust between two similar souls. "Just because I know wickedness when I see it and can handle it if it comes my way, that doesn't mean I'm part of it. You know those men pretty well?"

"I do."

"Then you're either a lawman or another outlaw." Looking him up and down in a manner that seemed oddly suited to the setting of a bedroom, she said, "I don't see a badge on you."

"I'm no lawman."

"Then the fire in your eyes means you probably mean to kill those two. Not that I'm opposed to the idea, but I'd like to know if anything along those lines might be happening. These walls are thin and won't do anything to stop a bullet. I'd rather be somewhere else in that instance."

"I'm not out to kill anyone." Seeing Heather's patiently raised eyebrow, he added, "But you might want to clear a path up here. Come to think of it, is there anyone else I should be concerned about?"

"Not for the moment. The other girls tend to other business at this time of the day, but they'll be back tonight. I don't know, but there could be someone in one or two of the rooms across the hall. They're rented, but there's no way of knowing if they're occupied right now short of me busting in there. Management tends to frown on that sort of thing."

"They should be fine. Has either of those two men made any requests? Either to you or maybe to the bartender?" When Eli asked that question, he was specifically thinking about Jake asking to be notified if anyone came sniffing around for him or Hank. Jake would also want to know if someone matching Cody's description had stopped by, but Eli didn't want to lead Heather into telling him something he wanted to hear. There was more money in his pocket, after all, and he couldn't blame her for trying to separate him from as much of it as possible.

"Requests?" she asked without so much as a glance toward the pocket containing the rest of the money. "I can ask a few people who would know more about things like that."

"I'd appreciate it."

"Appreciate it how much?" Now she reached out to stroke the pocket containing that money in such a way that Eli thought he should pay her for that alone.

"Depends on what you bring me," he said.

"All right, then. Wait here and I'll be right back. Shouldn't be long."

The moment Heather left the room, Eli cursed himself for a fool. Even though he thought he could trust her to do what she'd said, there was still the outside chance that she was more spooked than she'd been leading on and would come upstairs with a lot more than just a few pieces of information. The commotion caused by him being escorted from the billiard hall by the bartender or another man whose job it was to clean house was simply more than Eli could afford.

Fortunately for him, the lower floor was open enough for every sound to echo and the enclosed stairwell was narrow enough to catch the noise and direct it upward. Eli poked his head outside Heather's room where he could listen for any possible trouble. The sound that caused him to jump came from a direction he hadn't been expecting. One of the doors farther down the hall was coming open. As far as he could tell, it was on the side of the building facing the McKane building. Eli ducked back into Heather's room, pulled the door shut, and held on to the handle so he could keep it ajar without it being obvious to whoever was stepping out for a stroll.

Eli eased the .38 partly from his holster using his right hand. His eyes narrowed and he held his breath as light footsteps tapped against the floor in a line that would bring the walker directly in front of him within the next few seconds.

The person moved past Heather's door, allowing Eli to get a look at the walker's back. In less than a second, he recognized the man outside, which prompted him to swing the door open, reach out, and grab the other man by the arm. Although surprised at first, the man recognized Eli as well.

"Now, ain't this a kick in the pants?" Jake said as he pulled his arm free of Eli's grasp.

CHAPTER 22

"Howdy, Eli," Jake said in a cordial tone. "Didn't think I'd be seeing you so soon."

"Didn't think you'd be seeing me at all is more like it," Eli snarled.

"Oh, I wouldn't put it that way."

"You left me back at that ranch. Why'd you do that?"

Dropping his voice to a cool, deadly pitch, Jake asked, "What would you have had me do? Stay in that death trap until the cross fire got so bad a dog couldn't have crawled away on its belly?"

"You could have at least tried to fetch me. All I saw was you and Hank turning tail to save your own hides."

"And when did you see that? Before you charged that fella that had the drop on you or in the half a second of consciousness after you got whacked by that lawman?" Jake's eyes narrowed as he took a quick look at Eli's gun belt. He pulled his arm loose, placed a hand on his holstered Smith & Wesson, and took one step back. "Is that why you snuck up on me like that? Because you wanted payback for what happened back at that ranch?"

"If that's what I wanted, do you think I'd be talking to you right now?"

"If you were Hank, probably not. You bein' you, on the other hand . . ."

"Why'd you leave me, Jake? And don't give me any garbage about there being too much shooting for your liking."

"Jobs turn sour sometimes. You know that."

"Sure I do, but we always clean up our messes."

"What about Dave Garza? He rode along with us on that first general store we robbed after you joined up. The store owner grabbed a shotgun, fired some lucky shots, and brought half of his family raining down on us with rifles of every make and caliber. We had to skin out of there real quick, and if we'd turned around to go after Dave, we all would've been caught or killed. They were looking for us, just like those guards and lawmen were looking for us back in Seedley."

"Dave was with the gang about three days before I was, and you were the only one who remembers his name. Nobody else even liked him."

Jake shrugged. "We still had to leave him behind. That's my point. It happens."

"I've had plenty of time to sort through what happened at that ranch. Plenty of time spent in a cage with my thoughts. Nobody even tried to come back for me or fire a single shot at the men who pinned me down. You and the others may just as well have been on your way out before I was bushwhacked!"

Jake sighed as his face took on a more contemplative and melancholy expression. His hand remained squarely on the grip of his gun. "Can you really blame us?"

"You're damn right I can. I was the one who got his head cracked open. I was the one who was locked up like an animal and I was the one who nearly got his neck stretched!"

"You're also the one who got away to have this conversation right now," Jake said with a raise of his eyebrows. "Ain't that something?"

Eli wasn't even close to being affected by the change of tone. "That doesn't matter. I was left to my own devices. Anything I did after that is my affair."

"All right, then," Jake said. "How's this?

You're the one who put us all in jeopardy by acting as if bullets bounced off your skull. Either that or you're the one who didn't much care whether you lived or died."

"What?"

"Don't try to act like you don't know what I'm talking about, Eli. We've all seen it for some time. Even Cody saw it and his head's full of rocks."

"Saw what?"

Jake leaned forward a bit, as if to narrow the world down to just him and Eli. "Saw that look in your eyes whenever a gun went off. While we were looking for a place to find cover or kill the man pulling the trigger, you were charging into the path of the bullet. You're the first one to step up when another man draws his weapon."

"When Hank does something like that, it's a good thing," Eli pointed out. "Why should I be chastised for it?"

"Because Hank's returning fire. He's looking for a resolution. That's what all of us are doing. We're trying to get our job done and get away so we can come up with another job."

"So, what do you think I've been doing?"

Now Jake began pacing within the room. "That's what I've been trying to figure out. Near as I can tell, you're trying to get to the end of this life so you can see what else is next. Considering the sort of mud hole this world can be, I don't rightly blame you. Still, that kind of behavior don't exactly make it easy to be around you sometimes. If you weren't such a good thief or close to magic when it comes to cracking a lock, I would have cut you loose after our first few rides together. And don't give me that horse manure about you getting those headaches. It takes more than that to make a man charge into gunfire with a smile on his face."

Eli's voice was so weak, it almost seemed to be detached from the lungs that gave it life. "That's not true."

Shaking his head, Jake replied, "We all choose this way of life for a reason. Some men have demons. Some are too stupid to know any better. Some are just too mean to live like civilized folk. But you're different. You're a smart fella, Eli, and you see a lot more than most anyone else around. That's what makes you such a good thief. That's also what made you lose hope."

Eli turned around, the desire to get Jake out of his sight overpowering the instinct to keep the gang leader where he could keep track of him. "What would you know about that?" he snarled.

"Because I make it my business to size a

man up in a short amount of time. It's how I ran at the front of an outlaw gang without getting shot in the back. It's how I know which people to threaten, which to sweet-talk, and which to kill."

"Is it also how you decide who you'll cut loose so they could be jailed or worse?"

Surprisingly enough, when Eli turned back around, he saw Jake was nodding. "Yeah," the gang leader said. "It is."

"So you handed me over to those men from McKane Trust and Loan?"

"Where'd you hear about that?"

"Never mind," Eli snapped. "Is that what you did or isn't it?"

"They don't work for the McKane Company, but they do represent some mighty big interests in this territory and several others along with a few states back East."

"Don't make me ask again," Eli said as he closed his right hand around the grip of his .38.

Without wavering, Jake said, "They made an offer to Hank when he was scouting that iron wagon in Omaha. I don't know if Hank approached them or if he was found out, but the offer was made for us to hand over one of our own in exchange for allowing us to ride away."

"Ride away from what? We hadn't even

fired a shot at that wagon when Hank was scouting."

"We'd been burning a path through three territories in as many months," Jake mused as if he were fondly remembering a string of pretty ladies he'd courted. "Some of those payrolls we helped ourselves to were connected to larger companies, and rich men can afford to cast their gaze in a whole lot of directions. It was only a matter of time before some of those rich men decided to get together and do something about men like us. But there was money that never stopped flowing from one town to another." Jake was actually laughing when he added, "I heard tell that some larger company was shipping their money to one spot for safekeeping, so I thought I'd hit it. I already had Hank to do my scouting and a few men like Cody drifting in and out of the gang to add firepower. All I needed was someone to crack open the safes and lockboxes. That's where you came in."

The two men were slowly pacing in a circle, always keeping each other in sight. "It turned out better than I could have hoped," Jake continued. "The only thing that changed from job to job was that a few more guards were tacked on for us to burn through or a bigger safe was wrapped around all that cash. You saw to them safes and the rest of us burned through the guards."

"You never thought those rich men would catch on?" Eli asked.

Jake rolled his eyes at that and said, "It was bound to happen. If we could keep nabbing that money, there was no reason to stop."

"It wasn't that much money. We usually walked away with enough to live on and gamble or waste on liquor and women, but not much more than that."

"The money ain't the point! You know that! It's not as if men like us will just get enough stashed away and go buy a farm," Jake said as if he were spitting out each distasteful word. "That company pegged us as foolish cowboys without the gall or brains to hit them more than once. Every time we took one of them strongboxes and you cracked it open was sweeter than the last! I saw that in your eyes too, so don't deny it. In fact, the only thing that ever gave you any joy apart from drinking enough whiskey to ease them headaches was cracking open a lock of some sort. It's what you were made to do."

Unable to deny that statement, Eli said, "Every time we took a strongbox, that company took more notice of us."

"Eh, they don't matter. I never even cared about the name of that company until I was told about that place across the street."

"We don't need to know the name of the men we steal from," Eli said. "What matters is when too many of those men get together to hunt us down. Too big a price on our heads could be a death sentence. You let us all ride straight into the fire, Jake."

"One man's fire is another man's incentive. I've ridden with gangs that had the run of a town or two and all it did was make them lazy enough to be picked off by any lawman with enough sand to come looking for them. That company, whatever it's called, was full of itself, had too much money, and needed to be taken down a peg. We got to pluck some low-hanging fruit until it was time to find a way out. Handing you over just happened to be that way. The man who spoke to Hank while he was scouting that iron wagon laid it all out for him. A bounty was about to be placed on our heads that was big enough to bring every scalp hunter this side of the Mississippi after us. It was also big enough to put a sizeable dent in those rich men's coffers. If we agreed to part ways on their terms, they'd steer us toward someone else's low-hanging fruit and they wouldn't have to pay up on that bounty."

Eli scowled. "The head of some fat company came up with this?"

"No!" Jake said with a smile that bordered on triumphant. "It was the men hired to provide security for them rich men. The ones conducting business here in Cheyenne. They got sick and tired of losing men and chasing us all over creation. I'm betting things would have been different if they'd found all of us sniffing after that iron wagon instead of just Hank. Since they couldn't clean us out then, they did the next best thing by striking a deal."

"And handing me over?"

"That was a way for them McKane fellas to save face and make it look like they did something to earn their fees. They capture one of us, get their hands shook when the robberies stop, and get to be the ones hired by those rich men to guard the funds being brought into Cheyenne. Actually," Jake said with a beaming smile, "it ain't a half-bad plan."

"It is when you're the sacrificial lamb."

"Yeah, well, that's a mighty big shame." The two men had come to a stop with Eli's back to the door and Jake's to a window. "You became a dangerous man, Eli, and not in the good sense. You took on that ghostly look in your eyes that a man gets when he forgets his reason to keep living. That sort of thing happens to most of us at one time or another. But you hung on to it. I think it's because you look around so much."

"What?" Eli let out a frustrated breath. "This was a bad idea to talk to you like this. There's nothing you can say to make things right. I suppose I just wanted to hear what was going through your head when you hung me out to dry after I thought we'd become something close to friends."

"You never thought that," Jake said. "We were good partners. That's all it ever was. You're always looking at things so closely. You figured out all you needed to know about me after the first day or two we rode together. I could tell that much just like I could tell you never stopped looking at every last thing around you. When you're fidgeting with the tumblers of a lock, that's a good thing. When you're studying every aspect of this harsh world and everyone in it, that ain't so good. Sometimes you gotta let things slide. Like that Amazing Willhelm dandy we saw at the Birdcage when we went through Tombstone. Remember him?"

Although he'd been ready to draw his pistol and put an end to the ill-advised conversation, Eli was intrigued by the random change of subject. "You mean the fella who did them tricks?"

"That's the one. He made cards disappear from one hand and they'd show up in another. He wasn't that good, but he was a hoot to watch."

"He was terrible," Eli grunted.

"That's because you were watching too hard," Jake said while pointing a finger at him. "Sometimes you just need to kick your feet up and let some things pass. You never let anything pass, Eli. That's why you're always troubled and that's why getting gunned down might seem like a real good way to put this harsh existence behind you."

"Jacob Welles, known murderer, bank robber, and horse thief, is trying his hand at philosophy. Now, *that's* a hoot."

"You might not wanna die, but you ain't too fond of livin'," Jake said simply. "I seen that plenty of times in the faces of men like me who want to ride hard and go down in a blaze of glory. It's a hell of a way to leave a mark on this world. Get one thing straight. I didn't want to hand you over to them company men. That is, not until we took down that iron wagon. Until that day, I was about to tell Hank to stick his plan where the sun don't shine and find another piece of fruit to pluck. But when you rode up to the side of that wagon, stared into that opening, right down the barrel of the rifle being pointed out of it, and didn't get yer head blown off, you were disappointed."

Eli started to interrupt, but was cut short by a swiftly raised hand. Holding out that hand as if he were stopping someone from crossing a street, Jake said, "And when you had the drop on that man back at that ranch, you hesitated. You hesitated when you had a clean shot. A shot that could have allowed you to get back on your own two feet and get to the rest of us. The Good Book says the Lord will help thems that helps themselves. I was right there and if I saw you make the first move to help yourself, I would've helped you. What I saw was a man at the end of his rope with no interest in pulling himself up. I got no use for a man like that in my gang other than as something to trade to get the rest of us out of hot water. Was that the answer you were after when you dragged me into this room?"

"Actually . . . yes. It was." When he heard footsteps coming up the stairs down the hall, Eli figured the rest of the answers he'd been after would be on the way as well. Surely Heather would have found someone in the billiard hall who knew something useful.

"So, where does that leave us now? More importantly," Jake added with a mischievous smirk, "are you gonna tell me how you got out of that jail cell?"

"Maybe some other time. I assume you're in town for the money that made it to McKane's Trust and Loan, so let's see what we can see about that place."

"How'd you know to look for us here?"

Jake's growing curiosity didn't bother Eli as much as the approaching footsteps. They would arrive at the door in a matter of seconds, and there was no telling what Jake would do once he got his hands on Heather.

"I'll tell you about it once we're done with this job," Eli said. "Until then, you'll just have to trust that I need money and —"

"And some men to watch your back if them law dogs come after you again, huh?"

"Right," Eli said in a voice that was loud enough to carry through the door. "Just move along now." Hoping Heather heard him and heeded his advice, Eli lowered his voice once again. "Move along with the task at hand, that is."

The footsteps outside paused near the door and then moved along. Eli let out a relieved exhale.

"You ain't gonna put a bullet through my back, are ya?" Jake chided.

"Not until this job is over."

The gang leader laughed and began moving toward Eli as well as the door. "I should get back to my room. Cody should be back any time and I think you'll like what he's bringing along with him."

Not only were the footsteps still moving along the hallway, but they were too slow for Heather to be anywhere but directly in Jake's line of sight the moment he emerged from the room. Before that could happen, Eli grabbed the handle. "I thought I heard someone out there," he said to Jake. "Why don't I surprise Cody myself?"

Before Jake could say anything or move in closer, Eli squared his shoulders to the door to block as much of it as possible from the gang leader's view. He then pulled the door open and thought of what he might say to Heather to get her into another room without tipping his hand to Jake. Whatever words he might have prepared became lodged in his throat when he saw someone else standing outside the room.

"There you are," Saunders said with a relieved smile. "Did you find Jake yet?"

"You should probably move along," Eli stammered, still hoping to salvage the situation before it toppled out of his reach.

"I couldn't find anyone outside and thought you might need some backup," the sheriff said. "We might as well stick together."

Everything behind Eli was deathly still. He took a quick glance over his shoulder to find Jake standing a few paces behind him and angled so he could see the hallway over Eli's shoulder. "I remember you, law dog," Jake said. Shifting his eyes to Eli, he added, "Now, this is another surprise."

Judging by the look on Jake's face, he didn't enjoy this surprise nearly as much as the last one.

CHAPTER 23

"He a friend of yours, Eli?" Jake asked.

Eli felt all of the warmth drain from his body. While some folks might have compared that to someone walking over his proverbial grave, this seemed more as if someone had found that grave, stood on it, and done a raucous jig. "He's the one that told me you came to Cheyenne."

"That's a shame. Figured you were just smart enough to track me down." Jake nodded slowly and flexed the fingers poised above his holstered .44. "Guess I gotta cut you loose a second time."

Saunders stood in a sideways stance while looking over Eli's shoulder into the room. "Not if I have anything to say about it," he announced. "I made him come with me to find you. He didn't have a say in the matter. Both of you are coming back with me to answer for what you done. There ain't nothing to say about that either."

As Jake glared at the men in front of him, Eli could hear another set of footsteps coming down the hall from the direction of the stairs. “Heather!” Eli shouted, since there was no more need for subtlety. “Get away from here!”

Rather than retreat, the footsteps charged toward the door.

Saunders pivoted on the balls of his feet to face the end of the hall.

Most disturbingly, Jake didn’t budge.

In the hall, two bodies collided like a pair of rams locking horns over a disputed mate. It didn’t take long for Eli to realize that one of those bodies was most definitely not Heather’s. It was the patch over one eye that caught his attention first, telling Eli that Hank had gotten the drop on Sheriff Saunders.

Knowing Jake wasn’t above taking a shot at an enemy’s open back, Eli skinned his gun and twisted around to catch him in the act of drawing his Smith & Wesson. Jake snarled a string of obscenities at him, even as a wild shot from Eli’s .38 hissed past his left side. Both men dived for cover behind the biggest thing in the room, landing on the floor on either side of Heather’s bed.

Jake’s foul language continued as he pumped a few shots under the bed and into the floor to cause a commotion in the room below. Since one of those rounds sent splinters flying only an inch or so away from him, Eli rolled away from the bed and scrambled to get his feet beneath him.

At the door, Saunders was fighting for his life. Even though he'd already drawn his Army Colt, Hank was too close to put it to much use as anything other than a club. He fired a shot at first, which only sailed past its target and down the hall to set off a chorus of women's screams. From then on, Saunders pounded the side of the pistol against Hank's shoulder, back, ribs, or anywhere else he could land a blow. When he attempted to knock the Colt against Hank's temple to put the outlaw down, Hank pressed his face against the sheriff's neck to allow the weapon to sail over him while only scraping the back of his head. Not one to waste an opportunity to do some damage, Hank sank his teeth into the lawman's neck in a crude but effective attack.

Saunders wailed in pain, feeling a rush of blood through his veins that gave him the strength to straighten up and carry Hank along with him as he rammed himself and the outlaw into the closest wall.

"Traitor!" Jake hollered while quickly

replacing the spent rounds in his .44.

Taking a moment to think back, Eli figured he had two shots left in the .38 he held. The second pistol was fully loaded, so he drew that one in preparation for a switch once the first cylinder was emptied. Acrid smoke filled the close quarters of the bedroom and burned his eyes as he pointed his right gun at Jake.

Every jostle threw his aim off-kilter.

When he pulled his trigger, stuffing exploded from the mattress Jake was using as cover.

With every explosive bark from Jake's .44, the world became that much more chaotic.

Eli dropped to one knee to present a smaller target. Although it had been a wise move to get away from the bed, there wasn't anywhere else for him to seek refuge. When his first .38 went dry, he dropped it and tossed the second across his body in a move he'd practiced enough times for it to become second nature.

Feathers and stuffing from the mattress hung in the air around the bed to turn the already smoky air into a murky soup. Jake stood up to get a better look above the thickest section of the gritty cloud. His gun hand was already coming up and his eyes searched for a target.

In the hall, Saunders still had his hands full. Blood streamed down the side of Hank's head from a nasty gash created by the lawman's bludgeoning attacks. Like most head wounds, it looked worse than it was, and since it hadn't put the outlaw down yet, it wasn't bad enough to do the trick any time soon. Saunders shoved Hank away and twisted his body to take a vicious swing at the outlaw, but Hank dropped down to let the sheriff's fist pound against the wood directly over his head.

Eli watched those things happen through the open doorway as if the fight were slowly spooling out in a dream. More accustomed to close-quarters fights, Hank had abandoned his firearm in favor of a blade, and being a killer with blood that was colder than the bottom of an ice floe, he had no qualm with hopping to one side so he could get a clear view at the sheriff's back.

If Eli took his shot now, he was certain he could get Jake before that .44 spat any lead in his direction. Making a subtle adjustment by shifting his hip and redirecting his arm, Eli used every bit of focus at his disposal, squeezed his trigger, and put a round into Hank's side just as the blade was about to be sunk into Saunders's body.

Hank yelped more out of surprise than

pain as the impact of the gunshot spun him away from Saunders and sent the blade flying from his hand. That gave the lawman enough of an opening to turn and face him for a more fair fight.

The .44 in Jake's hand went off.

A bullet slammed into Eli's upper body, followed by a searing hot pain that dug into his flesh before the chunk of lead found its way out again. Suddenly Eli didn't have the strength to move. He didn't even have the strength to stand, so he fell straight down and hit the floor in a heap.

The moment his cheek touched the dirty wooden slats, Eli became a simple observer without the ability to study angles or read the situation as it unfolded.

Footsteps thumped against the floor.

Boots filled his line of sight.

A familiar voice rumbled above him like a storm.

"We could'a been rich, you and I," Jake said to Eli. "But you wouldn't be happy until you had your damn blaze of glory! At least I can do that much for ya."

The next few seconds were mostly silent.

Something scraped in the vicinity of the doorway, but that might as well have been twenty miles away as far as Eli was concerned. There was a dull thump mixed with a crunch that was a lot closer. Eli briefly considered the notion that the sound could have been all he'd heard of the gunshot that ended his life.

When a pistol dropped to the floor directly in front of Eli's face, he reconsidered that notion.

Straining to get a look at the pistol, Eli could see it was a bloodstained Army Colt. Soon a scraped and equally bloody hand came down to retrieve it.

"Can you stand up?" Saunders asked.

The air still stung Eli's nose and clung to the inside of his mouth in a gritty film. When he tried to prop himself up, his entire body was set aflame by agony that extended in every direction from the fresh wound in his upper body. "No," he grunted while allowing himself to fall back down.

Rough hands rolled Eli onto his side and began tugging at his shirt. Eli couldn't tell much more than that because his senses were dulling to make his entire world one swirling blur.

"Looks like the shot isn't so bad," Saunders said.

"Feels bad to me," Eli groaned.

"It's messy, but the bullet went all the way through."

"What about Hank?"

"He's gone. Dead," Saunders quickly added. "Took every last bullet I had, but he's done for. That's why I didn't have any rounds left to help you."

"Where's Jake?"

"Out cold. I threw my gun at him."

Eli chuckled, which was one of the most painful things he'd ever done. "That's the best you could do?"

"Saved your sorry hide, didn't it? Let's get you up. Miss, we need a doctor as quick as you can find one."

Since his body had gone mostly numb, Eli didn't feel much of anything as he was hefted to his feet. Whatever he saw was smeared on the edges like a painting that had been left out in the rain. Heather was nearby, staring at him with eyes that were wide enough for him to see even with his current impediments.

"Are you all right?" she asked.

"He sure won't be unless he gets a doctor right *quick!*" Saunders roared.

She turned and hurried from the room.

When Eli was turned around so Saunders could bring him to his feet without aggravating the wound, he saw Jake lying across the bed. The gang leader was sprawled on the mattress with both legs dangling over the side. Blood from a gash on his temple stained the linens in a spreading crimson blossom. At least that explained why he hadn't heard the outlaw hit the floor.

"Is that . . . the only way you . . . know how to fight?" Eli asked. "Knocking men unconscious?"

Saunders pulled in a labored breath and shifted so Eli's arm wrapped more securely around the back of his neck. "Seems to have worked this long. Why put an end to a good thing?"

"Shouldn't you put some handcuffs on him? That's another one of your strengths, isn't it?"

"Shut yer mouth before I knock you out again. Already know just the spot to hit."

Eli no longer had the strength to hold his head up, so he allowed it to droop forward. He expected to fall to the floor as well, but Saunders wasn't about to let that happen.

Pain shot through Eli's body like a hot poker that had been jammed into his bullet wound and shoved all the way through to the other side. His eyes snapped open and were immediately closed by a rough hand that pressed against his face to push him down.

"Hold him steady!" an unfamiliar voice demanded.

"I thought you said the bullet was out of him!" Eli recognized that voice as Saunders's.

"It is, but it grazed a rib on its way out. There's chipped bone stuck into a few places that needs to be removed. Just hold him steady and let me do my job!"

"I think he's waking up, Doc."

"I don't care if he's trying to dance — hold him *still!*"

Eli felt another jolt of pain, accompanied by the presence of something cool and metallic within his side. He couldn't pinpoint where the tool was, but it was somewhere along the same path taken by Jake's bullet. When the tool found what it was after, Eli heard a crunch that filled his entire body.

"Got it," the doctor said. "Keep holding him steady."

"What do you think I'm doin'?"

"Steadier! This isn't going to come out easily."

The doctor was right about that. The bone fragment must have been lodged into a sensitive spot, because Eli felt it the instant it was moved. There was a stabbing pain, followed by a welcome wash of cold and an even more welcome blanket of unconsciousness.

"You know where you are, son?"

Although Eli still felt as if he were slowly falling through empty space, he knew one thing for certain: Whoever was talking wasn't his father. It took some effort, but he managed to open his eyes and get a look at a man with a round face, kind eyes, and sweaty brow. "Cheyenne?" he mumbled.

The kind man nodded. "Can you tell me what street we're on?"

"I . . . couldn't have told you that when I was upright and feeling fine."

Saunders stepped into view and said, "He's got that right. This one's nothing more than a robber who looks for money that needs to be stolen."

Despite the humor in the sheriff's tone, the man with the round face didn't find it amusing. "He's taken a blow to the head and has lost a lot of blood. I was merely checking to see if there was any memory loss or other side effects."

Gently rapping Eli's shoulder with the back of his hand, Saunders said, "He means he wants to make sure nothin' was rattled loose in that head of yours after you fell. You feeling all right?"

Eli rubbed his head. The movement caused some degree of pain, but not as much as he'd been expecting. When he went through the arduous motions of sitting up, he was partially hampered by thick layers of bandages wrapped around his torso. They didn't exactly restrict him, but were tighter than a bear hug. "Guess so. Feel pretty good, actually. That doctor did a real nice job."

"I would be that doctor," the man with the round face said as he shoved Saunders aside to get a closer look at his patient. "And yes. I seem to have done a good job. Sheriff Saunders tells me you suffer from some other sort of ailment. What is it?"

"Doesn't matter."

"It may affect your treatment."

Eli locked eyes with the doctor as best he could and said, "Just patch me up and let me deal with the rest."

"Fine," the doctor said grudgingly. "I suppose all I could have done was offer some medicine or possibly a suggestion for treatment. I'm not exactly a specialist."

"Kind of modest, ain't ya?" Saunders said. "After his being out for four days, I was beginning to think Eli was done for."

"Four days?" Eli said as he sat up. He grabbed his head with both hands when he felt the room start to tilt around him. Although his hands did nothing to cure the dizziness that had set in, they did feel enough stubble on his cheeks and chin to verify what he'd heard.

The doctor touched Eli's forehead and muttered, "Cooling off. Not so clammy. All good signs."

"You hear that?" Saunders said while smacking Eli good-naturedly on the shoulder. "Good signs!"

"Don't do that," the doctor scolded.

As the doctor checked him over, Eli looked at Saunders and asked, "What about the others?"

"Hank's dead," Saunders replied. "That one wasn't going to come with me any other way. Jacob Welles was handed over to some federal marshals who were after him for God only knows how many counts of murder or thieving."

"And what about me?"

"Since the marshals didn't ask about you, I didn't tell 'em. There were plenty of other men who rode with that gang, but Jacob Welles was the leader and when I tossed in Hank as a bonus, those marshals were pleased as pigs in slop. You'll answer for your crimes, but it'll be in a little town about ten miles outside Sherman. Friend of mine keeps the peace out there and owes me a favor. He'll see you get treated fair."

"I'm still to hang, then?"

The doctor seemed startled by that question, but continued what he was doing.

"Not unless they started hanging folks for cracking open safes or getting their heads busted open. That's all I can vouch for personally. There's more, I'm sure, but you paid your penance in other ways."

"You sure about that?"

"No," Saunders quickly replied. "I'm gambling. You'll do your time and mend your ways. I've seen enough to give me faith in that much. I'll be keeping an eye on you, Eli. Don't give me an excuse to drag your worthless hide into another cage."

"I'll do my best."

"Yeah, well. That's about the most any of us can do."

CHAPTER 24

Eight months later

Eli stepped out of the Wicksham Jailhouse a free man. He'd never been to Wicksham before Saunders had delivered him there like a package wrapped up in so much rope and chain. He'd never even heard of the small town northwest of Sherman, and that didn't matter since he never planned on going back.

It had been a long and quiet stretch of time while he'd been locked away. Summer had turned into autumn and was now deep into winter. Throughout his days behind those particular bars, he'd met more drunks and vagrants than he could count, along with several young cowboys that had been caught in their first attempts at stealing or firing a gun at something other than an empty bottle. The sheriff there was a thickly muscled fellow named Mark Beauchamp, who, as far as Eli could tell, hadn't drawn his pistol more than the one time it had taken for him to fire a few shots into the air on New Year's Day. When Eli left, Mark waved and wished him well.

Eli didn't have anywhere else to go, so he headed down the street to a stable that rented horses so he could propose working out some sort of arrangement where he could do some odd jobs in exchange for something to ride out of town. As he started walking down the wide main street, Eli had no trouble spotting a cart drawn by one horse with two people in the seat. He approached the cart and tipped his hat to one very familiar lawman.

"Still watching over me, Vernon?" he asked.

Saunders nodded once and shifted in the seat. "Too cold for that. Mark's been sending the occasional progress report my way. Heard you were a model prisoner."

"Would've been better if there was any decent food."

That comment was directed at the person sitting beside Saunders. Lyssa Beihn smiled and pulled her shawl a bit tighter around herself. It was bitterly cold, even for February, and specks of blowing snow hit their faces like tiny knives. "If I'd known you were here all these months, I would've brought you something," she said.

Saunders held both hands in front of his mouth, blew some steam onto his palms, and rubbed them together. "Which is why I never said a word. Eli had to serve his time properly, without anyone making it easier on him."

"It was easy time regardless," Eli admitted. "Suppose I have you to thank for that."

"You saved my life," the lawman said. "And you proved you deserved a second chance. Despite what some wide-eyed optimists might tell you, not everyone deserves those. While I'm on that subject, I figure you deserve this." Saunders reached inside his coat and removed a sealed envelope, which he tossed to Eli.

After peeking inside the envelope, Eli said, "What's this money for?"

"It ain't much. It's some of what was left from that box your friend Cody dug up."

"We must have spent most of that money before I got shot."

"All right, then. It's some of the reward money that company was handing out for the capture of Jake, Cody, and Hank. Dead or alive. Thought you'd rather think it was from someplace else."

"Money's money," Eli said dryly. "Long as I won't go back behind bars for taking it, it's fine by me."

"Well, I thought you'd want to see another friendly face. That's why I brought her along." Leaning down to extend a hand, the sheriff added, "Thanks for being one of the few gambles that pays off."

Eli shook his hand, which brought him close enough to catch a whiff of the fragrant scents of Lyssa's hair and skin.

"You two like a moment to catch up?" Saunders asked.

Lyssa was first to reply. "I would. Very much."

Saunders helped her down from the seat until Eli could take her arm and make sure she didn't slip on the cold ground. Wickham was quiet at its rowdiest times, and since the snow had fallen, every step echoed across the frozen Kansas landscape like boulders being dropped from a cliff. Once he had the cart to himself, Saunders snapped the reins and rode down the street to have a few words with his fellow lawman.

"So," Eli said while walking in the opposite direction as the jailhouse, "you remembered me."

Stuffing her hands as deeply into her coat pockets as they could go, she replied, "I was told you were locked up, but not where. After a while, I stopped asking."

"And here you are."

Her smile was thin and shaky, but not from the chill in the air. "When Vernon told me I could see you soon, I wondered if I was crazy for being so excited."

"Why would that make you crazy?"

"Because I barely know you. It was pleasant enough talking with you, but that was only a short amount of time and then you were gone. What could possibly come of some short-lived fancy that started on a whim?"

"Doesn't seem short-lived to me," Eli said in a quiet voice that seemed to carry for miles in the calm, snowy breeze. "From the first moment I saw you, it seemed like you were always supposed to be by my side. I've heard people speak about knowing when they found someone special. That kind of joy seems like one of the only truly beautiful things left on earth, and yet when we found it, the first thing we tried to do was brush it aside."

"We?" she asked with a smirk.

Eli nodded. "Wouldn't you say?"

"Yes," she replied in a tone that might not have been heard if not for the calmness surrounding them. "But there's more than one beautiful thing on this earth."

"Maybe, but they all seem to pale since

I've had you to think about."

"I don't know what I'm supposed to say to that."

"Say that you came out here with the sheriff to do more than enjoy a cold winter's ride." Eli clasped her hands delicately at first, as if he were holding something precious that would break if he got overly excited or careless. "Ever since I first saw you, I knew I wanted to be anywhere I was close enough to see your face. Before long, I stopped trying to figure out why it happened or how smart it was to act on it. A friend of mine once told me I spent too much time studying the world, and maybe he was right. I notice a lot of ugly things and even more that are just plain and ordinary. When you see so much of that, it gets tedious. Life loses its flavor. Things hurt worse than they should. I ain't never seen anything like you, Lyssa, and I never felt the way I do whenever I get the honor of looking into your eyes. I don't much care for an explanation of why it happened or how. I just know that it did and I don't want to throw it away."

She blinked a few times and drew a long breath before saying, "Vernon told me about what you did. How you helped bring in those killers that used to be your friends."

"I did it because I wanted to be the sort of man you deserve to be with," Eli said before he had a chance to think about it. "I don't know how we'll pay our way, but it won't be through me stealing. I promise you that. I put all of that behind me."

"You did all of that with the sheriff on account of how you felt when you looked at me?"

"I know it sounds crazy, but yes. You're the fire in my chest that made me want to get out of that jail cell instead of rolling over and waiting to be hanged. The fire that made me want to start trying to live. You know what I mean?"

Lyssa nodded.

"I probably couldn't live in Seedley, though," he sighed. "Not since there are probably still those there who want to see me hanged."

"I have family in Colorado. Do you like the mountains?"

"Never been to the mountains, but I think I'd like them very much. Care to take a gamble on me, at least for the duration of a ride to Colorado? If you change your mind, I can put you on a train to wherever you'd rather be."

She nodded again. The gesture gained momentum as tears showed at the corners of her eyes to glisten in the harsh winter sunlight. "I don't think it'll be a gamble." With that, she placed her hands on either side of his face, pulled him close, and kissed him gently.

It was a kiss that let Eli know he would be warm for the rest of his days.

ABOUT THE AUTHOR

Ralph Compton stood six foot eight without his boots. He worked as a musician, a radio announcer, a songwriter, and a newspaper columnist. His first novel, *The Goodnight Trail,* was a finalist for the Western Writers of America Medicine Pipe Bearer Award for best debut novel. He was also the author of the *Sundown Riders* series and the *Border Empire* series.

The employees of Thorndike Press hope you have enjoyed this Large Print book. All our Thorndike, Wheeler, and Kennebec Large Print titles are designed for easy reading, and all our books are made to last. Other Thorndike Press Large Print books are available at your library, through selected bookstores, or directly from us.

For information about titles, please call:

(800) 223-1244

or visit our Web site at:

http://gale.cengage.com/thorndike

To share your comments, please write:

Publisher
Thorndike Press
10 Water St., Suite 310
Waterville, ME 04901